M000306269

Hot Shot

Hot Shot

An American Royalty Romance

Robin Bielman

TULE
PUBLISHING

Hot Shot
Copyright © 2020 Robin Bielman
Tule Publishing First Printing January 2020

The Tule Publishing, Inc.

ALL RIGHTS RESERVED

First Publication by Tule Publishing 2020

Cover design by Lee Hyat at www.LeeHyat.com

No part of this book may be used or reproduced in any manner
whatsoever without written permission except in the case of brief
quotations embodied in critical articles and reviews.

This is a work of fiction. Names, characters, places, and incidents are
products of the author's imagination or are used fictitiously. Any
resemblance to actual events, locales, organizations, or persons, living or
dead, is entirely coincidental.

ISBN: 978-1-951786-30-4

Acknowledgments

Thank you to the Tule team for your awesomeness. Sinclair, Meghan, Jane, Jenny, Lee, Cyndi, Nikki, Helena, and Marlene, I'm so grateful for your partnership, unwavering help, and dedication.

Thank you Nicola Armstrong for beta reading and offering the best advice and input. I appreciate your help and continued support more than I can say.

Thank you Kelly Reynolds and Nathan Zachary for your podcast love for this series. You guys rock! I will forever remember the smiles you put on my face while I listened to you talk about these books. Everyone needs to listen to Kelly's Boobies & Noobies podcast! It's fun, informative, honest, and all about romance. Wishing you loads of success in the coming years, Kelly. And Nathan, best wishes with your acting career.

Thank you so much Sarah Ferguson and Social Butterfly PR for your help and guidance! I'd be lost without you.

Thank you readers, bloggers, and bookstagrammers for everything you do! A few of you have been with me since the very beginning – Elena, Rachel, Kim M., Nicola, and Shari, you ladies hold a very special place in my heart and I'm forever grateful. Claire, Lori, Kim C., Cheryl, Irene, Shelly, Amber, Bette, Vee, Jessica, and Courtney (I really hope I didn't forget anyone), thank you so much for spending time with my characters and writing reviews. I adore you all and am appreciative beyond words.

Thank you Tule Book Club! I couldn't ask for a nicer reading group to be part of. And hugs and thanks to my Illinois Book Club ladies – I love "seeing" you gals and am so grateful to you for inviting me into your living room!

Thank you to my author friends, you mean so very much to me. xoxo

And lastly, thank you to my family, most notably my hubby, for supporting me and loving me every single day.

Dear Reader,

Drew's book is here and I'm so excited for you to read it. I've loved writing about three brothers and a close-knit family with a special grandmother who keeps her grandsons on their toes. Grandma Rosemary is one of my favorite characters I've ever written. I was lucky enough to grow up with one very exceptional grandma. She was the heart and soul of our family and I miss her every day. Grandma Mae cooked us delicious meals, spent all her free time with us, guided and loved us, and always spoke her mind. Which, in her later years, we often chuckled or groaned over. ☺

In writing this final book in my American Royalty series, I knew I wanted Drew and Rosemary's relationship to be a focal point. Who doesn't love a matchmaking grandmother? Enter Alejandra, the perfect girl for Drew, only there's a little obstacle in their way to happily ever after. Along with Drew and Alejandra, older brothers Ethan and Finn are back to offer some advice to their baby brother. Does Drew take? Of course he does. He idolizes his siblings (just don't tell them that). Family is a recurrent theme in all of my books, and the Auprince clan is one I so love. I hope you do, too.

Thanks so much for reading!

xoxo
Robin

Chapter One
Surprise

Drew

NORMALLY, I'M A good listener, I really am. But ever have the feeling something is about to go awry? The temperature in the room goes up a notch. The air thickens. The tiny hairs on the back of your neck stand up. That sort of thing. My marketing and publicity manager, Luna, is talking about ways to up the hotel's wow factor this summer, and I can't concentrate on a thing she's saying.

We're sitting at the lobby bar, an ocean breeze blowing in through open shuttered doors and beams of light glittering off the sun-drenched pool right outside, so in theory, the vibe is perfect Sunday morning chill. Fresh-squeezed orange juice sits in front of us. A steady stream of guests make their way to and from brunch at the restaurant across the foyer.

There's no reason for my Spidey senses to be on alert.

It's probably just the hangover I'm trying to ignore. Word of caution—Moscow Mules should not be consumed one after another after another, no matter how good the friend is you're celebrating. I press a couple of fingers to my temple in hopes of pushing the headache away. Doesn't do the trick.

Luna waves a hand in front of my face.

"Sorry. What?" I ask.

"Did you hear anything I just said?" Her sympathetic tone is appreciated. Her first words to me twenty minutes ago were: "You look like shit."

"I did, but how about repeating the highlights?"

"I said we'll continue with an upscale, luxurious feel rather than a wild party atmosphere and make the cabanas and daybeds available to non-hotel guests starting at one fifty. Lounge-style music by our house DJ will play Fridays, Saturdays, and Sundays from noon to eight p.m."

"Sounds good." To the best of my knowledge, no other hotel in the area is doing something like this, which means I'm all over it. The Surfeit is my baby. A Santa Monica Beach boutique hotel that caters to an affluent LA and out-of-town crowd. The pool deck is sophisticated and adult only, a magnet for singles and couples interested in family-free fun with a classy atmosphere.

I've worked my ass off the past eighteen months to make The Surfeit *the* place to be. Some of the best hotels in the world are here in SoCal, including those owned by my family. Auprince Holdings is at my back if I need them, but there's nothing I want more than to make my first privately owned and operated venture a huge success without any extra assistance from my father.

"I also think themed social hours will give guests some great visual material they'll want to post and share on their social media channels," Luna says next.

"Do we need a designer for that?"

"Yes."

"Let's try it one weekend and see how it goes before committing."

"Done." She types notes on her iPad while I finish my OJ then cover a yawn with my hand.

There's a definite nap in my future, lack of sleep no doubt contributing to my inattentiveness. And by future I mean as soon as I stand up from this barstool and head upstairs. I don't normally take residence at the hotel, but renovations at my house have made it necessary for the foreseeable future.

I'm ready to call this meeting and thank Luna when a flash of red catches my attention. I squeeze my eyes shut, thinking back to last night when my friend's business partner's sister decided I was next on her to-do list. We didn't do *it* for a few reasons (all mine), but she did crash in my suite because I didn't want her driving home or catching an Uber given how drunk she was.

"Hey, good morning," she says, sidling up beside me at the bar.

"Morning."

"I'll talk to you later, Drew," Luna says, making a quick escape. Sisterly amusement is painted across her face as she mouths, *Call me if you need me.*

"Thanks for letting me stay last night," Red Dress says.

"No problem." I'm ashamed I can't for the life of me remember her name at the moment.

"I also owe you an apology. I may have come on a bit

strong last night."

"Apology accepted. And I'll forget I nicknamed you Octopus." I give her a smile. The woman is attractive and nice enough, but as of last week I've taken an oath of celibacy. Until I find someone I want *more* with—and someone who doesn't look at me with dollar signs and hollow stars in her eyes—I'm done messing around.

She laughs. "I *was* pretty handsy."

"I understand the appeal," I tease.

"Of course you do," she says with lightheartedness. "You're not the West Coast's most eligible bachelor for nothing." At my shrug she adds, "Take care."

"You, too."

Not my most friendly conversation, but I've learned if I offer even a hint of encouragement, I'm bombarded with advances I didn't mean to give a green light to.

I cut myself some slack given I *was* a gentleman last night and get to my feet. Light-headed from the sudden movement, I sway and grip the edge of the bar before turning to lean my back against the polished wood, elbows on the countertop. I'll just take a minute before walking anywhere. It wouldn't do to have the owner of the hotel stumbling through the lobby. Add abstain from alcohol to my recent pledge.

My gaze catches on a petite older woman impeccably dressed in her favorite shade of green, with dyed dark blond hair and bright blue-gray eyes zeroed in on me.

"Hello, Grandmother."

"You forgot we were meeting this morning, didn't you?"

Rosemary Auprince is a freaking mind reader whether I welcome it or not. She's always been super in tune to my two brothers and me, and being the youngest I feel like I get it the worst. Granted, I am her favorite, so she especially likes to mess with me. In the most loving way, of course.

"It may have slipped my mind." I pull out a barstool for her. The bar isn't open yet so we have the area to ourselves, which is exactly how she likes it. I'll put a call into the kitchen to have breakfast brought to us here.

"You look a little peaked this morning. Feeling all right?" she asks as she takes a seat. "Because I forgot to take my vitamin C this morning so if you're sick, I'll catch up with you another time."

Tempting, since I really do want to collapse back in bed, but lying isn't my style. "I'm fine, just hungover."

She gives me *the look*. The one that says she's trying to piece together whether a woman was involved in last night's festivities. This is because my grandmother has decided to play matchmaker for her only remaining single grandson. With Finn happily married to Chloe, and Ethan head over heels in love with Pascale and her daughter, Rylee, suddenly interfering with my single status is her favorite hobby.

It's time to fill her in on my dating sabbatical so she quits with her meddling. The only person in charge of my love life is me. It's a delicate situation, though. I don't want to hurt her feelings. I don't want her to think I don't appreciate her, because I do. The fact that she's 0 for 2 should discourage her, but instead it's only spurred her on. She's not a quitter. But it's not like she personally knows the women she sets me up with. They're granddaughters of friends or business associates whom she hears about and then believes might be my perfect match.

Good intentions aside, she's got to understand she isn't doing me any favors.

"So…" she says, "hook up with anyone while inebriated?"

Yes, my grandmother went there. Not for the first time. Not for the hundredth. And no doubt, not for the last.

I inwardly laugh at her use of the term "hook up." She prides herself on being up with all the lingo. I really should have told her I had a fever or mouthed I'd lost my voice when she first asked about my well-being. Not that it would have mattered since she has a mischievous streak a mile wide and enjoys making her grandsons squirm with discussions related to sex, especially if she's the only one talking.

"Mémère," I say, watching her eyes soften at the nickname, and then because I have no intention of answering her question, I change the subject to another favorite topic of hers. "Did you get your invitation?"

She arches a brow. She's on to me—she's always on to me when I use that term of endearment—but she'll let it slide for now. "It arrived yesterday and I loved it."

"I'm glad." Her eightieth birthday is next month and we're throwing her a party. We can afford to hire the best event planners, but my mom enjoys things like this so she's doing a lot of the planning herself. I won the coveted (not!) position of assistant to Mom. Finn is one of Major League Baseball's best players and on the road for games much of the time so he gets a free pass on many family obligations. And Ethan is the oldest and thus gets out of things he doesn't want to do by pulling the older brother card. "You hungry?" I ask, remembering we'd made plans to eat breakfast together.

"Starving. I'll have my usual, please."

I put our orders in—avocado toast for her, eggs and bacon for me—and then stare out across the lobby for a moment. I'm still not over the weird vibe causing a prickling sensation on the back of my neck.

"Now that invites are out, care to elaborate on the details?" she asks. It's killing her that we've kept most everything about her party a secret.

"Nope. We want you to be surprised."

"I hate surprises."

"That's why it's not an actual surprise party."

She *tsks* then pulls her cell out of her handbag. She scrolls up to unlock the screen, makes a face like someone ate her last hard candy, and takes a selfie. Next, she buries her nose in the phone like she's a teenager who can't be bothered with a face-to-face conversation.

"What are you doing?" I ask, curious *and* highly entertained. It's never a dull moment with her.

"Posting to Insta." She types something with superior speed for a grandmother. "Party pooped by my grandson. Hashtag grandma problems." She puts the phone down. It immediately lights up with notifications. My grandmother has a ridiculous amount of followers.

I shake my head in amusement. I'll comment later. She

loves when I do that.

"So," she says, "there is one thing I must discuss with you in regard to my birthday party."

"Okay, shoot." I can concede one thing for the matriarch of our family. She is, after all, the coolest grandmother out there. Plus, giving her this will hopefully keep her happy for the rest of the month so I can stay focused on the hotel. Sold-out rooms aren't enough to get me where I want to be.

"I've arranged a date for you. Marin is—"

I lift a hand. "Stop right there." Marin is someone we both actually know. She's Grandmother's best friend's granddaughter, and the girl who tortured me as a boy with stories of monsters in the closet. Swear to God, I didn't open mine for a month after that. And then only because my dad used his extinguishing powers (it's a real thing when you're seven) to obliterate said monsters. She tormented me with tales of people being buried alive when we were teenagers. And a few years ago she shared how she is psychic and can see dead people. These are traits I'm sure would make some lucky guy happy, but I'm not that guy. I literally break out in a sweat just thinking about having a conversation with her, which for the record, is always one-sided since she likes to talk. I'm man enough to admit I prefer romcoms to anything supernatural or creepy. So there is no way I'm agreeing to this.

No matter how unhappy my grandmother looks as our breakfast arrives.

Alejandra

I CUT INTO my French toast, head down, so my sister doesn't see how I really feel about her boyfriend. Brunch would taste so much better if it was just her and me, but at the last minute Landon decided to crash our celebration, bringing us to a fancy Santa Monica hotel for breakfast instead of the two of us going to our favorite café on Wilshire like we'd planned.

It's not that the guy is horrible or anything. He treats my sister well, which is the most important thing. He just likes to go on and on about all his material possessions, which off the record, he sometimes comes by illegally. I cringe at the thought. I know a thief! I about died when Gabby shared that crazy piece of information. "He works in a gallery and sometimes does things off the book or fraudulently," she said. "It's not like he walks up to someone and steals from them," she said. "He does what his boss tells him to do," she said.

I said, "Are you out of your flipping mind?"

She laughed and told me I needed to live on the wild side more.

Can I be charged as an accessory after the fact? Does knowing how he got the money for his flashy black sports car make me an accomplice in some way?

Most importantly, how rude of my sister to tell me. I did not need to know the man sitting across the table from me does illegal things.

Also. I can be wild when I want to be.

"A toast," Landon says lifting his glass of champagne.

"To Gabriela and her first film gig."

I'll drink to that. I lift my mimosa and grin at my twin sister. She's wanted to be a hairdresser on a movie set for a long time and her dream has finally come true. As different as the two of us are—in looks, temperament, and choice of men—we're both driven to succeed.

"I've reached my goal; now it's time you reach yours," she insists.

"Fingers crossed," I say, literally crossing my fingers under the table.

While Gabby went to cosmetology school right out of high school and has been working at a salon for the past six years, I got my master's in social work and am the activities director at my home away from home: the Davis Senior Community Center. The center opened twenty-five years ago on land generously donated by the Stuart Davis family, but we're running short on funds to keep the full-service facility going. And we have a balloon payment due August first. The developer who purchased the building next door is eyeing the property and the city only cares about the best financial gain.

I care about every single one of my seniors and will fight tooth and nail to keep the center open for them.

"You should think out of the box for ways to raise money," Landon says.

Am I crazy or does that sound like he's suggesting something nefarious? Gabby, though, is looking at him like he's a prince granting me his military legion to get what I need. If she has such faith in him, maybe I shouldn't jump to conclusions so quickly.

"Okay. Like what?"

He surveys the room before his gaze settles on something in the direction of the lobby. "See those blue crystal vases?" He nods toward a trio of beautiful sapphire-blue beveled-cut vases holding fresh flowers visible through large open shuttered doors.

"Yes," I say.

"If I'm right—and I usually am—those are limited-edition Baccarat and each one is worth more than thirty grand. You could take one. Sell it."

I bring my fist to my mouth. How dare he say something like that. It's one thing for my sister—and best friend—to overshare info with me. It's quite another for him to bring his lawbreaking tendencies to my face.

Gabby laughs and gives him a playful swat on the shoulder. I'm sure she's going to say, "Don't be ridiculous," but instead I hear, "That's not a bad idea."

Um, what the what? I can't even right now. They're joking, right? This celebratory breakfast has taken a weird turn and I want to finish my French toast then go work on a legal way to get my funding.

At my silence, Landon says, "I'll steal it for you."

"You can't be serious," I argue.

"They probably wouldn't even notice it was missing. And it's not as if a swanky hotel like this can't afford it. I could have a buyer for you by the end of the day."

I stare at him then my sister. She shrugs. "It's not like it would hurt anyone," she says.

An incredulous gasp slips out of my mouth. Yes it would. "Have you lost your sense of right from wrong?"

"Allie." My sister puts her hand on my arm. "It was just a silly idea. We're trying to help."

"By doing something illegal? Not to mention if you got caught, you could go to jail."

"I told you Miss Goody Two-Shoes couldn't handle this," Landon says.

A sharp, unwelcome pain slices down the middle of my chest. All my life I've been the *good one* while Gabby got to be the carefree one, allowed to make mistakes and take risks. All of a sudden, I'm sick of it.

"You don't think I could go pick up that vase and walk out the door with it?"

"I don't know. Can you?" Landon challenges, a smug look on his face.

I have no intention of stealing the vase but I get to my feet. Let him think me capable for a minute. Without a word, I stride toward the glossy wood table where the vases sit. They really are pretty, filled with an overabundance of white flowers, and curiosity gets the better of me. A vase this expensive must be bolted down, right? I run a finger over the beveled glass as caper music—ala *Ocean's Eleven*—plays in my head. (I mean if I'm going to pretend to do this, I've got to have a soundtrack.) Cool to the touch, I shiver and decide I'll try to lift it up. That ought to be enough to shock my sister and Landon. I put both hands on the vase.

The feeling I'm being watched—and not by Gabby and her miscreant boyfriend—raises goose bumps on my arms.

Mierda. I've been caught touching something I shouldn't be! I pull the old, don't-move-and-maybe-I'll-become-invisible routine. It lasts for all of two seconds, my natural tendency to own up to my actions taking over.

Slowly, I turn my head to the side. A man at the bar is watching me. Keen, light-colored eyes, straight nose, lips quirked in surprised interest. His attention dips to my hands.

On this very expensive vase.

This is bad.

Super bad.

I drop my hands and fight the urge to flee, instead playing off my actions like it's no big deal and leaning my hip against the table, arms crossed. *Nothing to see here!*

He gets to his feet. Determination rolls off him in waves likes he's brandishing a sword and one false move and I'll be pinned against this table.

I stick to my spot, chills racing up and down my spine. Not because I've been caught harmlessly touching the vase, but because I know him. Not *know* him, know him. I only know his name. *Drew.* He's the guy.

The gorgeous and charming blue-eyed devil who tried to knock the angel off my shoulder.

And almost succeeded.

Chapter Two
Like At First Sight

Alejandra
Nine months ago...

"CHEERS TO GABRIELA and Alejandra!"
I clink my shot glass against my sister's and our friends' Jane and Sutton's. "Happy twenty-fifth birthday! Love you guys!" Jane half-shouts. The bar is crowded and loud, and one of the hottest spots in Los Angeles. It's also way out of my price range, but Gabby can be very persuasive, especially when it's a special occasion.

"Love you back," Gabby and I say in return before the four of us toss back our tequila and slam the glasses down on the stainless steel bar top.

The alcohol goes down smoothly. Sutton tosses her red hair over her shoulder and orders another round from the very cute bartender. That I notice he's attractive is uncomfortable, even though it doesn't have to be.

Two months ago, my boyfriend since high school, Matthew, moved to New Zealand. We were very much in love, inseparable, each other's first everything, and on the night when I thought he might propose, he told me he'd been

14

offered a dream job—almost 7,000 miles away.

Being the wonderful guy that he is, he wanted us to talk about it together. Being the wonderful girl that I am, I wasn't going to hold him back. This was an opportunity for Matthew to be a civil engineer on an important environmental project in a country he'd visited as a child and loved so much he couldn't wait to go back one day.

We had a very mature conversation, talking for a really long time about what this meant for us, and ultimately we—mostly he—decided it would be best to break up. I felt like barbed wire had been shoved into my chest cavity. He didn't ask me to go with him. He didn't say twelve months will fly by and we can FaceTime every night so let's give long distance a try. "I love you, Alejandra," he'd said, "but this feels like the right thing to do. The assignment is for one year. No matter what, I will meet you at eight o'clock on the rooftop of the Observatory on July twelfth and if we're both still single, then we'll pick up where we left off." He looked at me so lovingly and added, "We've only been with each other. This break will be a chance for us to spread our wings and be sure about our future."

I knew he had a point. I knew long-distance relationships were difficult. But I would have tried. Instead, he left me so he could do something new in a new place, and since kissing him goodbye at the airport, I've barely looked at another guy.

Until tonight. I toss back my second shot, feeling unsteady for noticing the bartender.

Our appetizer platter arrives next—truffle mac and

cheese, pulled pork sliders and sweet potato fries—and smells delicious. I was too busy to eat lunch today so I'm eager to get food in my belly before the tequila sinks in. I pass down the small round plates to Gabby, Jane and Sutton. They serve themselves generous helpings before I do the same. We eat in comfortable silence, our appetites winning over conversation.

"How did your breakfast date go the other day?" I ask Jane a few minutes later.

"Really good," she says. "We had three rounds of coffee and delicious French toast and she texted me yesterday to ask if I'd like to go out tomorrow night. I said yes."

"That's great."

"Want me to do your hair?" Gabby asks.

Jane stops mid-fry-to-her-mouth. "Would you?" she says hopefully. She has naturally curly hair and is always trying to tame it.

"Of course."

"Oh my God, I love this song!" Sutton drops her fork on her plate. "Let's dance!" She hops off her barstool, her shoulders already swaying to the music.

Gabby and Jane quickly follow suit, taking several dancing steps away from the bar before realizing I'm still in my seat. My sister looks expectantly over her shoulder before remembering my predicament and glancing down at the clunky orthopedic boot on my foot.

"It's okay," I call out. "Go dance!"

"You sure?"

"Yes." I wave her away with my arm. I don't love the

idea of sitting at the bar by myself, but I'd hate to keep her and our friends tethered to me more. Gabby smiles and turns on her high heels.

One more week and this boot is finally history. I tore my plantar fascia sprinting to catch Mrs. Kindred before she toppled off the stationary bike during our weekly Senior Cycle class. Mrs. K. has already broken one hip. I didn't want her breaking the other. She felt terrible for causing me to worry and rush to her side, but I told her the same thing I tell all my seniors: it's my pleasure to look out for her.

"Get you another drink?" the bartender asks as he gathers our empty plates.

"Water would be great, please."

He fulfills my request before moving down the bar. As I take a sip, I look toward the dance floor. It's packed so I only catch a glimpse of Gabby's dark hair. I peer down at my stupid boot. It's not like I couldn't go out there and make the best of it, but I'd feel awful if I inadvertently caused someone around me to take a misstep or trip.

Instead, I let the electronic dance music wash over me. I ever so slightly bob my head from side to side. The bar isn't huge so when the front door opens my attention naturally swings to two men who walk in. Both are tall, dressed in classic dark suits and ties. I can't help but notice they're good-looking. The hostess grins at them with enthusiastic familiarity. The threesome talks for a minute before the two guys step away from the desk to take in the room with their heads confidently held high. When the one with light brown hair sweeps his gaze in my direction and we make eye

contact, I immediately turn my head to stare at the condensation on my water glass.

Pretend condensation.

There isn't any.

The ice cubes are very interesting, though. A few seconds
of weirdness go by.

"Are these seats taken?" a man asks, his voice nothing
special.

I peek out of the corner of my eye. He isn't one of the
two men who just walked in and I'm not sure why, but relief
flows through me, my shoulders relaxing. A woman stands at
the man's side.

It wouldn't be polite to save the seats next to me when
there's no telling how long Gabby, Sutton, and Jane will be
on the dance floor so I say, "No. All yours."

"Thanks."

After the couple sits, I can't help but scan the bar in
search of the two…businessmen, I'm guessing. It's Thursday
night, a little past nine, and office buildings take up much of
the block. Romeo One and Two looked a couple of years
older than me so having a drink after a long day at work
seems like a plausible explanation for their arrival. I cover my
smile with my hand. Romeo was the name of our dog
growing up and is also the nickname Gabby and I give hot
strangers. More than a time or two our grandmother looked
at us in total confusion when we slipped "Romeo" into a
conversation.

The two men are standing and talking with a small group
of twenty-somethings at a table near the front window. The

one who I made eye contact with, let's call him Romeo One, is in profile. Strong, clean-shaven jaw. Straight, slightly sloped nose. Nice ear. *Nice ear?* I'm about to look away when he turns his head and once again we lock eyes. The corners of his full mouth lift.

Wow. His easygoing smile causes a definite disturbance in the air, one that sweeps unwelcome but pleasurable curiosity over me. His perfect white teeth gleam, even from across the room.

I return to my enthralling glass of water. Take a sip to cool the places my imagination wants to run without my permission. He probably flashes that smile to everyone he meets and I just happened to be sitting in the right place at the right time. Besides, this guy is the complete opposite of Matthew and I still love Matthew. Ten more months will fly by.

I let the dance music that continues to pour through invisible speakers flow over me again. The great beat means I'll most likely be sitting here alone for a while. I'm tempted to pull out my phone so I have something to do, but I don't. I can handle the bar scene without a safety net.

When laughter erupts from somewhere behind me, I naturally twist around, thankful for something to check out.

A pair of light-colored eyes immediately meet mine. Romeo One is looking at me. Make that staring at me—like I'm the most interesting thing in the room. I absently rub the side of my neck where my skin is warm to the touch.

He's moved to another table where something is apparently very funny. A girl taps him on the shoulder, but his attention stays on me. I manage to keep my focus on him, too.

Until the beautiful face of my sister pops in front of me, snapping the invisible tightwire between me and Romeo One and breaking our connection. *Thank you, Gabs.*

"Hey," Gabby says bouncing into my personal space. Her cheeks are flushed from dancing. "You doing okay?"

"Yes. You?"

"I met a guy!" Her smile is huge. "He started dancing with me and his name is Landon and he is really yummy." She glances over her shoulder toward a guy at the edge of the dance floor. He lifts his chin at us. "That's him," she says dreamily.

He's not my Romeo, but then Gabby and I have never had the same taste in the opposite sex. A good thing, I guess. "Go back out there. I'm fine here. Where's Sutton and Jane?"

"They're dancing with one of Landon's friends. Come join us." She reaches around me to drink several gulps of my water.

"I still think I should stay here." I lift my leg and shake my boot.

"All right. I'll check back in with you in a bit then!"

She's gone before I can reply.

I watch her reconnect with Landon and then get swallowed by the dance crowd before my eyes flit back to Romeo One. He's sitting at the table now, talking, and holding everyone's attention. He finishes speaking, leans back, and someone else picks up the conversation. Not two seconds have gone by when he turns his head and, once again across the crowded room, his notice lands on me.

My heart thumps a beat faster as we continue to take each other in. There is something about a man in a suit that is really sexy. And when that man has loosened his tie and his shirt collar is open around the neck, it's even sexier. I can't be sure from this distance, but it appears the light blue button-down matches the color of his eyes.

His gaze dips to my body. He tracks slowly down then back up. My little black dress is my favorite thing to wear on a night out. Matthew used to say I slayed in it, and I agree. From Romeo's deliberate perusal, I think he likes it, too.

I've never been on the receiving end of a look I feel between my legs and in my breasts, and I do my best not to wiggle. I dart a glance away, only to come right back.

Which is very unlike me. I don't maintain eye contact with sexy strangers. *That's because you've had a boyfriend for the past seven years. Now you can do whatever you want.*

I bite my lip. His mouth curves into a small, but powerful smile.

This wild, untamed sensation inside me is completely foreign and I have no idea what to do with it.

The man next to me bumps my boot as he gets up off his barstool to walk away. "Sorry," he says.

"It's okay." The timing is perfect. I swivel in my seat and rest my elbows on the bar. I need a minute—or a thousand—to decompress. I'm flattered and I guess a little intrigued, and certain Romeo One is way better at this game than I am.

"Is it okay if I take this seat?" a man asks. The masculine voice is deep, seductive.

Friendly.

That's what resonates deep inside me, and I don't have to think twice about my answer. I also don't have to turn my head to know who's asking. "Sure."

"I'm Drew," he says as he gets comfortable beside me.

I take a moment to breathe in his clean, spicy scent before I look at him. "Alejandra."

"It's nice to meet you, Alejandra."

"You, too." Up close, he's even better looking. Eyes a shade of blue green I've never seen before, neat hair longer on top than the sides, broad shoulders that fill out his tailored suit coat. I'd venture his outfit cost more than my monthly mortgage.

He notices my glass of water and waves a hand at the bartender. A thick black watch peeks out from his sleeve. His hand is big, capable-looking. "Can I buy you a drink?"

With the way my pulse is racing, he absolutely can. I may need several to calm my nerves. "I think I saw a blood orange margarita on the menu."

"Good choice."

"Hey, Drew," the bartender says. "What can I get you?"

"Two blood orange margaritas, please. On the rocks."

"You got it." He drops a cocktail napkin in front of Drew and one in front of me.

"You seem to know a lot of people," I say.

"A few. What about you?"

"I'm here with my sister and two friends. They're on the

dance floor."

"It's lucky I got to you before someone else, then."

I cant my head down. It's a good thing my light brown skin doesn't give away my blush easily. Are there other people here? All of a sudden it doesn't feel like it.

"Looks like you took one for the team," he says next.

"What?"

His knee taps mine as he swivels and nods to my boot.

Oh, that. I grin. What a nice way to put it. Not only is Drew the hottest-looking man in this bar, but he's decided I'm caring rather than klutzy, something no stranger has done in the five weeks I've been injured. "Team captain right here," I say.

"Your T-shirts have a 'W' on them, don't they?"

It takes me a second to follow his train of thought. *Wonder Woman.* "Laying it on a little thick, aren't you?" I tease.

He smiles and I'm hit not only with flirty intensity, but sincerity, too. He might be coming on strong, but his compliment is genuine. "Is it working?"

Yes. No.

I'm saved from answering aloud when the bartender places our drinks on the bar. Drew picks up his glass and holds it in the air for a toast. I raise my glass next to his. "Cheers," he says.

"Cheers." I take a giant sip, and in my haste almost spill it down the front of my dress.

Drew is more graceful with his, and I can't help but stare at his lips as they wrap around the rim of his glass. Without permission, my mind wanders to what it would be like to have his mouth on mine. To have his lips on other parts of my body. While we explored each other's naked bodies between the sheets.

He raises an eyebrow and I immediately lock down any and all sexy thoughts. No way can he guess I'm imagining what he's like in bed.

Right?

I have no idea what has come over me. I've never been so *aware* of another person before. This is all Matthew's fault. He's supposed to be here with me tonight celebrating my birthday. Not sending a *happy birthday* text with an alligator emoji. Although the cute little animal did make me smile. It's our special thing. *See you later, alligator.*

"Dude!" Romeo Two approaches and pats Drew on the back. "You lucky bastard," he says, eyes trained on me. "I can't believe what I'm seeing."

On autopilot I glance down my body. Everything looks fine. He's seeing *me*, so what gives?

"Alejandra, this is my friend, West."

"Hey," West says, a grin on his face like he knows something I don't.

"Hi." I turn my attention back to Drew. "Have we met before?" I'm good with faces, so I don't think so, but—

"Only in Drew's dreams," West announces.

Drew glares at him. "Jesus, West, can you go find somewhere else to be please?"

"Alejandra," West says, "don't let my best friend down." He squeezes Drew's shoulder, a good luck gesture, I think, and takes off.

"I'm confused," I say, setting my forearms atop the stainless steel bar and fiddling with the napkin under my drink.

Rather than explain right away, Drew watches my hands. "I like your tattoo."

"Thanks." The delicate ink at the base of my finger is special and important, a constant reminder of strength and hope.

"It's some kind of flower?"

"A lotus. It represents our ability to prosper even in adversity." I bend my wrist up and straighten my fingers to give him a good look. "I put it there because the vein on our middle finger leads straight to the heart."

Drew lifts his gaze back to my face. "You're more than meets the eye," he says warmly. "But here's the funny thing. I have a huge crush on Zoe Saldana. We're talking massive infatuation, and you—"

"Look like her younger twin sister."

"Yes." His voice is adamant and intimate at the same time. "You've been told that before."

"Many times." I take a sip of my drink, intrigued by this turn of events. Drew sought me out because I look like his favorite celebrity. Since the real Zoe Saldana is married, he's probably thinking I make a decent runner-up. To sleep with? Have a one-night stand with?

I'd like to think I could put Matthew in the back of my mind and go through with something like that, but the truth is I'm not that kind of girl.

"That bothers you." He runs a hand through his thick light brown hair. "Shit. I apologize if I've offended you in some way. That's the last thing I wanted to do."

"Don't think anything of it."

"You've got me completely off my game," he admits.

I laugh. He looks at me quizzically and I laugh harder. That I've flustered him in some way is ridiculously gratifying in the most nerve-racking way possible. He's flipping gorgeous, friendly, and I'm guessing fantastic in bed. If he was on his game, we'd probably be halfway to his place by now despite my reservations and attachment to Matthew. My cheeks heat at the thought.

He moves a little closer, bends his head so we're eye level. "You have the sexiest laugh I've ever heard."

Okay, wow. No one has ever said that to me before. Then because his compliment is the nicest I've received in years, and I apparently want to distinguish myself as embarrassingly unimpressive, I snort. The sudden sound through my nose is mortifying. I cover my mouth with my hand and wince.

There is no way he doesn't walk away. I guarantee you Zoe Saldana doesn't snort.

He doesn't walk away.

Lifting his drink, he takes a sip, his eyes never leaving mine. Oh-kay, then.

I drop my arm and open my mouth to say something, but I've got nothing. I'm curious about this handsome stranger. He was unexpected, and maybe that's the only common thread we need for tonight.

"Let's get out of here," he says. With authority. And enough confidence for the both of us.

Don't let my best friend down.

Drew's proposition is nothing more than an invitation for sex and my pulse buzzes like a bumble bee. Temptation has never looked so good, but could I actually do it?

"Shit. Excuse me a minute," he says, his tone serious as he pulls his ringing phone from his pocket and stands. "I've been waiting on an important call. I'll be right back." He takes two steps then turns around. "Don't go anywhere." I'm left with a killer smile before he walks down the hallway toward the restrooms where it's much quieter.

While I wait for his return my mind goes to *what would Gabby do?*

She'd go home with him in a hot minute. But then she's always been the one to jump into things with both feet while mine stay planted firmly on the ground. One of us has had to. That doesn't mean she hasn't tried to drag me to the wild side over the years, but I can't do it. Even if deep down there's a part of me that secretly wishes I could.

"Hey!" *Speak of the devil.* Gabby leans her hip against the stool Drew vacated. "We're heading to a different bar. Come on."

"What?"

"Landon and his friend want us to join them at some other place. Everyone is waiting for us outside."

"I…" *Can't. Don't want to. Have other plans with someone who isn't Matthew.*

Gabby tugs on my arm. "Let's go. I really want you to meet Landon. I know I just met him, but I think he might be the one."

And just like that my decision is made for me. Gabby might be a serial dater, but her happiness ranks way over a potential hookup I'm really not ready for. "Okay, give me a minute and I'll be right there."

Her brows pinch together in confusion but rather than question my request she says, "All right. I have to use the little girls' room anyway. I'll meet you out front."

I tell the bartender I have to go and ask him for a pen. "Drew will be back to take care of these," I say, motioning to our margaritas. At least I hope he will. The bartender nods without a worry, so I won't worry about it either. I reach for a clean cocktail napkin. Flick the pen back and forth in my fingers for a minute.

Drew,
Maybe some other time...
Sweet dreams,
Alejandra

Sliding the note under Drew's drink, I glance toward the hallway hoping and not hoping to see him before I leave. Gabby emerges instead, and when she finds me looking in her direction, points toward the door. I slide off my stool without a glance back.

Chapter Three
Serendipity

Drew

THIS TIME WHEN the temperature in the bar jacks up and the air molecules seem to slow down, I know why.

Holy shit.

It's her.

Alejandra.

I can't believe we're staring at each other from across the room. I gave up on ever seeing her again. Tried to stop thinking about her.

Told myself the brief time we spent together was enough.

But here she is, looking more gorgeous than I remember—and it has nothing to do with the actress she resembles. Form-fitting yellow dress that falls midthigh, black hair spilling down her back, olive skin, almond-shaped eyes, a wide mouth I've stupidly fantasized about more times than I care to admit.

Alejandra, the things I've done to you in my sweet dreams.

A guilty look crosses her beautiful face as she tries to appear composed after dropping her hands from one of the limited-edition Baccarat vases my designer carefully chose for the lobby.

"Grandmother, excuse me a minute. I'll be right back." I've finished eating my breakfast. She's got one bite left of hers, and I can't let this opportunity go by.

I'm laser focused as I stride across the lobby, curious about what Alejandra is up to and anxious to reacquaint myself with her feminine scent. She's leaning a hip against the table, her arms are crossed, and she's dropped her gaze to the marble floor as I approach.

If she thinks that will stop me from saying hello, she is sorely mistaken. As if she can sense my determination, or better yet feel the magnetic pull between us all over again, she lifts her head. Eyes the color of melted toffee meet mine. Electricity sparks down my spine.

"Hi." I stop in front of her. Close enough to easily kiss her pretty lips if I wanted to. Yeah, nine months hasn't done much to cool my jets where this woman is concerned.

"Hello," she says. It's a standard "hello" rather than the breathy one I've imagined a time or ten.

"It's Alejandra, right?" Don't hate on me for playing it cool and not laying my cards too soon.

She frowns and for a second I feel like a total dick. But then her expression morphs into easygoing indifference brimming with poise, and she nods. It's hot AF watching her play off our chance encounter. "I'm sorry, I don't remember your name."

Sure, she doesn't. I fight a smile. "Drew."

"Right. Hi, Drew."

For several charged beats we size each other up. I have

never run into a female acquaintance less enthusiastic about my presence. It seems as though Alejandra wants to make a run for it. I can't have that.

"It's good to see you again." So good that my pounding headache has disappeared.

"You, too," she says absently before darting a glance over her shoulder toward the restaurant. "I, uh, have to get back to my sister and her boyfriend."

"You're here for brunch?" It doesn't go unnoticed she didn't mention a boyfriend of her own.

"Yes."

"How is it?"

She scrunches up her nose. "It's okay."

"Just okay?" I do not want to hear the food at Water's Edge is mediocre. My chef is one of the best. Sunday brunch is always busy, and I want every guest to leave here raving about their meal to their friends. Is the kitchen not up to par today? My grandmother enjoyed her breakfast. Mine was fine. *Shit.* Fine isn't good enough.

Alejandra deliberates something, her eyes flitting between me and the open shutter doors of the restaurant. "It's not the food," she admits, and I immediately relax. "It's my sister's boyfriend."

"Not a fan?"

"Not really."

"Is it serious?"

"You could say that. I'd rather have a tarantula crawling up my arm than hang out with him, and I hate spiders more than anything."

I laugh. She is sexy *and* adorable. "I meant is it serious between him and your sister."

"Oh." Her long lashes sweep down over the tops of her cheekbones. "I think so."

"That sucks then." I hit the jackpot with the women my brothers were lucky enough to land. I adore Chloe and Pascale.

"He's nice to my sister so that's all that really matters." She thumbs in the direction of brunch. "I really should get back now."

I really don't want her to walk away. "Was there something about the vase that you needed to check out?" Maybe she works as a designer or interior decorator. If so, I'll fire my current designer and hire Alejandra to help with the renovations on my house. The woman working for me now was recommended by my grandmother, so you know what that means, right? Big mistake, as the woman is not my type no matter how often Grandmother likes to go on about how great she is and that love happens all the time between people who work together, just look at Finn and Chloe.

"The, uh, vase?" Her voice cracks.

"The one you were touching."

She takes a step away from the table like it just burst into flames, and once again glances over her shoulder. "Oh, that. Uh...I wanted to check it out, I mean see if it was you know..." I raise my eyebrows. "It's so pretty and I wondered if maybe...if maybe it was...available for sale." A visible swallow makes its way down the long column of her neck.

I have no idea what to make of her nervousness—and

obvious lie—but I'll play along if it keeps her in my company longer.

"Do you know if they sell art pieces from hotel lobbies?" she continues, looking around the room. "I mean generally speaking, I don't think they do, but my sister's boyfriend works in a gallery and they're always buying new art." Her voice rises an octave on *buying new art*. "I'll just go ask the front desk and maybe they can leave a message for the hotel manager or something."

I smirk. She has no idea who I am and it feels fantastic. "I'll wait for you here."

"You don't need to do that." She transfers her weight from one foot to the other. She's wearing white flip-flops with a sunflower on each. Her toes are painted light blue. Along with the dress, she is the embodiment of sunshine and blue skies.

"I do actually." If truth be told, I have a list of needs: her phone number, her full name, her availability for our first date.

She looks slightly panic-stricken then gives a small shake of her head. Not to me, but to a girl I'm guessing is her sister, rising from a table in the restaurant. The girl sits back down.

I take Alejandra's elbow in order to find us some privacy. Her skin is soft, warm. Her floral scent is heady. "Come with me," I say, not sure where I'm leading her to.

"What are you doing?" She tugs her arm out of my hold. "Are you security?"

"What? No. Why would you ask me that?"

We stand still and take each other in, confusion swirling between us. We are clearly on different pages here.

"Hello."

Oh, shit. I forgot all about my grandmother. God, I suck at the moment. I turn my head to look down at all five-foot-one inches of her. Her focus, however, is narrowed in on Alejandra.

"Hi," Alejandra says with a friendly smile that's come out of nowhere. It certainly wasn't pointed in my direction.

"I'm Rosemary, Drew's grandmother."

"Hi, Rosemary. I'm Alejandra. It's nice to meet you." She looks between my grandmother and me with kindness. "I apologize if I kept him from you. I was just saying goodbye."

"I hope not on my account," Grandmother says.

"No. I—"

"What a beautiful brooch." Grandmother nods to the vintage glass bead and diamond flower-shaped pin on Alejandra's dress.

Alejandra crosses her arm over her chest and lightly touches the jewelry. "Thank you."

"Not many young women wear them anymore."

"It belonged to my mother. And before her, my grandmother."

Belonged. The word hints at loss and I don't like the way that makes me feel. Alejandra's eyes soften, but I can't tell if it's in remembrance or gratitude. Maybe both. *Fuck.* She's what? Twenty-four? Twenty-five?

"That makes it even more beautiful," Grandmother says.

"Drew wore my diamond earrings for a little while." She puts her hand to the side of her mouth to mock whisper to Alejandra. "Between you and me, he looked really pretty, but that wasn't the look he was going for."

Alejandra giggles at the same time I groan. "I never would have pictured you with pierced ears," she says to me.

Meaning she's pictured me other ways. Good to know.

"He and his friends wanted to be the next big boy rapper band."

"Oh really?" Alejandra asks in amusement, her eyes shining.

"It's boy band *or* rapper," I say. "And I think—"

"Drew has some magic fingers," Grandmother interrupts.

Alejandra chokes while I cringe. I can't believe she just said that. Actually, I can, but talk about uncomfortable innuendo. "Grandmother," I admonish with a nice tone.

"*What?*" she says innocent enough, but I'm not sure I buy it. This kind of teasing is right up her alley. "You are an accomplished guitar player and it's a shame you don't play anymore."

That she knows of. Sometimes late at night when sleep eludes me...

"I'm sure if you asked him to play something for you, he would," Alejandra offers.

She's not exactly wrong, but put an idea in my grandmother's head and she's relentless, and I stopped playing for a reason. One my family doesn't know about.

"Alejandra, you are a genius. It just so happens I have a

birthday party coming up and I would love for my grandson to show off his musical talents at the event."

I know Alejandra didn't mean any harm, and that she knows nothing about my past, but being reminded of the last night I played and what my ex-girlfriend Miranda did, brings up bad memories. So, while I know it's wrong, I feel the urge to retaliate. To take the focus off me and put it on Alejandra.

And that's when a brilliant idea hits me.

"It's funny you should mention your party. I hadn't had a chance to tell you, but..." I step next to Alejandra and put my arm around her. We've been friendly enough that I don't think she'll mind the cozy position. "Alejandra is my date." *So much for lying not being my style.*

She stiffens in my hold. Her jaw drops. Before she can contradict me, I add, "She's something special and running into each other this morning was just the opportunity I was looking for to introduce you two."

"That's not true," Alejandra says, clearly puzzled by my announcement.

"You two are dating?" Grandmother asks, disregarding Alejandra's confusion with—dare I think—approval in her voice. She sees something in Alejandra, too.

"No," Alejandra says at the same time I say, "yes."

I curve my hand tighter around her waist and give a squeeze. *Please go with me on this and I promise to make it good for you*, the action implies. We turn to look at each other, mere inches separating our faces. I lose my train of thought for a second as I fall into her fathomless brown eyes. We both blink, and it's then that I know I've got her. She may have voiced her objection, but in those beautiful depths lies desire. Interest.

"What we mean is we've been off and on, but we're definitely back on now."

"We are, are we?" Alejandra challenges, and not necessarily in a playful way. *Shit*. I'm making things worse, which is the last thing I want to do. Not that I expected her to react with lovesick eyes and gratitude, but a little more willingness would be nice.

"That makes me so happy," Grandmother says, freeing me from Alejandra's glare.

"It does?" Alejandra asks, her expression morphing into surprise as she meets my grandma's sparkling eyes.

I hate to tell her it could probably be any woman—or man for that matter—standing beside me earning my grandmother's approval.

Damn. This doesn't feel as good as I thought it would. The truth is, I'd love to date Alejandra. For real. She knows that, right?

"Yes," Grandmother says. "I've done some matchmaking for Drew the past few months, and now I know why he's been so resistant."

Alejandra darts a quick side glance at me.

I give her my winningest smile. It has minimal effect, but then she wiggles her nose like she's trying to keep her expression neutral, and I suspect she's more affected than she's letting on.

"It will be lovely having you at the party. Let's make this Insta official, why don't we?" Grandmother pulls her phone out of her purse and squeezes in between Alejandra and me. "Drew, your arm is the longest; you take the picture please."

"Um…" Alejandra starts.

I take the phone to do as I'm told.

"Say cheese!" Grandmother says, putting one arm around Alejandra and the other around me. She takes the phone back after I snap the photo, inspecting it before her thumbs move quickly across the screen.

"Wow," Alejandra says. "You're great on your phone for—" She stops abruptly, catching herself.

"Someone my age?"

"Yes," Alejandra answers honestly, which makes her even more appealing. Most people would have tried to backtrack or come up with a white lie. "And you're on Instagram?" She watches over Grandmother's shoulder. "That's impressive."

"It's my favorite social site." Grandmother stops typing and looks up in thought for a moment before returning to her post. "Hashtag glad grandmother."

Alejandra smiles. "Do you post often?"

"Every chance I get." She tucks her phone away and turns to me. "I'll let you and Alejandra get back to your conversation. Thank you for breakfast."

"My pleasure. Anytime."

"Alejandra, I look forward to seeing you again soon."

For a few painful seconds, I think Alejandra is going to set the record straight, her silence hanging in the air like an ax about to come down and split my story into two unforgiving pieces. But then the strangest thing happens: palpable affection for my grandmother soothes her tense demeanor, and with thoughtful consideration she says, "I look forward to seeing you, too."

Whatever the hell just happened, I owe Alejandra big time.

I kiss Grandmother's cheek goodbye. She's almost out the front door of the hotel when she does a one-eighty. Sudden skepticism materializes across her nimble expression. "Breakfast next Sunday. The three of us." With that, she spins back around and leaves.

There is no pulling the wool over her eyes. She's as sharp as they come and knows every damn time one of her grandsons stretches the truth. It's hilarious when it happens to my brothers. Me? Not so much. I open my mouth to smooth things over with Alejandra and thank her for playing along, but I don't get the chance.

"What were you thinking? *No puedo creer que hayas hecho eso!* This is not okay. You lied to your grandma. *Esa dulce mujer cree que estamos saliendo!*" Alejandra talks so fast that her words blend into one long sentence, most of which I don't understand. "How dare you—"

I press two fingers to her mouth to quiet her. "I'm sorry." The sincere apology earns me a slow blink. I drop my arm, fairly sure she'll let me continue without interruption. "I acted without thinking and apologize for dragging you into something you didn't agree to beforehand."

She crosses her arms over her chest and regards me with uncertainty. I can't say I blame her. What I did was very underhanded, but I'd do it again in a heartbeat. I saw an opportunity for more time with her, so I took it. I'm always a straight shooter rather than sneaky, but this beautiful girl, who smells like sunshine and carries herself with grace and warmth, has me acting out of character, my stomach in knots.

"Do I want to know what you said in Spanish?" I ask with my most pleasant tone, hoping to lighten the mood.

"I said 'I can't believe you did that. That sweet woman thinks we're dating.'"

"Would that be so awful?"

She narrows her eyes. "How do you know I don't have a boyfriend?"

"Do you?"

She lets out an exasperated breath. "I... No, but it's complicated and I'm uncomfortable with what you just did."

"Why did you go along with me, then?"

"Because..." Alejandra rolls her bottom lip between her teeth. "Because I didn't want to disappoint your grandma."

"I sincerely appreciate that. And again, I'm sorry. For what it's worth, I would very much like to ask you out on a date."

"Drew—"

"Fate brought us back together, don't you think? It would be a shame to ignore it."

"I don't believe in fate," she says to the floor. Then raising her head she adds, "Besides, I don't even know you. You could be a serial killer who chops his victims into tiny pieces and then goes fishing and uses the body parts as bait."

I get it. On top of being upset, she's unsure of me. Rightfully so. And I don't like that I've made her feel this way. "You're right. Not about the serial killer part," I rush to say, tongue-in-cheek. "So let's remedy that. What do you want to know about me?"

"How about—"

"Oh my God, you're Drew Auprince, aren't you?" the woman who I suspect is Alejandra's sister asks as she comes to stand beside us. She openly runs her eyes up and down my body. Normally, a woman's attention doesn't bother me, but standing next to Alejandra, I'm uneasy with the appraisal.

"I am. And you are?"

"Gabriela. Alejandra's sister."

"Nice to meet you." I shake her hand.

"I can't believe you didn't tell me you knew him," Gabriela says to Alejandra.

"I don't really." When Gabriela frowns at Alejandra, Alejandra adds, "It's a long story. How do you know him?"

"He's from one of the most prominent families in the country. I've seen his picture like a hundred times. He owns this hotel."

Alejandra's jaw drops. "You own this hotel?" She looks everywhere at once—me, the vases, her sister, the restaurant, the vases, back to me.

"Guilty."

"I have to go," she says nervously.

"Wait." I put a hand on her arm. "Can I please talk to you for another minute?"

She considers my request, rolling her bottom lip between her teeth again. I can't stop staring at her mouth. Her lower lip is plumper than the top, and I want to tug on it, too.

"I'll meet you back at the table," Gabriela says. "No rush. I just wanted to make sure everything was okay."

"It is, thanks. I'll be right behind you."

As soon as Gabriela is out of earshot I say, "Have dinner with me tonight. You can ask me all the questions you want."

"I don't know."

"Come on. What's the worst that can happen?"

"You say nice things and I want a second date."

"That is definitely going to happen so prepare yourself," I say with a heartfelt smile. I have never in my life had to work so hard to get a girl to like me. I should probably cut my losses and tell my grandmother things didn't work out. I'm a grown man and can show up to her birthday party without a date if I want to. The problem is I like a challenge and I haven't had one in a very long time.

More than that, though, I've never been more attracted to a woman. Alejandra has a gentle, yet sensuous way about her that calls to me like nothing I've ever experienced before.

"You've put me in a terrible position," she says.

I think she's referring to my grandmother. That she's concerned about her adds another checkmark to her growing list of qualities. She's family-oriented, and my family means the world to me. There isn't anything I wouldn't do for them.

"I promise to put you in much better positions in the future." A few of those being in bed. Against the wall. Bending over my favorite chair. I'm getting ahead of myself.

"You..." She shakes her head, as if to clear her mind of

dirty thoughts. *Good to know we're on the same wavelength.* I may not be her favorite person at the moment, considering how I pretty much roped her into a date, but she's not immune to me. "Wait. What am I thinking?" she says. "I have to work tonight."

"Tomorrow night then."

"I can't." I wait for her to elaborate. "I'm working every night this week," she says with a mix of disappointment and relief. "Looks like you need to find another date for your grandma's party."

No so fast, beautiful.

"Can I ask you a question?" I nod to Luna as she walks by with a clipboard in her hands. I've had a discreet eye on everything going on in the lobby while talking with Alejandra.

Alejandra twists a strand of hair at the nape of her neck around her finger. "Okay." There's a small slice of reluctance in that four-letter word—almost enough to get me to change my mind about us. *Almost.*

"Take my grandmother out of the equation. If we'd run into each other again and talked for a few minutes and I'd asked you out on a date, would you have said yes?"

She looks somewhere over my shoulder, waging some internal battle, I'm guessing. Delicate lines crease her forehead before she resumes eye contact. I don't believe there is a lying bone in her body so I hold my breath while I wait for her answer.

"Yes," she relents.

"I'm happy to hear that because that night in the bar wasn't enough, Alejandra."

Chapter Four
Sexy Surprise

Alejandra

I BLOW A stray hair off my forehead and hurry around the dining table at the senior center. All afternoon I've been off, my mind replaying my encounter with Drew over and over again until I'm practically dizzy. I shiver every time I think about his catching me touching that vase and then striding toward me like he was starved for my company, not pushing for an explanation for my unusual behavior. I can't believe we were face-to-face again. I can't believe after nine months he still makes my heart flutter. I stumble in my flip-flops, stubbing my big toe. "Sonofabiscuit."

"I heard that."

I know. That's why I said 'biscuit.' Ignoring the stab of pain in my foot, I lift my head and smile at Rhoda. I'd noticed her walk into the room when I placed the last bowl and spoon on the table. "Hi, there!"

"You okay?" she asks.

"I'm fine. How are you tonight?"

"Wearing sensible shoes." Rhoda is my no-nonsense senior. She takes her usual spot around the pinewood table, places her handbag at her feet, and puts her copy of *A Summer in Europe* by Marilyn Brant in front of her.

Book club is one of my favorite days of the month at the senior center. I started the club two years ago, motivated by my love of reading, and to honor my grandmother who had recently passed away. Much of my teen years were spent with my nose in a book after I discovered one of her Harlequins in her nightstand. She and I read and talked books constantly after that.

I rub at the ache in my chest. Those memories make this night a little harder than all the other nights I think about my *abuela*. I miss her so much.

Mrs. K. and Ethel walk in next. "Hi, guys!" I say. Mrs. K. was my third-grade teacher, hence the reason I don't call her by her first name. I just can't do it. It doesn't sound right. On their heels are Gloria and Claire. The ladies talk animatedly as they get situated around the table.

The large, open-concept room includes a kitchen where we offer meal and nutrition programs and cooking classes, a dining area, and a mix of couches and upholstered chairs arranged around game tables. Now that everyone is here, I excuse myself to grab the little surprise I have for them. In addition to the gelato we'll have after our discussion (we always tie in a special snack to the book), I bought them each a summer tote at the arts and crafts fair held at the library last weekend. The canvas bags are cute as can be in stone-washed colors and perfect for the grocery store or farmer's market or anything else they want to use them for.

I'm halfway down the hall toward my office when I hear,

"Hello, I'm looking for Alejandra."

I freeze while a bushel of butterflies takes residence in my stomach. Drew's here? I can't believe he came to my place of work. My heart resumes its quick beat. When he asked me where I worked I didn't think that meant he planned to stop by, and I'm not sure how I feel about that. On the one hand, I'm excited. I've thought about him a lot over the past nine months. Wondered what might have happened if I hadn't left the bar when I did. I walked away from a sexy, charming, happy-birthday-to-me present, and I'd be lying if I said I didn't sometimes regret it.

On the other hand, he's the only man to tempt me since Matthew left, but now with a mere month to go before Matthew and I meet up, shouldn't I be focused on that? I don't know what's going to happen when we meet on the rooftop of the Griffith Park Observatory, and after all this time I'm not sure what I *want* to happen, but staying faithful a little longer is much safer than starting something with a man who likes me because I look like his celebrity crush.

I did my due diligence after leaving the hotel earlier, and googled Drew as soon as I got home. Like Gabby said, Drew Auprince is American royalty and his family is one of the wealthiest and most influential in the world with their hotel empire. He and his older brothers, Finn and Ethan, are admired by people everywhere. Since the day he was born, Drew's been under a special spotlight.

In addition to news clippings and magazine articles about his tight-knit family, there were photos of him with beautiful women. He's had several girlfriends, and when I'd felt an unwelcome stab of jealousy, I'd closed my laptop, done with my research.

"She's running book club tonight. Down the hall and in the community room," our receptionist says loud enough for me to hear.

"Thank you."

I resume walking, mentally preparing myself for his handsome face and magnetic personality. This is my workplace. I'm a professional here and can handle Drew or anyone else who walks through our door.

He rounds the corner, our eyes meet, and I take back my previous statement. I have very little control over my thoughts and body where Drew is concerned, and instead of being levelheaded, I'm immediately drawn to him in a very unprofessional manner. Like I'm starved for sex when I've been perfectly fine without it since Matthew left. Drew's dressed in olive-green dress pants and a light blue button-down with the sleeves rolled to his elbows. His hair is perfectly messy. He's so effortlessly sexy, I suddenly don't know what to do with myself. I end up crossing my arms.

"Hey there," he says.

"Hi."

"I'm here for book club." His smile lights up the hallway. I check behind me to make sure no one's been struck senseless. It's all clear.

"Says the man who just found out about it," I tease.

"Hey, I'm nothing if not adaptable."

"Come on," I say, for the sole purpose of leading him away from my reader posse. Introducing him to the group feels too personal too soon. Plus, he smells really good and there is no way my romance readers won't comment on his scent. It's their favorite hero quality. We've debated for hours on what exactly musk smells like. "I'll show you to my office so we can talk and then you can go," I add over my shoulder.

God, he's handsome, plays on repeat in my head for the hundredth time today as he follows me. I step into my office, twisting to walk backward toward my desk. "I'm surprised to see you."

"I wanted you to know how sincere I am and thought one more face-to-face before our date on Thursday night might not be a bad thing."

Our date. It was easy to say yes to him, but there's nothing simple about it and the emotions twisting my stomach in knots. I pride myself on doing the right thing, and being drawn to Drew when I'm still connected to Matthew feels a little wrong even though I'm free to do whatever I want.

It's just a date, I remind myself.

"You're the activities director," he says, having noted the placard on my door.

"Yes."

"How long have you worked here?"

I take a seat at my desk. He sits across from me in the mustard-yellow chenille slip-covered chair I picked up at the Rose Bowl swap meet. "A few years. I started as an assistant while I was in grad school."

He looks around the room. At my bookcase filled with well-loved novels, framed pictures, and small knickknacks.

At the antique coatrack in the corner where I hang all sorts of clothing items. And at the distressed-wood bulletin board where I post cards, notes, inspirational quotes and cute magnets.

"Nice office."

"Thanks. So, about your grandma," I say, hoping to fix that white lie.

His friendly gaze settles back on me. "Her eightieth birthday is a few weeks away. She is smart, funny, sly when she wants to be, and full of more love than she knows what to do with. I hope I'm half as sharp as she is when I'm her age. She also likes to butt into her grandsons' business and lately that means she's been playing matchmaker for me."

I can't help but smile at his sweet words and the fondness in his voice. "I meant we should probably come clean."

"Probably." Drew glances at the photo sitting on my desk of me, Gabby, Diego, and our grandparents taken on their fifty-fifth wedding anniversary.

"Those are your grandparents?"

"Yes."

"Does your grandmother ever try and set you up?"

I shake my head. "She passed away two years ago. My grandfather right afterward." We knew he wouldn't want to remain on this earth without the love of his life.

"I'm sorry," he says, reaching across the desk to squeeze my hand. The gesture catches me off guard and feels nice, so when his touch lingers longer than necessary, I don't pull away.

"I miss them a lot," I say, suddenly overcome with emotion. "Besides my sister, my grandmother was my best friend. She taught me so much and loved to just sit around and read and talk. She gardened a lot, too, and sang to her vegetables. She said it made them healthier. She doted on my grandpa and whenever he could he held her hand, even at home when it was just the two of them watching cooking shows. They were each other's one true love." I let out a breath. "Sorry, I don't know why I said all that. It was more information than you needed to know." My cheeks heat in embarrassment. I haven't rambled on like that in a long time.

"Please don't be sorry. I'm glad you told me. I could listen to you talk for hours."

I get to my feet and pick up the canvas bags stacked on the floor. "Hours I don't have."

"After your book club, then."

"How about we save further discussion until our date?" I'm tired and more than a little confused about my reactions to him. I just want to go home and crawl into bed.

"Fair enough." We walk out of the office and toward the community room. I pause midway so Drew can head back to the reception area.

He eyes me carefully and I wish I knew what he was thinking. "Have a good night."

"Thanks, you too. Bye." I spin around and steel myself not to look over my shoulder. "Sorry to keep you waiting," I say to the book club upon my return. "I got you each a little something to celebrate the start of summer in a couple of weeks." I hand out the bags to thanks and bright smiles and then drop into my seat. "What did you think of the book?"

Unanimous love and gushing ensues. I knew they would enjoy it. The book includes a wonderful cast of older characters and the European setting is incredible. It's like you're in the pages of the book. Add in a spunky heroine and a sexy British hero named Emerson, and it was an unputdownable read. We discuss the story, starting at the beginning. We always break down our discussions to beginning, middle and end.

I've just mentioned how much I'd love to go to Italy one day when five pairs of eyes sweep over my head. "Well, hello there," Claire says.

Oh.

No.

I don't need to turn to know who is standing behind me.

"Hello, ladies. Pardon the interruption, but I couldn't end my tour of the center without checking out your book club," Drew says.

He stayed to tour the center? Not even Gabby has done that. In my periphery I see him move deeper into the room. Matthew has, though. Matthew has spent time here with me and my seniors. That he still pops into my brain like this means something, right?

"What brings a handsome young man like yourself to our senior center?" Ethel asks.

"Not what. Who."

All eyes swing back to me. "Alejandra Cruz, you didn't tell us you were dating someone!" Mrs. K. accuses.

"I'm... We're..." I raise my head to Drew. He arches an eyebrow. I am not going to exaggerate to these kind women.

"We haven't officially gone out yet."

"Honey, you better lock him down before someone else does," Claire only half-whispers from beside me.

"I'm all for Alejandra sealing the deal," Drew says.

Unfamiliar warmth flickers in the pit of my stomach. Maybe Drew likes me for more than what he sees on the outside?

"She is a catch," Mrs. K. says.

"We've been hoping she moves on from Matthew," Rhoda announces. "He broke her heart even though they both agreed to break up."

"Okay!" I jump to my feet. This is what happens when you drink wine at book club after the boy you've loved since you were seventeen moves to another country. You spill your guts to grandmother figures because you miss yours. "That's enough. Drew doesn't need to hear anything else."

"Actually, I'd love to know more about Alejandra," Drew says, earning "*awws*" from the group.

"Can I talk to you, please?" I ask under my breath. I take Drew's arm and lead him over to the kitchen so we're out of earshot before I continue. "You need to slow down. You may be used to relationships happening at warp speed, but I'm not. You can't just show up here and be all charming and smiley and ingratiate yourself with my seniors in under one minute."

He angles his body so we're facing each other. He's several inches taller and I have to look up to meet his unshakable blue-green gaze. "I'm happy to hear that."

"That we need to go slow?"

"That you think I'm charming and like my smile," he says without an ounce of modesty. Then he grins and I want to be mad, but I can't. The corners of his very nice mouth meet the corners of his sparkling eyes and it's ridiculously appealing.

"You're too much," I tell him.

"Of a good thing."

I shake my head. "Confidence definitely isn't a problem for you, is it?"

"When I see something I want, I go after it," he says, his voice a little deeper, a little more indecent.

My heart beats faster. I'm a lightweight when it comes to guys, Matthew being my only boyfriend. Love was a one-time event for my parents and my grandparents and I thought I had that with Matt. *Think* I have that with him? In the texts we've sent to each other to keep in touch, we've remained friendly, but superficial, and my feelings have definitely adjusted, but deep down there is still love. He's been such a huge part of my life, there for all my biggest moments—graduations, first job, first promotion. And he got me through my greatest losses—our dog Romeo, both my grandparents.

"But," Drew adds, interrupting my thoughts, "I hear you and will back off."

Why does that suddenly bother me? "Thank you," I say then quickly glance away before I'm drawn deeper into his hopeful gaze.

"Alejandra?" He waits for my full attention to return to his. "Is Matthew an issue?"

I blink at his question. Could he tell where my thoughts had strayed? And darn Rhoda for mentioning my ex in the first place. "It's complicated," I say. Now is not the time or place to talk about it.

"Was it complicated nine months ago, too?"

"Yes."

"Is that why you left the bar?"

I shake my head. "No, my sister dragged me away."

"Dragged, huh?" He's pleased by that.

Which makes me happy. I never wanted to hurt his feelings and that he's seemingly thought about me as much as I've thought about him triggers the same charged awareness I felt that night.

"I left you a note. I hope you got it."

"I did." For several heady seconds we stare at one another. "I'm glad 'some other time' is here."

He remembers what I wrote. And despite my conflicted feelings... "I am too."

"I'm going to take that as a green light, then, and confess I can't promise I'll always remember to be on my best behavior."

"What does that mean?"

"It means I've wanted to kiss you since that night, and if the opportunity presents itself, I'm going to take it."

Tingles race down my spine. I wanted to kiss him that night, too. Badly. "You don't strike me as a man who takes without permission," I assert, surprising myself. "And I think you've figured out I don't give it easily."

His eyes drop to my mouth. "But when you eventually

do, and trust me you will, the fireworks are going to be explosive."

How can he sound so full of himself yet so humble at the same time? "You're impossible."

"And apparently forgetful when I'm around you, which is why I interrupted your book club. This morning, and then again when I got here, I forgot to get your number." He takes his cell out of his pocket and types in my digits as I rattle them off. "I'll phone you so you've got mine."

"Excuse me," Ethel says, coming up behind Drew and startling me enough to jump away from him. "We're ready for gelato now."

"But we're not even halfway through the book," I say.

"We thought we'd change it up tonight. Drew, would you like to join us?"

He casts a quick glance at me and when I shrug he turns his entire body to Ethel and says, "I'd love to."

Ethel gives a thumb-up to the other book club ladies then turns to walk back and I don't know whether to laugh or to cry. The group doesn't mean any harm, but the last thing I'd wanted was for them to meet Drew, wasn't it?

I pull the gelato out of the freezer.

"Can I help?" he asks.

"No, thank you."

I move around the kitchen, keeping my back to him. Not to be mean, but to take a breather from him. I fill my hands with two types of gelato, two ice cream scoops, and a box of wafer cookies.

"Alejandra, let me help." He reaches for one of the gelato

cartons and I let him take it because it's *cold*. He lifts the cookies from my arms next.

"Thanks," I say, still not looking at him.

We both dish out the sweet treat. He's got the coffee flavor. I've got the chocolate. As I serve Ethel she leans over to Claire and whispers, "He smells really good." *Yes, he does.*

Mrs. K. and Rhoda make room for Drew to sit between them. He joins in the discussion, listening as the women talk about the plot and characters before he entertains the over-seventy group with stories of his travels in Europe. It's safe to say as book club comes to an end, everyone is enamored with him.

Except me.

Or so I tell myself.

Chapter Five
Team Drew

Alejandra

TUESDAY MORNING GABBY and I are at home listening to music. She's sitting at the kitchen table dressed in a cute coffee-colored jersey mini dress and on her computer filling out paperwork for her new job while I'm on the couch in cut-off shorts and my sunflower tee, attempting to knit my first scarf. Whoever said 'anyone can easily knit a scarf' was lying. Or maybe it's just me and my two left hands. I'm still enjoying the process, though, and the color makes me happy. Pale yellow, like melted butter.

"Holy shit," Gabby says.

Our house is small: one story with three bedrooms, two bathrooms, and a family room and kitchen. So even with Carrie Underwood's vocals filling the air, I hear my sister loud and clear.

"What is it?" I ask.

"Get your ass over here and see."

It's not the best place for me to stop knitting, so I bring the scarf with me, plopping down on the chair next to my sister. The table is pushed against the wall, underneath a window. I glance outside at the tree-lined street. The sky is overcast, typical for early June.

Gabby turns the screen of her laptop toward me.

"Holy shit," I echo, my knitting project slipping through my fingers and onto the floor as I stare at the photo of me with Drew and his grandmother in the lobby of his hotel. The picture is on the celebrity news site, PEOPLE.com. (One of Gabby's daily internet stops. She loves to stay up on celebrity news.) The headline reads: Drew Auprince With His Grandmother and Mystery Woman on Instagram—Is it Love?

"You didn't tell me you guys took a picture!" Gabby accuses.

"I assumed you and Landon were keeping an eye on me the whole time." After leaving the hotel and getting a few minutes alone with her, I filled Gabby in on everything else that happened with Drew.

She scrolls down so we can read the post. It talks about the Auprince family and Rosemary's popularity on Instagram. The reporter mentions Drew's status as one of the West Coast's most eligible bachelors, his hotel, and his brothers. She hypothesizes on the caption Rosemary included and how it implies she's giving her approval to the relationship between Drew and me.

Sweat breaks out on my forehead. My heart races. We're not in a relationship! We've just met. Or re-met. You know what I mean.

"Do you think anyone will figure out who I am?"

"Let's hope so."

"*What?* No. I do not want that happening." I shake my head. "We haven't even gone out yet, Gabs. This is way out of my comfort zone."

"Exactly." She lifts her phone off the table and opens Instagram. "This is your walk on the wild side and it's amazing. Now let's find out what's going on." She locates Rosemary's account, follows her (of course), then thumbs to the photo and brings it full screen. "There's over five hundred comments! You need to grab your phone and see if you've been tagged."

I turn and reach up onto the counter where I left it to charge. I have a private account on Instagram with less than a hundred followers and I'm happy to see I haven't been tagged. "No one has linked to me," I say. My racing heart slows.

"Bitch," Gabby mutters under her breath.

"*What?*"

"Some girl left a racist comment." Gabby scrolls through more comments.

I pick up my knitting, content to let my sister give me more details, if need be. It is weird that a picture of me with Drew and his grandma has been seen by presumably thousands of people, and for a second, even though I'm sitting in my tiny kitchen with my sister and no one can see us, it feels like all eyes are on me. Scrutinizing me. I shake it off, turn my phone face down on the table and rub my thumb over my lotus tattoo.

"Screw you," Gabby says to another commenter. "And you. God, people can be such dicks."

For a minute I'm back in middle school, being judged and bullied by the popular girls. Gabby was sent to the principal's office numerous times for fighting back (often on my behalf), but not me. I always stayed on my best behavior. I saw the pain in my grandmother's eyes when she had to meet with the principal over Gabby's conduct.

"Most of the comments are nice," my sister informs me, her nose buried in her phone. "You should follow Drew and his grandma. I bet they'll follow you back." She side-eyes me when I don't answer right away. "You're not going to, are you?"

"I might, just not yet." I have to think about it for longer than two minutes, first.

She turns her phone screen to me. "Here. Check out some of the comments."

I read no further than the first one that catches my eye: *Whoever she is, she's beautiful. His last girlfriend was blond and plastic-looking. This one looks like that actress Zoe something.*

"What's wrong?" Gabby asks.

"Drew only wants to date me because I look like his favorite actress."

"You don't know that."

"Gabby, he said as much the first time we met."

"But now he's getting to know you, and trust me, he'd be an idiot not to fall for the person you are on the inside, too."

"You're my sister, you have to say that."

"No, I don't." She gets a thoughtful look on her face. "I know it's hard for you to trust someone after Matthew left like he did, but so far the guy seems genuinely into you."

I could argue with her that it's because he wants in my pants, but the more I think about it, the more it's clear I haven't given Drew enough credit. "You're right."

"Always am." She logs out of her computer, cutting off the music. "I have to get going. Don't worry about the picture okay? I love you." She kisses my cheek.

"Love you, too. Do you hear that noise?" I put my knitting on the table. "It sounds like running water."

We get to our feet and walk toward the sound. Three steps into the family room, we're met with water under our feet. It's coming from the hallway. "Holy shit!" Gabby says, surveying the scene from beside me. There's at least an inch of water.

"A pipe must have burst in the bathroom."

"What do we do?" Gabby shrieks.

"I don't know! Turn off the water?" After our grandparents passed away, the house was left to me, Gabby and Diego. A small mortgage remains that we've been able to cover without help from Diego since he lives an hour away, but something like this could set us way back.

I run toward the bathroom in my bare feet, sloshing water on the walls as I go. This is bad. This is really bad.

"I'm going to go get Mr. Hernandez," Gabby shouts from behind me. He's our neighbor and the resident handyman, bless his heart.

Sure enough, the leak is coming from somewhere behind the toilet, I think. It's hard to tell for sure with gallons of water pouring onto the floor. The entire house is flooding and I don't know how to stop it.

Mr. Hernandez does. He knows how to turn off the water main but the damage is done. Water is everywhere. The next hour, or maybe it's two, goes by in a blur as more neighbors come to our rescue with instructions, guidance, and support. I find our insurance information and make a phone call. As I hang up, my cell rings. I answer it without looking at the screen, thinking the adjuster forgot to tell me something.

"Hello?"

"Hi, Alejandra."

Tears prick the backs of my eyelids at the sound of Drew's solid and friendly voice. Which is silly. And confusing. "Hey, Drew." My voice is shaky.

From my spot at the living room window, I look around. Landon is here, at Gabby's side, helping her salvage whatever she can from her room. A van has arrived, and several people in matching monogrammed shirts pull large fans from the back of the vehicle. There's a bird in the tree outside the window, sitting on a small nest I hadn't noticed before. Keeping her eggs warm while my bare feet are freezing cold.

"I called to see if you're okay. I saw the photo of us with my grandmother got some media attention. I'm sorry about that. Usually, I fly under the radar."

I sniffle.

"Shit. I'm really sorry. Please don't—"

"It's not the picture," I say. "A pipe burst and our house just flooded."

He lets out a disheartened breath and curses. "You and

your sister are okay, though?"

"Yes."

"What's your address? I'm coming over."

I wipe at the corner of my eye. "You don't need to come over."

"Yes, I do. The address?" His tone leaves no room for argument so I give him the address.

A few minutes later I'm still standing at the window when Gabby wraps her arms around my shoulders from behind. I reach up and hold on to her forearm. "We can't stay in the house while all the cleanup and repairs happen," she says.

"I know."

"I'm going to go stay with Landon. You're welcome to stay there, too."

"Thanks, but I think I'll call Jane or Sutton." If Diego lived closer I'd stay with him.

"I understand." She sounds disappointed.

"It's only temporary," I say to make her feel better. To make me feel better, too. This has been our home for twenty years. The only one to hold all my memories. I don't remember Puerto Rico.

"I know. Will you call now? Landon needs to get going as soon as I'm done packing a few more things and I don't want to leave until I know where you'll be."

"Sure."

She kisses my cheek, says, "Thanks," and walks away.

I call Jane first. Her cousin is flying into town from Florida tomorrow—a surprise visit with no end date. Jane's apartment is really small so cramming three of us into her one-bedroom place is not going to work. She tells me I'm still welcome, but I tell her I'm going to call Sutton, so no worries. Jane would no doubt want me to share her room and give her cousin the couch, which would mean listening to her snore and getting no sleep and I need uninterrupted Zs or I'm very grouchy. (FYI, she gets very touchy when we tell her she snores and argues she does not.)

Sutton answers her phone on the second ring. "Hey, chica!" she says.

"Hey," I say in return and then tell her about the flood.

"I'm so sorry, Allie."

"Thanks. So, Gabby and I have to move out of the house for a little while and I was wondering if I could come stay with you?"

She sighs. "You know I'd have you stay with me in a heartbeat, but…"

"But?" My stomach drops. I thought for sure it wouldn't be a problem. I have nowhere else to go. The last thing I want is to stay with Landon.

"I got a kitten!" Sutton shouts. "She is the cutest thing ever and just sort of fell in my lap. I wasn't planning on getting a pet, but I walked by one of those adoption setups yesterday afternoon and she was the last one left and I couldn't resist."

"What's her name?" I ask.

"Fluffy," she says, and even though I can't see Sutton, I know she's making an apologetic face. Because Fluffy implies the kitten has lots of fur and I'm very allergic to cats.

"Well, I look forward to meeting her."

"Sorry."

"Don't be. I'll figure something out."

Sutton tells me a little more about Fluffy and then we hang up.

The hardwood floor is already buckling in several places as I walk through puddles to my bedroom. The cleanup and restoration crew the insurance company sent over is sweeping water out the front door, placing the large fans around the house, and taking assessment of structural damage.

Fortunately, the water barely reached inside my room so I pull my dry suitcase out of the closet, put it on the bed, and start filling it with clothes. My back is to the doorway when I feel a presence behind me. I can't explain how I know it's Drew and not any of the other half-dozen people in the house, but I do.

"Alejandra," he says.

I turn. "Hi." With all the wet ugly in the house, he is a gorgeous and welcome sight dressed in a charcoal button-down and black dress pants that he's rolled up to his knees. No socks. No shoes. I can't help it. I smile in appreciation at him. "Welcome to Flood Central."

His eyes drift over me, head to toe. I'm not sure if he's checking me out to check me out, or scanning my body for signs of injury. Maybe both. "One of the guys outside told me what happened."

"It's an old house. Some things are bound to break."

He moves closer, looking around the room. "What can I do to help?"

"Nothing, but it was nice of you to stop by."

"Oh, hey," Gabby says, coming to a halt inside my room, Landon beside her.

"Hi, Gabriela," Drew says before putting his hand out to Landon. "Hey, I'm Drew."

"Landon, Gabby's boyfriend."

Gabby looks up at Landon. "Would you mind running out to pick up the two plastic bins without me?"

Landon looks a little put out, but when Gabby adds, "Pleeease," he says he'll be right back. "Make it four," she calls after him. "In case you need one or two," she says to me.

"Thanks." I know why she sent her boyfriend away—she wants to find out why Drew is here and most likely meddle. She loves the idea of me finally dating again. She hasn't been Team Matthew for a while.

"Of course. So, Drew, what brings you by? I don't think you just happened to be in the neighborhood."

"No. I called to check in with Alejandra and she told me what had happened."

"And you immediately came over?" She moves her attention to me and her dark eyes say, *See, I told you he likes you.*

"I did."

"So what happened with Jane and Sutton?" she asks, clearly fighting an I'm-always-right grin.

"Jane's cousin is coming to visit for an unknown amount of time so that's not an option, and Sutton got a kitten yesterday."

"She did?" Gabby says excitedly then, "Shit. She did?"

she repeats much more downbeat.

"What's going on?" Drew asks.

"We need to move out of the house for a little while," Gabby says. "I'm going to Landon's, obviously, but Allie doesn't want to go there so she was hoping to stay with a friend."

"You could stay with me," he says without hesitation.

I laugh. *Yeah, right.*

Gabby bounces on her feet and says, "That's a great idea."

"No, it isn't," I say in all seriousness.

"Would you mind if I spoke to your sister alone?" Drew asks Gabby.

"Not at all." She spins around and disappears faster than I can blink, leaving me to fend for myself with Mr. Hotshot Hotelier. *Traitor.*

I sit on the side of my bed, next to my suitcase.

"I think I've proven to you I'm not a serial killer who chops up his victims and feeds them to the fish as bait," he says, drawing a tiny smile from me. "But this is a big deal, so..." He holds up a finger in the universal sign of *one minute*, and with his other hand pulls his phone from his pocket to make a call.

What is he doing?

He holds the phone in his palm so I can see the screen and puts the call on speaker. The name in the top left corner is G-ma.

"Hello, Drew," his grandma says.

"Hello, Grandmother. Quick question for you."

"I have a quick answer."

"I need a character reference. Can you give me one in, say, ten words or less?" He winks at me. Winks! And apparently winking does it for me because I have to press my lips together to keep a bigger smile from taking over my face.

"Of course I can." She clears her throat. "Drew is honorable, trustworthy, considerate, and he only wet the bed until he was seven."

I suck in my bottom lip while Drew closes his eyes and shakes his head.

"That was a little more than ten," Rosemary says.

"Yeah, thanks for that," Drew says amicably. Mostly. "Hanging up now. Goodbye."

"Bye, darling," she gets in before the line goes silent.

"That was—"

"We can't conclude on that note," Drew interrupts before I get a chance to comment on the glowing reference. He locates another number on his phone, presses the call button, and puts it on speaker as he takes a seat beside me on the bed.

"Hi, Drew," Chloe says. I know it's 'Chloe' because that was the name at the top of the screen while the phone rang.

"Hey, Chlo, how are you?"

"I'm great. Hey, did you see the picture Grandma Rosemary posted got picked up by *People*?"

"I did. Think you can post something else to take some of the heat off?"

"Only if you tell me who the mystery girl is and why I had to find out on social media that my brother-in-law is apparently off the market."

"Her name is Alejandra and it's an interesting story I promise to tell you when I see you next." Drew's gorgeous eyes, more blue than green at the moment, are steady on my dark brown ones.

"Okay. Consider the heat cooling."

"Thanks. You're the best. Think you can do me one more solid and while I've got you on speaker, sing some of my praises so my friend Alejandra knows what an upstanding guy I am?"

"Hi, Chloe," I say.

"Hi, Alejandra. Drew, you have a lot of explaining to do."

"I know, but we're in a bit of a hurry so…"

"Drew's intelligent, helpful, and unselfish," Chloe says with affection. "Dependable. He likes to tease, but deep down he's serious about most things. He loves his family and his work and he will never eat your last cookie. How's that?"

Drew raises his brows at me.

I nod. How can I argue? That he'd go to all this cute trouble to convince me to stay with him makes it hard to say no, but…

"Thanks, Chloe. I think that did the trick. Talk soon." He hangs up, happy lines creasing the corners of his eyes and mouth.

This is still a crazy idea. And very unsettling. It was one thing to look forward to a date with him. Quite another to live together, even temporarily.

My stomach tightens. I hadn't realized how much I was

looking forward to being with him until I said it to myself.

"I think I've more than proven myself now."

"Agreed, but staying with you is—"

"A great idea. I've got plenty of room. And besides that, it's the least I can do to say thanks for helping me out with my grandmother."

I'm about to ask if he's told her the truth, but then I realize it doesn't really matter because what started as a fib is the truth now. At least most of it.

I take a minute to think about his offer. He probably has a house so big we'll be lucky if we run into each other. And just like that, my apprehension disappears. We won't be in close proximity, just under the same roof. That's doable. And selfishly, it means I don't have to stay at Landon's.

"You saved me from my grandmother's matchmaking and that's a huge deal," he adds. "One day I'll tell you about the woman she wanted me to bring to her party." He shudders. "And you're saving me from women who see me as a meal ticket rather than a guy to share a meal with."

"That's awful."

"Believe it or not, I was about to take a break from dating before running into you again."

"Really?" My stomach flutters at the idea he broke his pledge because of me. Because I mean more than just a quick hookup.

He shifts at the foot of the bed and our knees brush. "Yep. So, you see, you're doing me some serious goodwill agreeing to go to my grandmother's party with me. Not to mention agreeing to a date before then, and giving you a place to stay would make me really happy."

I want Drew to be happy. And sharing meals with him beyond our two planned dates would be no hardship. "Okay. I'll stay with you. Thank you. Wait. You don't have a cat do you? I'm super allergic."

"No cat." He stands. "Now let's get you packed."

Chapter Six
Close Quarters

Drew

I WAVE MY arm out the car window, motioning to Alejandra to park her car in the spot beside mine before I hop out of my BMW while she pulls her MINI Cooper in, turns off the engine, and exits the vehicle with confusion on her face. We're in the small underground parking lot of the hotel that's reserved for upper management, so her uncertainty is justified. I probably should have told her I'm living here while my house is being remodeled, but I didn't want her to say no to staying with me. A house speaks *friend helping out another friend*. A hotel room speaks *let's get into some sexy mischief together*.

For the record, I'm all for the latter.

Not that I'll tell her that.

She stressed taking it slow and it's finally penetrated my thick skull. On the drive here I told myself to chill with any romantic ideas. I'm just so unused to the slow lane that I feel like I'm flying by the seat of my pants when it comes to this gorgeous woman.

"What are we doing here?" she asks, surprised.

"This is where I live—at least temporarily. My house is under renovation for the foreseeable future."

"Drew."

"Alejandra."

"I can't stay in a hotel room with you."

"It's a suite. So you can. And you will." I open her passenger-side door to grab one of her bags.

She hip-checks me, knocking me off-balance, and almost catches my arm in the door when she slams it shut. For someone several inches shorter and dozens of pounds lighter, she packs some serious power.

"Hang on just a second," she asserts. "You have to admit, this was a sneaky thing to do."

"I don't know if I'd go that far. You didn't ask where I lived, and I just kept my current address to myself."

She grumbles something under her breath in Spanish and starts to round the back of her car. I gently grab her wrist to stop her.

"Wait," I say. "I'm sorry. I didn't mean to sound like a jerk. I honestly didn't think this was that big of a deal."

"Well, it is. This is your hotel, Drew. Not your home. People are going to see me coming and going all the time."

"Only if you want them to."

"What does that mean?"

"Private elevator." I nod toward the steel doors that leads straight to the penthouse. On the other side of the small parking garage is the communal lift.

Some of her anger visibly deflates. "This is too much."

"It's not. Not for you. And I'd offer you your own room

if it made you more comfortable, but we're currently sold out."

"Are you like this with everyone?" She crosses her arms over her chest.

No. Yes. I don't bloody know. What I do know is I like being around her and I'll do whatever it takes to keep her close. My watch beeps with a reminder that I've got a meeting in—I glance at the time—thirty minutes. Alejandra raises her eyebrows. "I'm meeting with my marketing team in half an hour. How about you come upstairs and if you hate it, you can come right back down and make other arrangements?"

She thinks about it before finally saying, "Okay."

We walk to the elevator and I press in the key code. "Zero-seven-one-two," I tell her. The doors immediately slide open, and I follow her fruity vanilla scent—I think it's her shampoo—inside. "Very few people know that code, by the way, so if you're making a mental list of pros and cons, count safety in the pro column."

"Noted."

I press the button labeled PH, and up we go. The hotel is only six stories so it takes but a second for us to reach our destination. "That elevator," I say nodding to our left as we step into a small foyer, "leads downstairs to the lobby. It's the same code we just used to come up. No codes are required to go down. And this door here—" I nod to our right "—leads to our temporary home."

"How long have you been staying here?" she asks.

"Couple of months." I open the door, motioning for her

to enter the large open space first. I've been in and around hotels my entire life. My family owns four hundred and seventy-six hotels in eighty countries and territories across five continents. For as long as I can remember, I've wanted to be part of the family business. Before I could even write, I'd follow my dad around our different properties with a clipboard in my hands and pretend to take notes. I'd greet guests in the lobby. Sit atop the concierge desk and tell anyone walking by about the best things to do (eat chocolate chip ice cream topped the list). Auprince Holdings is in my blood and in my heart and I'm grateful I get to do something I love.

So, it's always a rush when I watch someone else step into my world with fresh eyes.

"Wow," Alejandra says, "this is beautiful."

"Thanks. We designed it to feel like home at the beach. All the rooms on the property are this way, actually."

She takes in the polished dark wood floor, white shutters, overstuffed beige couches with navy striped pillows, cream-colored walls, and large potted trees in the corners with appreciative, almost dreamlike scrutiny. I smile to myself. She wanted to hate my current place of residence, but she doesn't.

"Mission accomplished," she says.

"So, you're staying?"

"Yes," she says without looking at me. Instead she walks toward the floor-to-ceiling window that takes up one whole wall with views of the beach. The sun hasn't broken through the clouds yet, but the picturesque coastline is still killer.

I try hard not to stare at her ass in her cut-off shorts and fail miserably. Shit. How am I going to keep my eyes off her? My hands? Shacking up together was not my smartest idea. I mean, what if she walks around in a towel? Or sleeps in next to nothing? *Drew, you are a glutton for punishment, man.*

She looks over her shoulder at me. I quickly lift my gaze to hers. "Thank you," she says. The soft, sincere acknowledgment lands directly in the center of my chest, and I vow to keep my dirty thoughts to myself and take this at her pace.

"You're welcome." I move in her direction. "So, quick tour before I head to my meeting. This is the kitchen, obviously." I gesture to my right and the full kitchen with top-of-the-line appliances that I've yet to use. "Dining room." I gesture to my left and the rectangular driftwood table that seats eight. "Sitting room." I put my hand on the back of the couch.

"This hallway leads to the master bedroom and bath." She follows me to my room. The penthouse is a corner unit and the master's full-length windows take up two walls. The toilet and shower have their own enclosure. A giant sunken tub sits off to the side of the room. Before I let my mind wander to naked bath time with Alejandra, I steer her back into the hallway and the common area. "This way leads to your room." We round the dining table and walk down the second hallway, circling the suite rather than going across it.

"You have a full bathroom here." I flick on the light so she can take a peek. "And your bedroom is here." I step through a separate doorway to show her a large room with a king bed, comfortable sitting area, workspace, and one floor-to-ceiling window. Our rooms share a wall.

"This is beyond generous. Thank you, again."

"No problem." We walk back toward the main living area. "There's also a small laundry room off the kitchen. And speaking of the kitchen, feel free to use it as much as you want."

"I will."

"You like to cook?" I lean against the side of the tiled counter. Cooking is not my thing. At all. My brother Ethan gives me shit when I show up at his house on Saturday mornings for a home-cooked breakfast, but what neither of my brothers know is I had a kitchen disaster that scarred me for life. Don't laugh. I was seven and decided to make myself a milkshake. I put vanilla ice cream, caramel syrup, Oreo cookies and chocolate chips into a blender and pushed the button. *Before* I remembered to put the lid on. It was an explosion of epic proportions. Worse than the mess to the kitchen, though, was getting sprayed in the face. Ice cream went up my nose. Chocolate got into my eyes. I couldn't see, panicked, fell off the chair I was standing on, and hit my head on the counter behind me. Had a bump the size of a golf ball.

Since that day, I don't think I've touched an electric appliance.

The fiasco is a legit reason to never cook again.

"I don't hate it," Alejandra says. "But I do it more out of necessity than anything else."

"I get it." I glance at my watch. "I do need to get going. Would you like some help getting your bags out of the car? I can send someone up."

"No. I'm good."

"Okay. See you later, then."

"See you later."

I take the lobby elevator downstairs to the conference room. My hotel manager, Chin, marketing and publicity manager, Luna, a couple of reps from the PR agency Luna hired, and our event-slash-social planner, Jax, are already waiting for me when I take a seat at the table.

"Hello, everyone. Thanks for meeting this morning."

After exchanging pleasantries, we get right down to business. Our goal is straightforward, but not easy: develop a strategy to win next year's Best on The Beach award in Condé Nast's Best of the Best Hotel Awards. I want The Surfeit to be *the* destination for influencers, vloggers, and those seeking an upscale, yet relaxed vibe. To that end, we talk at length about working themed social hours into our Friday pool parties starting next week.

Customer service goes without saying, but it can never be emphasized enough so we identify our core strengths and weaknesses next. "Our digital presence is strong," I say, "but face-to-face communication with every single guest is what's going to help set us apart."

"An enhanced personal connection," Luna says.

I nod. "Exactly. Warm welcomes, attention to details, addressing requests quickly, and making guests feel like they're staying in their dream home. That kind of hospitality will remain with them long after they've left."

Further discussion takes place well past one o'clock so I

have lunch delivered. We take a twenty-minute break to eat and shoot the shit. I wonder what Alejandra is doing. If she's eaten lunch. I swivel my chair so my back is to the table and text her. *How's it going?*

Good. I'm at work so can't really talk. Is everything okay?

Fine. Just wanted to be sure you got settled okay.

I did. The three little dots wave across my phone screen. Stop. Wave. Stop. Wave. For someone busy at work she sure is taking her time texting me. Maybe I confuse her as much as she confuses me.

I'm not sure what protocol is, but with my sister I always told her when I'd be home, so I'll be home around nine tonight.

Could there be a more polite, courteous, respectful woman who sets my blood on fire? I don't think so. I reach for my water glass and down it, cooling my jets so I don't text back something like, *Protocol is you naked in my bed with my face buried between your legs.* Instead I text, *Thanks for letting me know.*

Before I can put my phone down to resume the meeting, another text arrives, this one from my brother Ethan. It's a picture of Rylee standing in front of a monkey exhibit at a zoo. The accompanying message goes like this... *Rylee says, and I quote: "Will you take my picture and send it to Drew and tell him he's a monkey butt?" <insert 5yo cackling>*

The kid is damn cute and wicked smart for her age.

Tell her thank you and the tickle monster will be waiting for her when she gets home. My brother, his girlfriend—Pascale—and her daughter Rylee are driving across the country on a month-long road trip. Rylee's favorite wild animal is a monkey and I may have called her a 'monkey butt' a time or two. She loves the different nicknames I throw at her.

I slip my phone into my pants pocket and ask if everyone is ready to restart the meeting. They are.

Luna offers up information on the trends in the marketplace and statistics on our guests. She cites the hotel's revenues and what's working and what isn't. As she speaks, I stand and pace around the table, trying to focus on her report, not thoughts of Alejandra or how much I want with her what my brother has with his girlfriend. Jax chimes in next with the schedule for upcoming weddings and other events, keeping in mind our brand and upmarket reputation.

My team is kickass and I tell them so before sitting back down and saying, "Before our next meeting, let's each brainstorm ways to take our customer's experience to the next level. Is there an unexpected touch or amenity not being offered by our competitors? Something no one else has done?"

"Summer is about sustenance of the body, heart, and mind in glorious SoCal and there's no better place than The Surfeit for fun in the sun," Luna says.

"You've been mentally working on that the whole meeting haven't you?" I tease.

"Maybe," she answers.

With that, I adjourn the meeting. Chin stays behind to go over some operational matters with me. "By the way," he says when we're finished. "Thanks again for the tickets to the Landsharks game. We had a great time and my son can't stop talking about Finn."

"You're welcome. I'm glad you guys enjoyed it." My

brother Finn is the best player in Major League Baseball this season (not for the first time). He's on fire, his stats confirming that even coming back from an injury, he's one of the most talented athletes to ever play the game.

Chin leaves me alone in the room, my thoughts going to my place in my chosen field. I lace my fingers behind my head as I lean back in my chair. *Positive mind. Positive vibes.* The poolside DJ and social hours are new, and maybe a little risky, but I've never played it safe in business. With white-sand beaches steps away and the glitz and glamour of Los Angeles a short car drive in the other direction, we're primed for prominence even though I feel like there's still something missing from creating an overall "wow" factor.

"Hey, Chin said I could find you here."

"Hey," I say turning to my best friend, West. "Did I forget we had something on the calendar today?"

He takes a seat at the table. "No, I was just in the area so I thought I'd stop by." West is dressed in his usual business best. Dark suit, white shirt, paisley silk tie.

"Scouting another piece of property?"

"Always. This one looks to be a done deal, I hope. I need it. Am excited about it." He smooths his tie down. His success with buying and selling buildings is exceptional. "How goes the hotel biz today?"

"Can't complain."

"Did you get the invite to Justin's party?" Justin is a friend from college and he just bought a boat. He's christening it with a get-together next weekend.

"Yeah. You going?"

"I'm going. And you're going. I'll find us a couple of dates to bring along."

"I don't need a date," I say. The only person I want to take anywhere is Alejandra. Will she agree to be my plus-one? I don't know. I rub a hand over my jaw. Two dates sandwiched around breakfast with my grandmother isn't exactly slow.

"Because…" West draws out the word, confusion creasing his forehead.

"Funny story." I haven't talked to him since getting reacquainted with Alejandra. "Remember the woman who left me at the bar at Swig?" I grumbled about it for weeks so I'm sure he does.

"Your Zoe Saldana look-alike? Of course I do. You cried like a baby for weeks afterward."

"I didn't fucking cry."

"Whined then," he says with levity.

"I ran into her again."

"No shit."

I tell him about finding her in the lobby and introducing her to my grandmother. I tell him I saw her later that night and that I like her.

"So what? You two are dating now?"

"Actually, we're doing more than that. She's staying with me for a while." I fill him in on the flood at her house.

"Are you out of your fucking mind?" he says with a mix of compassion and disapproval.

"No," I respond a little on the defensive.

He raises his eyebrows. "You are shit at reading people,

Drew. How do you know this girl isn't using you? It was one thing to take her home for a night. It's something entirely different to have her stay with you."

My ex, Miranda, makes an appearance in my mind. West is right. Even after what Miranda did to me, I do often give people the benefit of the doubt. I don't get any negative vibes from Alejandra, though.

"I don't care what you're thinking right now," West says. "You need to be careful."

"She's different," I say. "I had to practically beg her to stay with me."

"So she's beautiful *and* smart." His skeptical tone negates the compliment. "Look, just do me a favor and keep your wits about you."

"I will."

"Good." He studies me. Ten years of friendship has taught him a lot about my demeanor. "You really think she's genuine?"

"Yes."

"Then I hope you're right," he says, letting it go as we move on to the topic of work.

We talk sports and politics, too, and through the entire conversation there's a part of my brain that clings to thoughts of Alejandra. She's unknowingly become my favorite subject.

I bury the doubt West planted in the back of my mind. I'm not wrong about her. I can't be.

Chapter Seven
Getting to Know You

Alejandra

I WRAP MY yellow scarf around my neck. It isn't scarf weather, and my first attempt at knitting isn't anything to brag about, but that's okay, I'm wearing it anyway. I coat my lips with pink gloss next. Smile at my reflection in the bathroom mirror. "You've got this," I say to myself.

I grab my purse off the counter and before I talk myself out of it, stride toward the hotel room door. I'm about to open it when it swings wide, almost catching me in the forehead.

"Sorry!" Drew rushes to say as he steps into the suite. "I didn't mean to barge in. I thought you were working late tonight?"

"I was supposed to meet with our executive director to work on a grant application, but her son came down with a fever and she wanted to get home to him."

"I didn't realize the senior center relied on grants to maintain operation."

"It's one resource, yes. Most centers have to rely on two to six different funding sources. We've typically done well with state and local government funds, bequests, in-kind donations, and participant contributions, but this year is different."

"How come?"

"We have a balloon payment due."

He nods in understanding. "Let me know if there's anything I can do to help."

"Thanks." I have no intention of asking him for help. Not yet, anyway. He's been more than generous already, giving me a place to stay, and we still don't know each other that well. It would be rude of me to hit him up for a donation right now. I'm worried about the senior center, but it's my problem, not his.

"You off somewhere?" he asks.

"Dinner and a movie."

"Meeting your sister?"

"No. I'm going by myself."

"Great. I'll join you."

"That's okay, I'm good."

He looks at me quizzically, like he's not used to being told no. "No one ever turns you down, do they?" I ask.

"No."

"Well, I've got a list of things to do and try by myself." I take a seat at the dining room table, almost sitting on the book I forgot I left on the chair. Drew watches me place the paperback beside my current read on top of the table. After my breakup with Matthew, I decided it was past time I did more things on my own. I've prided myself on being independent, but I realized he was always there to lend a hand or accompany me somewhere. For the past several months I've been getting to know *me* better, discovering what I'm capable of, and it feels good.

Drew sits down, loosens his tie and the collar of his dress shirt. "Why alone?" he asks without judgment.

My eyes are drawn to his hand at his neck, working the material of his clothing with dexterity that makes me wonder what else his hands are good at. I lift my gaze to find him staring at me with unmistakable interest.

"Why not?" I question back, curious how he'll answer.

"It just seems out of character for you. From what I've seen, you have a connection to people. You certainly drew me in."

I swallow hard at his unexpected compliment and rearrange my scarf to give myself something to do. He's certainly captured my interest as well. "I guess this is out of character, but that's the point. Pushing myself out of my comfort zone."

"Is it a long list?"

"Kind of? It's all up here." I point to the side of my head. "And I add and remove things all the time depending on my mood. I've taken a dance class. Refurbished an old piece of furniture. Traveled solo to visit a friend in San Francisco. Hopped on a scooter with no destination in mind. Made this." I touch the end of my scarf. "Stuff like that."

"Well, then, I hope you enjoy your dinner and movie."

"Have you ever done either by yourself?"

"Dinner alone, yes. Movie, no. But then I don't get to the movies very often."

"Was it weird sitting at a table by yourself?" Eating alone feels harder than the other things I've accomplished.

He gets a faraway look in his eyes. "Actually, I wasn't alone for long." Of course he wasn't. "But I didn't set out to have company. Does it still count?"

"I think any amount of time alone counts." I stand. "I should get going. I'll see you later."

"Have fun."

"Thanks. I will." As the hotel room door clicks shut behind me, I decide tonight will be a fun night despite my hesitation. Attitude is everything, right?

A good thing, because dinner is a disaster and the movie is lighthearted and enjoyable until the hero dies at the end! Whoever in Hollywood thought that was a good idea was way off the mark. I'm still not over it as I park my car next to Drew's in the underground parking structure.

I press in the code for the elevator and the doors open. It's still surreal taking the private lift to the penthouse suite. If not for the unusual situation I'm in with Drew, I could never afford to stay in a hotel like this. His generosity is above and beyond and somehow I'll figure out a way to repay him. When I get to our room, I open the door slowly so as not to wake him if he's already asleep. Not that he'd hear me if I was loud since the suite is bigger than my entire house.

My house. I miss it. And I'm worried about it since there is a lot to repair. All the flooring has to be pulled up and replaced. The baseboards, too. Everything in the bathroom is being ripped out. New drywall is necessary in some places.

New paint. New fixtures. Thankfully, Gabby doesn't start her film job until the end of the summer so she's picking everything out that we need. She enjoys designing much more than I do, and more importantly she's excellent at bossing people around. We've been told renovations will take several weeks.

"Hey, how was it?" Drew asks, bringing my attention back to right now. He's sitting in the dark on the couch watching television.

I think he waited up for me.

Santo moly.

It's been almost a year since I've felt this kind of protectiveness. *Don't give it too much consideration, Alejandra. You don't know if he actually waited for you.*

I round the couch and plop down on the adjacent love seat. Once again, I have to move a book from underneath my butt. I put it on the driftwood coffee table. "It was terrible."

He flashes me his matchless smile, lit by the glow from the TV, but then he catches himself, my solemn opinion registering, and he drops the happy expression. He changes position so his body faces mine. He's still in his classic dress pants and his dress shirt is loose and rolled up at the sleeves. "Tell me about it," he says.

So, I do. I slip off my scarf, slide off my shoes and relax. He's easy to talk to and it feels like I've known him for years rather than months.

"I was in the mood for a meatball sandwich so I went to this little Italian place off Fifth Street that recently opened. It was crowded, but I snagged the last table by the window."

"Sounds awful so far," he teases.

"I'm getting to that part. My waiter turned out to be one of Landon's friends. He's an aspiring actor and flirt, and he likes to talk a lot. So, he's telling me about his latest audition when a girl storms into the restaurant, walks straight up to him, and throws her iced coffee in his face. He shouts, 'What the fuck?' She yells something about finding out he can't keep it in his pants, and then she looks at me and says, 'Is this the bitch you've been cheating on me with?'

"I'm still wiping off the coffee that splashed in *my* face when I look up. The girl is glaring daggers at me and what does the apparent cheater do? He says, 'What does it matter if she is?' So I tell her, 'No! He's only my waiter.' She's thankfully satisfied with that, and then she knees him in the balls and walks out. He bowls over in pain before turning to go place my order and clean himself up."

"Wow."

"Right?"

"How was the meatball sandwich?"

"Promise not to laugh?"

"Promise."

"There was a hair in it," I say with a straight face.

He keeps his expression blank too, until he can't hold it any longer and cracks up. It is pretty funny. *Now.* Telling him the whole story and hearing him laugh is exactly what I needed. I join in the laughter.

"Please tell me the movie was better," he says once we've quieted.

"Nope. I thought it was a romance and then the hero died near the end."

"Damn. Well, the good news is you can officially cross it off your list." He sounds proud of me, which is another unfamiliar gift as of late, and the awful parts of my evening are forgotten. This, right here, is what I'll remember.

"True." I look more closely at the television screen for the first time since I sat down. A baseball game is playing, the volume barely audible. "Who's winning?"

Drew goes back to watching the screen. "The Land-sharks. Eight to two. Finn hit a three-run homer in the fifth."

"That means there were two players already on base, right?" I move to the other couch so I can watch without craning my neck. I keep a respectable distance between us as I get comfortable with my legs crossed in my lap.

He gives me a quick side look. "Right."

"Do you watch all of your brother's games?"

"I try to." He shifts, putting his feet on the coffee table and settling deeper into the very comfortable couch cushions.

"Did you play growing up?" I ask.

"I did. Started when I was five and played through high school. I so badly wanted to be as good as Finn, but I didn't come even close. It was awesome watching him stand out and get scouted, though. And I played the younger brother card countless times to up my cool factor."

"*What?* You weren't cool as a kid? I find that hard to believe."

"Believe it. I was a total nerd. Wore ties and preppy sweaters to school. Talked business like I understood it. Which I did for the most part, but no one else cared. I was also small. Didn't have a growth spurt until my freshman year of college."

"So, no high school sweetheart?" I ask lightly. I bet there were still plenty of girls interested in him.

"Not a one. I made up for it later, though," he says with a cheeky grin. "What about you?"

"Matthew was my high school sweetheart."

"Oh. Okay. How long were you two together, then?"

"Seven years. We broke up amicably almost a year ago because he took a job in New Zealand."

A pained expression comes over Drew's face, but it vanishes quickly, leaving me to wonder if I imagined it. "I understand the complication a little better now."

"There's a little more to it." I bring my leg up and wrap my arms around my knee. "He's coming back. Next month."

Drew's jaw visibly clenches. "What does that mean?"

"Honestly, I don't know."

He considers my words, never breaking eye contact. I wish I could read his mind. I wish he could read mine and help me sort through my jumbled feelings.

"And Gabriela? She's older, right?" he asks, returning to the safer topic of family. I'm relieved, but also oddly not.

"We're twins, actually. Although, you're right. She is older by a couple of minutes. Which she loves to lord over my head."

He's quiet for a minute then, "Do you have any other

family nearby?"

"Our older brother, Diego, lives in Orange County. He's a teacher and overall great human being. Our parents died in a hurricane in Puerto Rico. Gabby and I were five. Diego was ten. We came to California immediately after that to live with our grandparents. They raised us and you already know they passed away. We don't have any other family."

"That's rough. I'm sorry. Do you remember much about your parents?" His soft, compassionate tone is potent. Maybe even more than the sexy, confident voice that filled my stomach with butterflies the first time I heard it in a crowded bar.

"Not very much, no. I remember my mom brushing my hair and reading to me, and my dad running beside me while I rode a red tricycle. I remember my parents' unending affection for each other." I look out the floor-to-ceiling window, into the darkness, grasping at the edge of another memory. "And my dad bringing my mom flor de maga all the time."

"Flor de maga?" Drew asks. He's completely ignored the baseball game playing on the television and listened attentively to me.

"It's Puerto Rico's national flower. It looks similar to a hibiscus. I think it must have been my mom's favorite."

"Those are good memories to have."

"They are," I agree.

"I know it can't really compare to losing a parent, but my grandfather passed away when I was young."

"I'm sorry. Was this Rosemary's husband?"

"Yes. He went into cardiac arrest and was pronounced dead at the scene."

"That's awful. Although in some ways, I think losing someone quickly is easier than watching them suffer through a long illness."

"I think so, too," he says and a bond of understanding connects us further.

By silent agreement we resume watching the game. The timing is perfect—it's the top of the ninth and Finn is at bat. Drew puts his feet on the floor and his elbows on his knees, leaning a little closer to the television, like maybe his proximity will help his brother in some way. "Come on, Finney," he says.

The first pitch is a ball. The second a strike. Ball. Strike. Ball. "Full count," Drew tells me, tension rolling off him. It's cute, how into the game he is. Finn swings on the next pitch, makes contact, but it flies foul. This happens two more times before he strikes out. "Damn it," Drew breathes out, falling back against the couch in defeat. He's obviously a huge fan of his brother's.

"It was a good at bat," I offer, drawing a smile from my couch mate.

"You're right, Al. It was."

Al? No one ever really calls me that. Not that I mind. I like it. I look away to settle down my wild thoughts. Nicknames are not a big deal.

"I meant to ask you what else is on your list." He twists, slipping one leg under the other and resting his arm along the top of the couch. His fingers almost reach my shoulder.

"If you don't mind me knowing."

I turn, too, but casually scoot away until my back hits the arm of the couch. It gives me a few more inches between us. "I don't mind. Let's see... Train for a half marathon."

"Only a half?"

"Yes, I hate running."

He laughs. "Then why do it?"

"To prove to myself I can, and keep my heart healthy."

"Good reasons. What else?"

"Read a book a week." I cover a yawn with the back of my hand.

"I'd say you're accomplishing that one." He glances at the books on the coffee table.

"Yeah, sorry about that. I have this habit of leaving books around. That way I always have one handy. And they bring me comfort."

He sits a little taller. "You're not comfortable here?"

"Oh, no. I am. It just feels even more like home now."

The room is dark, the glow from the TV the only light, but I think his eyes are sparkling. He likes that answer. "Sleep under the stars is also on the list. And teach myself an instrument."

"What instrument?"

"I'm not sure yet."

"Tent or no tent for sleeping under the stars?"

"No tent. I don't want anything blocking my view of the sky. I want it to be just me, a pillow, a blanket or sleeping bag, and a thermos of hot chocolate."

"You've put a lot of thought into this."

"That's me. Always thinking before I do something. So, that's on my list, too."

"Thinking?" he teases. He looks right into my eyes when he talks to me and it makes me feel important. All of a sudden I'm not the least bit tired and wouldn't mind staying up all night learning things about each other.

"Ha-ha. What I mean is, I want to jump into things with both feet more often. Have adventures and do things outside my comfort zone, maybe even something dangerous." I tilt my head and keep my eyes locked on his.

"You're talking an activity like bungee jumping?"

"Maybe." No chance in hell, but I like to think I'd be badass enough to do it.

"Do not tell my grandmother about this. She's been begging me to jump with her for her birthday. Ethan's jumped a time or two already so has passed. Finn is contractually prohibited from doing anything that puts his health in possible danger. And so that leaves me. And while I might be persuaded, it freaks me out thinking about my grandma doing it. She's too fragile. She might break a rib midair or something, I don't know."

That Drew is protective of his grandmother makes my heart swell.

"Are you sure she isn't teasing you?"

"I'm positive. She's having a late-life crisis or something. Last Thanksgiving, she took surfing lessons. Last month she went indoor go-karting. I admit she's in great physical and mental health for her age, but now is not the time to start pushing her limits."

"It's a good problem to have," I say.

A flash of guilt spoils his easygoing features. "I didn't mean to make you feel—"

"You didn't. I'm around seniors all day, Drew. They're my favorite age group. Your grandma seems like a firecracker and you're lucky she's not shying away from life. I hope there's some Rosemary in me when I'm her age."

His lips quirk. "I hope..." He trails off. "I'm sure you will. You are the woman who just had a date night with herself and survived it."

I press my shoulders back. "That's true."

His eyes dip to my chest. My white zebra-print off-the-shoulder blouse is loose so he can't see the effect his quick look has on my nipples.

"What about you?" I ask, drawing his gaze back up to mine. "Do you have any kind of list?"

"Right now I'd say it's all about the hotel. Sold-out rooms aren't enough to give me the reputation I want."

"Did you always want to be involved in the family business?"

"I did, yeah. I admire my dad more than anyone else. And I want to make him proud."

"I think you've probably already accomplished that. Besides The Surfeit, do you have a favorite hotel?"

He runs his hand along his jaw. "That's a tough question. Our property in Maui is pretty special because we gather there as a family every Thanksgiving."

Drew's phone, sitting faceup on the coffee table, trills and lights up with a text message. We both zero in on the device. A split second later, I wish I hadn't looked. The name on the screen clearly reads Dahlia. There's only one reason a woman would be texting him at ten o'clock at night.

"I'll let you take that," I say, putting my feet on the floor to stand.

"Wait. It's not what you think."

I give him a look.

"Okay, it is what you think, but I haven't seen her in a while and have no plans or desire to see her tonight." He flips the phone over rather than respond to the message.

"It's fine with me if you want to text her back," I lie.

"It's not fine," he argues. "I don't date—or see—more than one woman at a time. What kind of guy do you think I am?"

"I'm sorry. I didn't mean to insult you. I just thought…"

"You thought…?"

I blow a piece of hair off my face. "I don't know what I thought, but I don't want to tie your hands behind your back because I'm staying with you."

"Is that an option? Because I'm all for tying each other up," he fires back.

A hot and heavy sensation flares between my legs at his teasing words. My breasts tingle. I nibble my bottom lip while I try to think of a flirty comeback.

He saves me with: "I know you're out of practice, Al, so I'll spell it out for you. I'm a monogamous dater, and I'd venture you are, too."

I nod. "Yes."

"Good. So that means while we're dating, there will be

no seeing other people. You and I are going to have some fun. No stress. No doubts. And if something you're not sure about comes up, we'll talk about it. Deal?"

"Deal," I say, wondering how I got so lucky to meet this man.

"Let's shake on it." He extends his hand. I take it.

And even though we've touched before, this time is different, and his warm, masculine hand gives rise to sparks on my skin that thrill and scare me at the same time.

Chapter Eight
First Date

Alejandra

I HAVE NOTHING to wear.

Okay, not *nothing*.

But you know what I mean.

I stare at the pile of clothes on the bed—everything I brought with me from home—like maybe something new will magically appear, but of course it doesn't. Jeans and a cute top, or a dress? That's my dilemma since Drew didn't tell me where we were going for our date tonight. I deliberate for another minute before searching for the outfit I put on fifteen minutes ago: my lavender floral-print button-up mini dress. Finding it, I slip the soft cotton over my head and smooth it down before looking at myself in the mirror above the hotel dresser. With a V-neck and cap sleeves, it's sexy, but conservative. A good-enough first-date dress.

I'm going on a first date.

For the first time ever.

Matthew and I were friends before we became a couple and our relationship grew gradually from hanging out with friends to hanging out just the two of us at each other's houses. I can't pinpoint an actual first date that signified our togetherness. More like we just naturally settled into being boyfriend and girlfriend. We chose our anniversary date as the day we said "I love you" for the first time. Matthew took me out plenty of times after that, to restaurants and movies and concerts. But I've never had the experience of first-date jitters like I do now.

My hands shake as I put on my heels.

I've wrestled with my feelings all day, confused over how I can feel both guilty *and* excited. I can't deny I'm attracted to Drew and want to spend more time with him. But am I being fair to either of us when I don't know what's going to happen when I see Matthew again? Until I reconnected with Drew, I knew what I hoped would happen: that there would still be a spark between us and we'd resume our relationship and live happily ever after. My parents and grandparents married their first loves and that had always been my goal, too.

Goals change, Alejandra.

People change.

I push all thoughts of Matthew out of my head when I notice the bedside clock reads 8:29. Drew made our date for eight thirty, so I better get a move on. I grab my purse, make a quick stop in the bathroom to brush my teeth, then walk down the short hallway to the main living area.

The suite is quiet, the only light in the darkening room coming from the lamp next to the couch. "Drew?" I call out. No answer. And no noise coming from his bedroom. Did he forget? Get tied up with work? My heart sinks at both possibilities.

A knock on the door startles me.

Grateful for the distraction, I quickly answer it and find my date looking just as handsome as he did when he left this morning, with a bouquet of sunflowers in his hand. "Hi," he says.

"Hi. What are you doing out there?" I ask.

"Picking you up for our date. These are for you." He hands me the flowers. "I didn't know what your favorite was, but these made me think of you."

My cheeks heat at his sweet words and formality. "Thank you. Do I have time to put them in water?"

"Sure." He waits at the door while I move to the kitchen.

"Drew. Please come in," I say over my shoulder.

"You look beautiful," he says stepping behind me and reaching over my head to pull a pilsner-type glass off the top shelf of the cupboard and handing it to me. There's no vase that I can see.

"Thanks. You do, too. I mean…you know what I mean."

"Don't be nervous," he whispers in my ear, his warm breath heating up the side of my neck. *I am so nervous.*

I place the flowers in water, taking a moment to arrange them while I compose myself. "Ranunculus," I say.

"Ra-what?"

"Ranunculus. They're my favorite flower. But I love these, too."

"Good to know. You ready to go?"

I nod and he leads me to the elevator, his hand on the small of my back.

We reach the parking garage and he opens the passenger-side door of his car for me. Out of the corner of my eye, I catch him looking at my legs as I tuck myself into the comfortable leather seat. His notice puts flutters in the pit of my stomach. I'm really glad I decided to go with a dress.

"Where are we going?" I ask once we've pulled onto the road.

"It's a surprise."

Twenty-five minutes later we pull up to a building in downtown Los Angeles with a blue neon sign that reads *Library Bar.*

Turns out it's a scholastically themed hangout that is so cool I can't stop smiling. "Drew, this is fantastic."

The vibe is upscale with shuttered windows, wood-paneled floors and ceilings, and exposed brick walls. One entire wall is lined with vintage books!

"I thought for a girl who loves to read, this was a place you should see." He takes my hand and leads me through the main room, past a striking marble bar, to a smaller lounge-like area. We sit side by side on a leather couch next to a candle-filled fireplace and the wall filled with the weathered tomes that remind me of what an English library might have looked like in the past.

"I love it," I say as I look around. We're the only ones seated in this area. The rest of the place is standing room only, so I'm guessing Drew arranged for a bit of privacy for the two of us.

A man greets Drew with familiarity before handing us menus. "Enjoy your evening," he says.

I give the man a smile then look at the menu. The super fun and unique menu. "I think I need to take this home with me," I say excitedly as I pore over every word. At the top of the page it reads "The Hunger Games" then small plates are listed under "Prologue" and larger plates are listed under "Novels." At the bottom are three different kinds of french fries listed under "Excerpts." "That would be okay, right?"

Drew nods with a wide smile. "I'm happy I can already count tonight as a win." He leans back against the couch, not bothering with the menu. Instead his eyes are on me.

I beam at him. "Absolutely."

Drew

GOD, SHE'S GORGEOUS. Candlelight from the fireplace bathes her in an amber glow. Her dark hair falls in loose waves down her back. Her bare legs are crossed at the ankles and I want to put my hand on her thigh and move my palm smoothly under the skirt of her dress more than I want my next breath, but I won't. Whatever happens between us has got to be initiated by her.

Not that I don't plan to help influence her decision-making. I'm the man here with her right now, and while I've got her to myself, I'm going to do everything I can to make her happy. To make her see the connection we have is worth committing to. Since she told me about her ex, I feel like I'm competing with someone who can't defend himself, but then I remind myself he got seven years with her. Seven years of memories and experiences and nights in bed, and I don't care that he's on the other side of the world. His loss is my gain. I only hope Alejandra isn't still hung up on him. I mean, if she was, she wouldn't be here with me, would she?

"What looks good?" I ask. "My friend reserved us this prime spot to sit, but I need to walk over to the bar to order our food and drinks."

"We definitely need some fries," she says, looking over the menu with rapt attention. "I don't mind which kind, they all look good. Do you want to share things or get our own?"

"How about we share?" I can tell she'd like that.

"Okay! The shrimp and bacon skewers look yummy. And I'd love to try the crispy calamari. The grilled cheese looks good, too. Oh, and the charred brussels sprouts." She turns to look at me. "Is that too much? I forgot to eat lunch today."

"It's not too much." I love that she has a healthy appetite and whatever we don't finish we can take to go. "Can I get you a drink?"

"Sure. Surprise me." I also love that she's not picky and trusts me to choose.

"Anything you don't like?"

"Whiskey."

"Be right back." While I wait at the bar to place our order, a woman in a dark blouse and pencil skirt sidles up beside me.

"Hi," she says.

"Hi."

"I'm Tamar."

"Drew."

"Can I buy you a drink, Drew?"

"Thanks, but I'm here with someone."

"Someone special?" she asks, like she might have a shot with me if not.

"Yes," I say without hesitation then turn to the bartender who's ready with pen and paper.

"Lucky girl," Tamar says before she walks away.

Let's hope Alejandra feels that way. If not tonight, then tomorrow. Next week. Hell, just as long as she feels something for me before her ex gets back.

Our food will be delivered to our table, but I wait for our drinks. Glasses in hand, I return to the most captivating girl in the room. "For you," I say, handing her a cocktail as I sit.

"Thank you. What is it?"

"A Tequila Mockingbird."

"The drinks have fun names?" She takes a sip. "Mmm. It's really good. What are you having?"

"Adventures of Blackberry Finn."

"Two of my favorite books when I was young."

"Is there any book you didn't like?" I ask, fairly certain she's a lover of all fiction.

She thinks about it. "One or two required readings in high school, but I don't like to talk ill about anything someone has written." She takes another sip of her drink.

I smile at her. I'd bet my hotel she doesn't talk with disrespect ever. "I wrote a book once."

"Really?" She raises her eyebrows in suspicion.

"It was called *The Two Poopheads*. I was six and I bet you can guess who the book was about."

She laughs. *Aaand* my dick twitches. The sound of her laughter is so damn sexy and easy on the ears that certain parts of me especially appreciate it. "What did your brothers think?"

"Ethan read it and said it was shit, which at the time got him in big trouble, but now is pretty funny. He hadn't meant to make a pun. And Finn wasn't bothered by it. He was too busy playing outside."

"Did this book have illustrations as well?"

"*Pfft.* Of course."

"Does you mom still have it somewhere?"

"I think so. She's got boxes of stuff from when we were kids. Schoolwork, trophies, that sort of thing."

"My brother pretty much kept his distance from Gabby and me. He called us 'double the trouble,' and being five years older, he didn't have a lot of patience for us. We're a lot closer now that we're adults."

"Even though you don't look alike, got any funny twin stories?"

She gets a devilish look on her face that catches me completely off guard. "Well, there was this time when Gabby decided she'd had enough of me and only wanted to hang out with her friends. One night she had two girls sleep over and they were being mean to me and excluding me. It was right before Halloween and Diego had this creepy mask and rubber monster hands, so when they were raiding the kitchen for a late night snack, I put them on and hid under Gabby's bed."

"No way," I say, pleasantly surprised to find out there

isn't always an angel on her shoulder. I mean, sometimes it's fun to be bad.

She shrugs, like she did this sort of thing all the time, but I highly doubt it. "I waited until they were all back in the room and relaxed, and then I jumped out and scared the crap out of them. Gabby spewed her soda all over one of her friends. It was hysterical."

"Did your sister try and retaliate? Me and my brothers didn't let anything go without some kind of retribution, although they took it a little easier on me since I'm the youngest."

"She was really mad for the rest of the night, but the next day after her friends left she said it was funny. Then later she put the mask and hands on while Diego was getting ready for bed and scared him. He was pissed and banned us from his room. Which was just as well since it smelled like sweaty boy all the time." A look of nostalgia sweetens her delicate features. "More often than not, we did get along."

Our food arrives, and we dig in. The conversation continues to flow when our mouths aren't full, and by the time we've finished eating, I'm in deep.

Alejandra is smart, funny, kind—she gives me all the best bites of food—and so beautiful, I ache to be closer to her.

At the end of the night, though, as we stand just inside the suite and she gazes up at me with hesitancy, my heart takes a beating.

Will we ever be on the same page?

Chapter Nine

Tlc

Drew

"SHE GOT A better offer," I say.

Alejandra gathers her long, dark hair over one shoulder and not for the first time, I wonder if it feels as soft as it looks. She's sitting on the balcony, curled up with a book and a blanket. It's early Sunday morning, not even eight. Fog cloaks the coastline. "I'm guessing you mean your grandma," she says in her sexy barely awake voice.

I sit next to her on the sturdy, but comfortable outdoor couch. "Take a look." I show her my phone and the photo of my grandmother sitting in the passenger seat of an open-air Hummer, thumbs-up. The matriarch of our family is apparently ready for some off-road fun. "She's living it up on Catalina Island for a few days."

"Early birthday present?" Alejandra asks, smiling at the photo.

"I guess. She's definitely determined to live life to the fullest."

"I admire her." Alejandra's gentle tone fills the terrace with longing that tugs at my heart.

For my entire life, I've never been denied anything. And by that I mean if I worked for something, or saved for something, or expressed an interest in a place or object or activity, I've had the financial means and family support to make it happen. It's a luxury I'm beyond grateful for and I never lose sight of what really matters.

Despite having more money than we could ever spend, my mom has always kept us grounded, her humble beginnings never far from her mind. She taught me and my brothers to value the little things, she didn't spoil us, and she made sure we always had each other's backs.

Alejandra has two siblings, but damn if I don't want to keep her safe, too. Take the yearning she carries inside her and make her wishes come true. Not that she can't make her dreams a reality without me. She absolutely can. I'm simply dealing with primal masculine instincts I've never felt this strongly before.

For an unwelcome second, my ex, Miranda, floats through my mind. I hate when she creeps into my thoughts, and I blink away that miserable night.

"I admire her, too," I say. "She's been a great role model. She was CFO of Auprince Holdings back in the day."

"Really?"

"Uh-huh. She met my grandfather in an accounting class at Stanford. She didn't like him very much at the start, but for him, it was love at first sight. He made a bet with her. If he got a better grade in the class, she had to go out with him. And if she got a better grade in the class, he had to go out with her."

I watch the corners of her mouth slowly lift as she fully comprehends what I said. "That's one of the cutest things I've ever heard. Who won?"

"My grandmother got an A and my grandfather an A minus. By that point he'd almost won her over with his charm and constant compliments. She took him to dinner, he tried to pay, and she told him she could damn well buy him a burger and fries. They were inseparable after that and married right after graduation."

"So she's always been a force to be reckoned with."

"Oh, yeah." I lean back, look out over the railing toward the sea. My grandfather was taken from us too soon, but the life he had with my grandmother was an extraordinary one until the day he passed unexpectedly. And not because they had wealth. But because they genuinely adored each other. They laughed all the time. Didn't hide their affection for each other. Enjoyed simple things like walks outside and watching their grandsons swim in the swimming pool. I peek at Alejandra out of the corner of my eye. I can picture those things with her.

"Since breakfast was canceled, I think I'll go for a run," Alejandra says, interrupting my thoughts.

"Sounds good. I'll join you." Normally, I'm a treadmill guy but I'm all for mixing it up, especially with her.

She closes her book and gives me a slightly exasperated look. It's damn cute. "I didn't invite you."

"Is running with you off-limits?"

"It's on my list, remember?"

"This is training for your half marathon?"

"Yes."

"You know running with a partner is a great way to stay on track and keep up motivation," I say matter-of-factly.

"But when you run alone, you can better concentrate on your form and breathing. Plus, run at your own pace," she argues in return.

"True, but running with someone can also improve your performance. I bet you'd have a faster running time with me by your side."

"How do you know *you* wouldn't have a faster time running beside me?" she fires back.

I grin at her. "How about we find out?"

"O—wait a minute." She shakes her head. "You almost had me, but no."

I'd like to have her in more ways than one. "Fine, Miss Marathoner. Want to grab something to eat afterward?"

"Thanks, but I need to stop by the senior center."

"We can do that, too."

She still doesn't appear sold so I add, "And then go shopping? I could really use your help picking out a birthday gift for my grandmother." Truth right there. What do you buy someone who has everything? Plus, I've learned Alejandra has a soft spot for grandparents and I'm not above using Rosemary to score more time with her. She's been a little distant since our date. Since we said a simple good night and walked to our own rooms.

"Okay," she says, and I give myself a mental high five. Then she stands, the blanket falling around her ankles, and I almost swallow my tongue.

Her light blue tank top is thin. Her cotton sleep shorts are tiny. I can see the outline of her pert, round breasts, the curve of her waist, the contours of her hips. There's a lot of exposed skin—her arms, her thighs, a tiny strip of her stomach—that I want to touch and taste before stripping her out of her pajamas and exploring every inch of her.

"Drew? Did you hear what I said?"

I stop ogling her and snap my gaze up to hers. If she noticed my once-over, she keeps it to herself, her features neutral as she stares down at me. I hope she doesn't notice the rise in my pajama bottoms. Or maybe I hope she does.

"Sorry. What?"

"I said give me about two hours."

"Sure. No problem."

"And if I'm not back in an hour from my run, send a search party." She says this jokingly, but there's also a serious glint in her eyes. She wants to do this on her own, but she's still a novice runner.

"Will do. But make sure you take your phone with you."

"Are you always this bossy?"

"You brought up the search party."

She makes a face and turns to go.

I watch her walk away, leaning to the side so I can follow her movements inside the suite. I almost fall over in my attempt to keep my eyes glued to her fantastic ass. I'm acting like a perv and I don't care. I'm helpless around her. When she's out of sight, I get to my feet, walk directly to my room, strip, and get in the shower to rub one out. With one hand on the tile wall in front of me, and the other wrapped around my dick, I let the warm water rain down my body. I work my fist up and down my length, imagining it's Alejandra's lips on me. Her lush mouth sucking me deep, making me harder than I've ever been before. I close my eyes tighter. Move my hand faster. God, Alejandra, what you do to me. She's a goddess, and one more image of me pumping into her warm, wet mouth and I blow like a teenager getting head for the first time.

I LEARNED ON my tour of the senior center last weekend that one center can be vastly different from the next. The Davis Senior Center has five main programs: meal and nutrition, fitness and wellness, education, arts, and social and recreational. Alejandra oversees all of these. She plans them, coordinates them, reaches out to teachers and professionals in the community who can help with them.

As we trek through the 21,000-square-foot facility, she talks to every senior and knows every single one of their names. She's quick to smile, ask about grandchildren, compliment on agility.

We stop at a meeting room where she asks me to wait in the hallway so she can have a word with the director of the center. I can't hear what they're saying, but looking through the glass wall at their dour expressions, it isn't a welcome discussion.

"Is everything okay?" I ask when Alejandra rejoins me.

She takes in my whole face as she deliberates my question. Or maybe she's mulling over how much detail to tell me. I know the center is in financial trouble. After a long beat she says, "No, but I don't want to talk about it right now. Come see our little slice of outdoor heaven. Our gardening group is working outside and I want to be sure they've got everything they need. It's a new program."

It bothers me she's keeping it to herself, but I get it. With every business there are ups and downs. The hotel's first official pool party weekend hasn't garnered the attention I'd like. We're a few days away from the first official day of summer, though, so I'm hopeful the coming weeks see big gains in attendance and word of mouth.

We step through a sliding glass door out into a large atrium. A small group is working on a flower bed inside a brick planter box about eight feet long.

"Hi, everyone," Alejandra says. "Wow, this is looking great."

I take a seat on a bench and watch her do her thing.

"Jemma, you've got a hard-working group here," Alejandra says to the thirty-something woman overseeing the project.

"They are," Jemma says.

"Nice hat, Lynette," Alejandra says to a woman wearing a leopard-print wide-brim hat.

"Isn't it?" the woman replies.

"I didn't know you were a Lakers fan, Norm." Alejandra smiles at an older man, his hands buried in dirt, and the bill of his purple and yellow baseball cap slightly askew.

"I never told you about the time I had floor seats next to

Jay Z?"

"No, you didn't."

"Remind me the next time we play cards," Norm says.

"You got it." Alejandra says something to each of the other participants before looking over some gardening supplies, righting a bag of soil that has tipped over and then stacking several empty plastic flower containers. She chats for a few more minutes before sitting down next to me. She raises her face to the blue sky, closes her eyes. "Ahhh...fresh air, sunshine, and the smell of mulch."

Her ponytail hangs over the back of the bench. Her eyelashes brush the tops of her cheeks. She takes a deep breath and my gaze catches on the rise and fall of her chest in her plain white T-shirt.

Too soon, she jumps to her feet. "Okay, let's go shopping."

She's got me completely captivated, so I follow right along.

I drive us to Beverly Hills and score a metered parking spot on Beverly Boulevard. I hurry around the car to help Alejandra out of her seat, but she's faster than me and already closing the door behind her.

"Thanks again for coming with me," I say.

"You're welcome. Any idea what you want to buy?" She walks beside me down the sidewalk. The sun is warm, palm trees slightly sway, and plenty of people are milling about. We pass a mix of stores, from casual to expensive.

"None. What do you think she'd like?" Alejandra understands seniors so she's got to have some good ideas.

"Have you never bought her a gift before?" she teases.

"I have and it's always a struggle. I'm good at everything but gift giving."

Alejandra laughs. *"Everything?* You can juggle? Flame throw? Ride a unicycle?"

"Do you have a secret job with a circus and your mission is to recruit multi-talented performers?"

"Obviously," she jokes. Then, "I have no idea where that all came from."

"A hidden desire to work under the big top with me by your side, of course."

She snaps her fingers. "That must be it."

We turn the corner onto Rodeo Drive and window shop in the luxury boutiques until we come upon the Coach store. "How about a purse?" Alejandra says, stopping fully to admire the window display. "And then you could tuck little handwritten notes into the inside pockets. Tell her all the things you love about her."

"That's a great idea." And one I guarantee my brothers won't think of. Not that it's a competition. (It's a competition.) I open the door for Alejandra to enter the shop before me. Mahogany shelves, glass, leather, bronze, and mid-century furniture greet us. Alejandra strides straight to the wall of brightly colored bags.

She looks over her shoulder at me, her eyes sparkling like a kid in a candy store. "I feel like she needs something bold."

"To match her personality."

"Exactly." She turns back around to study the choices before us.

I stand beside her, leaving only a sliver of space between us, and pretend I'm considering which purse to buy when I'm really watching her out of the corner of my eye.

"They're all so lovely," she says.

You are so lovely.

"Hello," a saleswoman says. "Can I help you with anything?"

"Hi," Alejandra says.

"We're here to buy a gift, but I think we can manage on our own," I say.

"No problem. Let me know if you have any questions or need assistance as you look around."

"Thanks. We will," I say to be polite. Alejandra's got this.

"The red is stunning," Alejandra says as the woman walks away. "But so is the royal blue. Oh, but look at that one." She points to a coral-colored bag with leather flowers layered one over the other and sewn onto the outside.

I have no clue which one to pick, but Alejandra is enamored with them so I say, "Model them for me." In the back of my mind do I want to buy one for her, too? Yes. But I won't, because I have a feeling she'd be put off if I so much as even mentioned it. Doesn't mean she can't enjoy a little fashion show.

"Okay," she says excitedly. "I'll probably never set foot in this store again so you're on." She lifts the red handbag from its perch, her tongue darting out to wet her bottom lip. She holds the purse by the handle so it hangs at her thigh, then she twists her shoulders and drops her chin in a fucking adorable pose. "What do you think?"

In her white T-shirt, light blue jeans, and white tennis shoes, she is a red-white-and-blue dream come true, that's what I think.

"Not bad," is what I say. Because I can't have her deciding on the first bag she poses with. No way am I depriving myself of more handbag hottie.

She gives a little shrug. "My grandmother loved handbags." She puts the red one back and grabs the blue. "She never had a bag like these, but the ones she had she treasured." She slips the detachable leather strap over her shoulder this time, turns to give me her side. She bends her leg and quickly turns her head to the right to look me straight in the eye, a serious expression on her face, like she's striking a solemn pose, the kind you might see on a fashion runway.

"How does this one look?" she asks, unsmiling.

I hold her gaze for one second, two…and then we both laugh.

"Everything looks good on you," I tell her. "But I just remembered green is my grandmother's favorite color, so maybe we should find something in that shade."

She looks a little flustered by my compliment as she slides the purse off her shoulder and directs her attention around the store, in search of a green purse, I'm guessing.

"I'll put this one back," I say, taking the blue bag from her. Our fingers graze during the hand-off and we both startle at the electric shock. She practically elbows herself in the stomach pulling her arm back. Which tells me she agrees that wasn't just static electricity, but something more.

I don't bother to hide my delight while she appears adorably nerve-racked. I'm cool with her nervousness. I'm cool with everything about her.

Alejandra spots something across the room. "I think I see the one," she says. She walks toward another open display case, her steps faltering slightly halfway there, like she stepped on something, but I don't see anything on the floor.

She lifts up a handbag with a mosaic patchwork design in hues of bright green, blue, and purple. Clutching the bag by the leather handle with both hands, she places at her hip, tilts her head and smiles. She keeps that pose for a couple of seconds then releases one hand and holds the bag with her arm straight at her side. She struts away, pivots, struts back. It's the best runway walk I've ever seen.

"Can I get a repeat?" I ask for purely selfish reasons. She could be holding a blank piece of paper.

She grants my request, swinging her arm this time. It's the kind of carefree, happy walk that shouts confidence and delight. I'm tempted to ask her for a 'three-peat,' but refrain. When she's standing in front of me again, she brings the purse up under her chin, elbows out to the sides, and shows off her straight, white teeth. I snap a mental picture.

Twisting, she drops the purse and holds it beside her thigh to check herself out in the mirror. "This bag is bold *and* playful. I think Rosemary will love it."

"Sold." I lead us to the register and pay for the gift.

On the drive back to the hotel, I tell Alejandra about the birthday party. "Invitations recently went out, but we're keeping all the details a surprise."

"She won't hear anything from me."

"Thanks."

Once back in the suite, I notice Alejandra limp toward her bedroom. "Hey," I say. "Are you okay?"

"Fine," she answers without turning.

I've learned over the years that when a woman tells you she's fine, she is anything but. I follow, keeping several feet back. She leaves her door open so I lean against the doorframe to find her sitting on the upholstered bench at the foot of the bed taking off her tennis shoes, a look of pain on her face.

Slipping off a thin pair of no-show socks, she lets out a miserable breath. Next, she crosses her left leg over her right knee to examine the bottom of her foot and that's when I see the reason for her discomfort. A nasty blister the size of a dime.

"Ouch," I say, catching her attention.

"That's an understatement. It hurts like a mother."

God, she's cute. "A consequence of this morning's run, I assume?"

"Yes." She gently taps the blister. It's red around the edges. "I've never had a blister like this before. Do I pop it?"

I take her question as an invitation to look more closely at the unwelcome bubble and to offer my help. Scratch that. Give my help. I kneel down to take her foot in my hands.

"What are you doing?"

"Checking it out so I can give you a proper diagnosis." Her skin is soft, her toenails still painted a pretty blue.

She chuckles. "Oh, okay, Dr. Auprince. What's the verdict?"

"Well, typically you shouldn't pop or drain a blister, but this one is large and a ten on the pain scale from your description—" I glance up at her pretty face for confirmation; she nods "—so stay put and I'll be right back to take care of it."

By the furrow in her brow, I think she's about to argue with me, but when I kiss the top of her foot, her eyes widen in surprise, or maybe it's shock, and she bites the corner of her lip instead.

I grab the first aid kit under the kitchen sink, thinking about all the times Finn had blisters on his feet from his baseball cleats and me watching my mom take care of him. Next, I grab the sewing kit in the laundry room.

"So," I say, returning to the room, "how far did you run this morning to garner this kind of reward?"

She notes the kits in my hands and swallows. "Funny story."

"Yeah? Let's get you to the bathroom." I help her stand then hold her arm for balance as she hops on her good foot. "Have a seat." I motion to the marble countertop. She hoists herself up and sits.

I put my supplies down and roll up her pant leg then turn her so she can put her foot inside the sink.

She watches me closely, my every move. I'm not sure if it's because she's nervous or intrigued, probably a combination of both. Her lips are slightly parted, her breaths are coming a bit faster.

"Tell me this funny story while I get you fixed up." I

turn on the faucet, waiting for the water to warm.

"I tried to chase down a pickpocket."

"You *what*?"

"I was jogging down Ocean when this older woman sitting on a park bench started shouting and pointing at a guy running away. She said he'd taken her wallet out of her tote bag."

"And so you chased after him?"

"Uh-huh." She flinches when I clean her foot with soap and water.

"Sorry," I say, forgetting to be gentle at the thought of her getting hurt even worse if this guy had turned on her. "I'm guessing you didn't catch him."

"No," she says dejected. "I followed him for what seemed like forever before I lost sight of him."

"It's never a dull moment with you, is it?"

"Lately that seems to be the case." She looks away for a moment. "Interestingly, before I ran into you again, my life was very uneventful."

"You're welcome." I carefully pat dry her foot.

"For what?" she argues.

"Making your life more exciting." I sterilize a needle from the sewing kit with rubbing alcohol. "Obviously."

"Or more taxing," she playfully offers.

"The saying does go 'no pain, no gain.'" I cradle her foot in my hand. "This is going to hurt a little."

She pinches her eyes shut and wraps her arms around her middle.

"Al?"

Her long lashes slowly rise. "Yes?"

"Tell me if I do anything that's too uncomfortable and I'll stop. The poke with the needle won't be bad, but squeezing out the fluid will be."

"Please just hurry and do it." She clamps her eyes shut again.

This is going to hurt me more than it hurts you. I poke. I squeeze. She squirms and it about kills me. I leave the skin over the blister and wash the area again. Pat it dry. "Hard part's over," I say quietly. I apply antibiotic ointment. Cover the spot with a sterile bandage then loosely wrap gauze around her foot to keep the bandage in place.

"All done."

She opens her eyes, relaxes her arms and shoulders. "Thank you."

"You're welcome."

"Now what?"

I lift her in my arms. "Drew," she protests, but she laces her fingers behind my neck, lets her legs dangle.

"Now I carry you to your favorite reading spot."

"How do you know my favorite reading spot?"

"Because I pay attention." I deposit her on the arm chair and ottoman next to the couch. There's a clear view of the ocean. A blanket within reach. A book tucked into the side of the cushion.

I don't need affirmation I got it right. Her soft expression tells me I did. She looks between my eyes, thinking I don't know what. When she hastily drops her gaze and picks up her book with a quick, "Thanks," *I* think I should probably give up any hope of this becoming something more before she breaks my heart.

Will I though?

Not a chance.

Chapter Ten
First Kiss

Alejandra

I STARE AT the photo Matthew just texted. It's so green and beautiful. So far away. *Wanted to share the picturesque farmland where* Lord of the Rings *was filmed.* The last text he sent me came the night of mine and Drew's first date. Talk about bad timing. I didn't want to be reminded of him when I was having one of the best nights ever with Drew. I wish I hadn't looked at my phone on the drive back to the hotel, but I did. And it ruined what I'd hoped would happen when Drew and I walked into the suite: a toe-curling kiss good night. Guilt seized me instead, and we simply walked away from each other toward our own bedrooms.

The guilt isn't over just Matthew. It's over Drew, too. Am I a horrible person for liking him as much as I do when I can't say with one hundred percent certainty that Matthew and I are over for good?

I huff under the weight of my confusion. But then I look a little closer at my phone. I look and I look and I look, stuck on something besides the breathtaking scenery. On the right edge of the photo, barely there, is what looks like a woman's shoulder. I think Matthew took this picture from behind her and then cropped it before sending to me.

Matthew is sharing this view with someone else.

And it…hurts.

Is she a friend? Lover? Both?

I swipe up to close the text, unsure how I want to respond. Words were never this hard between us, but it's to be expected given our circumstances. Ultimately, if she's someone important, I'll find out soon enough. I put my phone face down on the coffee table and resume reading my book.

A few minutes later the sound of Drew moving about has me looking up to a vision that immediately makes my pulse race. In a very good way. "What are you doing?" I blurt out, caught off guard and *hot*, the temperature in the room increasing rapidly. It's Friday night and he has plans to have dinner with Finn. I'm having my sister, Jane, and Sutton over for a girls' night in. A very nice thing for Drew to agree to since I'm his guest here. We're navigating this temporary roommate thing relatively easily.

Or, we *were*. Before his nakedness intruded.

"Grabbing a bottle of water from the fridge," he says, seemingly unaware of how his being dressed in nothing but a towel is making me hot and bothered.

A tiny, white towel draped low around his waist! If sex appeal had a proper name, it would be Drew Auprince.

He has those sexy indentations that form a V on his lower abs. His chest is defined, his shoulders broad, his stomach packing a couple of mouthwatering ridges. And his biceps?

They're big and muscly and I'd like to have them wrapped around me.

Have I mentioned how hot it is in here?

Looking at him is almost too much for my little heart to handle.

"Naked?" I object to his state of undress and my tone tells him so. Not that I object, object. I, uh, like the view. Very much. But I'm all flustered!

He grins. Grins, the sexy jerk! Which makes this even worse. Because over the past week, ever since he took care of my blister, things have been intensifying between us. We've been caught looking at each other more, flirting, touching here and there.

"Is that a problem?" he asks.

"Um…define problem."

He laughs. "You know, you're lucky I have the towel on. Normally I don't bother."

My jaw drops, only he doesn't see it because he's walked past me to the kitchen. I turn my head to check out his nice round ass. I can't help myself. It's an involuntary response to his hotness. When he moves behind the counter, I force myself to resume reading. Not that I could tell you a thing about what's happening on the page.

On the way back to his bedroom, he stops in front of me. Thankfully, the ottoman separates us by a couple of feet, otherwise I'd be *way* too close to his family jewels. That I just thought *family jewels* means there is something definitely wrong with me. I'm naming the condition Drew Fever.

"Yes?" I say to page 167 of my book. "Did you need

something?"

He doesn't say anything so I'm forced to look up. And what do I find? Too much bare skin! Too much, too much, too much. Also, he's giving me *the look* again. The one that makes me ache between my legs.

And one more thing, I'm pretty sure he's intentionally posing. Flexing his muscles and angling his square jaw in such a way to make a woman sigh. (I do no such thing, but it's difficult.) His hand is curved around the towel at his hip—one quick flick of the wrist and I will see everything, that hand teases. I want to look away. I really do. But I don't. *I can't.*

"The fridge is stocked for you," he says, drawing my gaze back to his eyes.

"What do you mean?"

"Drinks and snacks for your girls' night. I asked Chloe what to get so you should be good."

"Drew, I can get my own food."

"I know you can." He shifts and all his muscles flex in a very distracting manner.

I start to sweat. My cheeks heat further.

He smirks in triumph. He knows. He knows what his nakedness is doing to me.

Well, two can play this game. I put my book down and get to my feet. "Thank you. I'm sure we'll enjoy everything." I reach for the top button of my sweater.

"*What are you doing?*" he asks, clearing his throat.

I continue to unbutton my black cardigan, silently shushing my nerves. Underneath the soft wool, I'm wearing a lace-trimmed white cotton camisole with a built-in bra. It covers me, but doesn't hide much. Including my pebbled nipples.

"I think I'll change into my pajamas before the girls get here," I say, slipping the sweater off my shoulders to dish some of his own medicine back at him.

Drew gets an eyeful before I step around him. I almost walk backward toward my room so he can look his fill, but I'd rather leave him curious than satisfied. "Have fun with your brother," I call out.

"Uh, you, too," Drew stammers. "I mean not with your brother. Have fun with your sister and friends."

The second I turn the hall corner and am out of sight, I sprint to my room, close the door with my foot, jump onto my bed, and roll around to extinguish all the excess nervous energy. How is it Drew can feel dangerous and safe at the same time?

I change into my pajamas and then open my laptop to do some more work on the grant proposal for the senior center. As it stands now, we won't be able to make our balloon payment. The developer eyeing the property is waiting in the wings with deep pockets and friends in high places. Not to mention the company knows exactly what to say to increase our director's stress level.

I stare at the lotus tattoo on my finger. I have to save the center. I just have to. I can't lose it, too.

An hour later I'm sitting on the couch with Gabby, Jane, and Sutton. We're wearing homemade honey masks on our faces and talking, eating the yummy assortment of food

Drew had stocked, and drinking vodka lemonades. The sun is setting outside the window, the final rays of a warm June day slashing across the large, but homey room. My own home is getting a beautiful facelift, the work progressing nicely when I checked in on it yesterday.

"Oh my God, look at this one," Sutton says, turning her phone so we can see the screen shot of Drew in a tux at a charity event. "He is too good-looking for words."

Despite my best efforts to avoid the topic of Drew, it's hard to avoid the topic of Drew when I'm staying in his suite and he's provided more food than I ever would have on my own, thus begetting discussion of his generosity. There's also the lingering scent of his aftershave or body wash or whatever it is that smells so fantastically incredible Sutton said it made her panties wet with one inhalation.

"Enough with the pictures," I say. "He's just a man."

Gabby shakes her head. "He is so *muy caliente* it should be a crime."

"Better not let Landon hear you talk like that," Sutton says. "He'll lose his shit."

My sister stays quiet, which is very unlike her. Sutton is right. Landon is the jealous type. He and my sister are also fighting more than usual. To cut through Gabby's funk, I say, "I saw Drew in nothing but a towel today."

Three honey-oatmeal faces turn to me. "*Muy, muy caliente*," I tell them.

"Tell us everything from the beginning," Gabby says, her posture perking up.

I relay what happened, my neck getting warm as I picture Drew and all his masculinity on display. When I've finished, I take a big gulp of my vodka lemonade. Drew is so much more than just a well-built man. He's kind. Intelligent. Confident yet humble.

"You need to have sex with him," Gabby orders. Yes, orders. She likes to do that.

"You do," Sutton agrees. "What happened today was foreplay."

"I concur," Jane says in her lawyerly voice. She pulls a wayward curl of hair off her cheek.

"He's into you," Gabby says. "I saw it the first time I met him at his hotel. And from everything I've seen since then and the things you've told me about him, *and* the way you say them, you're into him, too. You've had sex with one person, Allie." My sister thinks this is a bad thing, and as such, her tone drips with disapproval. "I know you still have feelings for Matthew, or you think you do, but you guys are not together. And before he comes back you need, yes need, to be with someone else."

This is easy for my sister to say. She's had lots of boyfriends and doesn't put the same significance on sex that I do. She gave her virginity to a boy she didn't even love, while I made Matthew wait for almost a year.

"Let yourself go for once," Gabby continues. "Sex doesn't have to be anything more than just sex."

"I hear what you're saying, but you know I don't work that way." I wipe the corner of my mouth where some of my face mask has gathered. "I really like Drew so if we have sex it's going to mean something to me."

"So, you're afraid you'll get hurt?" Jane asks.

"She's already hurting," Gabby says, taking my hand to give it a squeeze. "I know Matthew hurt you when he left and you're still not entirely over it, but don't deprive yourself the chance to be happy with someone else."

"That's just it. Drew definitely makes me happy and I think I make him happy, too, but he deserves someone who's all in, and I feel guilty for still hanging on to hope that Matthew and I will pick up where we left off."

"Do you really?" Gabby asks. "Not the guilty part—I know you feel that because you care more about others than you do yourself. I'm talking about the hope part. Because I don't think you hope that anymore. I think you're hung up on the idea that you've always believed in one true love and if it's not Matthew then you won't have it."

"I don't see the difference," I say quietly.

"What if Matthew isn't the person you're supposed to have forever with?" Gabby asks. "I don't think it's a coincidence that Drew came back into your life mere weeks before you see Matthew again."

"I don't think it is either," Sutton chimes in.

"This is the universe telling you something," Gabby continues. "There are other great guys out there and maybe you should keep an open mind."

"I'm trying," I admit. Drew *has* opened my eyes, but I haven't quite given myself full permission to let all these feelings free. From the second I saw Drew I knew there was something special about him, and that terrified me. It scared me to think what I've believed since I was seventeen—that

Matt and I would get married one day—wasn't true anymore.

"That's all any of us can do, Allie," Jane says.

"Here's an idea," Gabby offers. "Add sex with Drew to your mental list."

I narrow my eyes at her. She knows that everything I add there, I make happen.

"Don't look at me like that." She taps the side of her head. "Put 'single girl sex' here—got it? It's doable, Sis."

I chew on my bottom lip. "The truth is I don't need to put it on the list. I want to be closer to him." There. I said it out loud. Put it out there so I can't take it back.

"Yes!" Gabby pumps her arms in the air.

"But is it fair of me? I don't want to hurt him either."

"Trust me," Sutton says, "no man would say no to sex with you. And you aren't promising him anything by sleeping with him. As long as you mutually consent, there's no harm."

Gabby nods. "We can't predict the future, so the best thing to do is live in the present. Dating is supposed to be fun and sex is fun. I know you think so, too."

"True," I say, imagining the newness of being with someone like Drew will be way more than just fun.

"And you might not want to hear it, but I can guarantee you Matthew hasn't stayed celibate." Gabby reties the bun on top of her head.

She's probably right. I don't want to think about that, though. And it doesn't matter what he's done. He's free to do as he chooses. I close my eyes for a moment and wonder if he's had sex with someone else. Maybe more than one someone. And I know the answer, because I know him. *Yes.*

He likes sex. He's good at sex. And he's a twenty-six-year-old male.

"Sorry," Gabby mutters. "I just thought it should be mentioned."

"Thanks, you guys." I look at each of them, grateful for their friendship. "You've helped put things in perspective for me."

"We love you," Sutton says.

Gabby holds up her drink. "To sisterhood."

We clink glasses and move on to talk about their love lives. In the back of my mind, though, is Drew. The smile he gives so freely and readily. His deep voice. The pride he takes in his work. I may not know what the future holds, but I know I want Drew to hold me.

Drew

"I CAN'T BELIEVE I had to hear from Grandmother that you have a new girlfriend," Finn says. "I thought you were on a break from women? Or at least not jumping into bed with one right away?"

It's a legit question considering I usually—okay always—have sex pretty quickly, and the last time I had a heart-to-heart with my brothers we talked about how I wanted a meaningful connection with someone and so maybe some mental foreplay and anticipation would be a better way to approach my love life.

See, I've got my own list. In my search for *the one*, there are several boxes in my mind that I want to tick off on my girl-I'm-going-marry checklist.

Box 1: Be attractive. Don't hate on me for making this number one, I'm just being truthful here. I have to find my future wife beautiful, sexy, and fascinating.

Box 2: Be sexually open. I want someone who's not afraid to talk about sex—what we want and don't want, what we're willing to try. Likes and dislikes. Fantasies.

Box 3: Be confident. I've dated some clingy, irrational, materialistic, closed-minded, preoccupied-with-having-my-babies-before-we've-gotten-to-dessert women, and no thank you. I want someone honest, optimistic, self-sufficient. Honesty is key. Trust. I've been hit over the head—literally—with lies and trickery, and it still occasionally keeps me up at night.

Box 4: Be goal-oriented. I want a woman who has her own goals and doesn't look at me like a free meal ticket.

Box 5: Be kind. I want some who is nurturing, family-oriented, and thinks of others, not just herself.

Box 6: CLW. I'm not sure yet how I'll know, but I want the woman I Can't Live Without.

"I haven't slept with her," I tell Finn. We're in his kitchen sitting on barstools at the counter and eating a great meal prepared by his housekeeper, Sylvie. It's a rare night off for Finn, and when he's in town he likes to stay home. Chloe is bringing dinner to her best friend, Jillian. She and her husband just had a baby a few days ago.

"Yet you've been off and on for a while? Wow. I need to meet this girl."

My grandmother has a mind like a steel trap so of course she shared every detail about me and Alejandra. Or rather, what I told her about us.

"Yeah, about that…" I feel like shit for not coming clean with her yet, but I've been a little preoccupied. With Alejandra. So that should count in my favor, right?

Finn puts his fork down. "What did you do now?"

I stop midbite of my salmon. "What do you mean what did I do now? You make it sound like I'm always up to no good."

He raises his brows at me.

Okay, so maybe I like to be a pain in my brothers' asses. Isn't that what I'm supposed to do as the youngest? It's how I show my love for them.

"I may have misled Grandmother," I confess.

"May have?"

"Okay, I did. But it's only because she wanted to set me up with Marin Fitzpatrick."

"Isn't she a ghost hunter or something?"

"Yes, and then some."

Finn laughs. He knows how much I hate scary shit. "I see your dilemma."

"Thank you," I say adamantly and drop my fork on my plate. It clinks. "So when I ran into Alejandra again at the hotel while having breakfast with Grandmother, I fibbed about dating her so Grandmother would back off on the matchmaking."

"What do you mean by *again*?"

I tell him about meeting Alejandra last year and her leaving the bar without a proper goodbye. I admit to thinking about her often since then. "I couldn't believe she was in my hotel," I say, scratching the back of my head. "And I know it's cliché, but she drew me in like a magnet. It's not just her looks either. It's her…" I trail off trying to come up with the perfect word or words to describe this unique energy I get from her. "It's her moral fiber. She's uplifting and I feel like we're connected without even trying."

"So, why the subterfuge?"

"Because she didn't exactly feel the same way at the time." I'm definitely wearing her down. This past week we've flirted a ton. Talked and teased each other. I want to believe her ex isn't on her mind anymore because when I think about how he got to touch her, love her, look at her, go head-to-head with her, for *years*, it worries me. That's not something easily forgotten, and right or wrong, I dislike him for it.

Finn gives me a straight face for all of two seconds before he busts out with laughter that doesn't quit until I cross my arms and glare at him. "Finally, a girl who doesn't throw herself at you," he says.

"It sucks."

"Does it really?" Being a professional athlete, Finn is well acquainted with eager women, but when it came down to the woman whose heart he wanted, he had to give chase. Chloe didn't fall at his feet or even want to go on a single date with him. *Huh. I tuck away the parallel for safekeeping.* "Because in my experience a woman worth having is one who knows her worth and isn't easily swayed by a handsome face."

"You've swayed women with that face?"

"More than you, baby brother."

He's probably right about that, late bloomer that I was. There's also the four months in college where I barely left my condo. Miranda screwed me over and screwed me up. West got me out of my funk. He gave me his blessing to date his sister. I know that sounds weird, but it wasn't. It was an act of true friendship. I'd always had a crush on Tracy. She was—is a good person. She was safe when I needed safe. We dated for almost a year before deciding there wasn't the kind of spark we both wanted or deserved.

I know Alejandra is attracted to me (you should have seen her eyes widen and hear her breath hitch when I walked around in a towel earlier), but all of a sudden I'm gun-shy. *Fucking memories of Miranda.* Logically, I know Alejandra is nothing like her. But the fact is, I've only been dating Alejandra for a short time.

"You think Grandmother will be mad at me?"

"Probably."

"Gee, thanks."

"No problem."

"You're supposed to make me feel better, not worse."

"Do you need a hug?" He turns in his chair and opens his arms. He's half serious, half flippant, and I'm cool with both because a back slap from my big brother is needed regardless. Alejandra is under my skin and I hope I don't get burned.

We grasp hands and wrap our other arm around each other. "I'm kidding you know. Grandmother can't stay mad at any of us."

"That's true," I say.

"How is work?" Finn asks on the release. We switch gears to talk business and baseball and a little while later, I'm back at the hotel.

I expect to find everyone still in the suite as it isn't very late, but the room is quiet except for Alejandra cleaning up the kitchen. "Hey," she says, drying a glass with a dish towel.

"Hey yourself. I didn't expect to find your girls' night over so soon."

"Yeah, Landon came early to pick up Gabby, so then Sutton figured she'd go home to check on her kitten, and Jane's cousin is staying with her so…"

"So, lucky me I have you all to myself," I say without thought.

She turns her head away, but not before I catch a small twitch to her lips. "Thanks again for all the food. You've been so generous and I can't thank you enough for everything." She lifts up onto her toes to put the glass back in the cupboard. She's wearing her usual pajamas—cotton sleep shorts and a V-neck tee—and my gaze sweeps down from the curve of her neck to the backs of her calves.

"No problem."

"I saved you a piece of pie." She dries another glass.

"There's only *one* piece left?"

She looks over her left shoulder at me. "Yes, there's *only* one piece left. You know lemon meringue is my favorite so be grateful I saved you any," she teases.

I do know that about her. Discovered it the other day

when she was snacking on Lemonheads candy. "Here, let me help you with that," I say when she struggles to fit the last glass into the cupboard. Her stretch isn't quite long enough to reach the higher ledge.

My front presses against her back as I surround her, taking the glass from her hand and placing it alongside others on the uppermost shelf. The top of her head comes just under my chin. My blood heats. She's soft and warm and her hair smells fantastic.

I don't immediately step away. I physically can't. I'm lost in her feel and her scent and for a moment, I take it in. Commit these few seconds in time to memory.

When I do move, it's with a semi in my slacks. This is a recurring situation as of late.

Alejandra slowly turns around. Like a good boy, I do not dip my eyes to her chest. Nope. I keep them on her whiskey-colored irises.

"I'm going to do some work in bed," I say. And yes, some of that work will entail using my hand on my current problem. "We still on for our date tomorrow?"

She leans against the counter like she needs it for support. "Uh-huh." She's going with me to Justin's boat party tomorrow.

"Great. Good night, then."

"Wait." She wraps her slim fingers around my forearm. I'm wearing short sleeves and her touch burns. She takes a step closer. Her gaze slides to my mouth.

I don't move a fucking muscle.

I'm hot under the collar for no other reason than she's

looking at me like she might kiss me.

Do it.

DO IT.

Her face alights with gladness as if she heard my thought.

She's running this show so I hold my ground while she takes her sweet time inching closer. I watch her watch me until finally her long, dark lashes sweep down and over her cheeks and her lips meet mine.

I think I hear angels sing.

The problem in my pants becomes a bigger issue—pun intended, sorry angels—as her mouth presses against mine with the perfect amount of pressure to blow my mind. It's soft. But firm. Gentle. But demanding. She kisses me with tenderness. Care. This isn't a let's-go-to-your-bedroom-and-fuck kiss. This is a fairly innocent first kiss. A getting-to-know-you kiss, which is epically sexier and more consuming because it tells me she wants more at some point.

I kiss her back. I slant my mouth over hers, put one hand on her waist and the other on her cheek, and give as good as I get. She tastes like honey. Sugar and spice.

And so much more than nice.

She makes a breathy sound, grips the front of my shirt in her hands. She holds tight, but our kiss is relaxed. Languid. We explore without using our tongues and I'm surprised by the intensity of it. Sparks skitter down my spine. Pure joy blooms in my chest.

Before I'm ready, she puts on the brakes, stepping back and gazing up at me under heavy-lidded eyes. "Good night," she whispers then walks away.

I stay rooted to my spot until I hear the click of her bedroom door. I hope she locked it, because it's taking everything I have not to follow her and continue the hottest kiss of my life. *Patience*, man. There's no rush.

Chapter Eleven
Second Date

Alejandra

M Y FIRST TIME on a boat is as I predicted: fun but nauseating.

How can I smile nonstop and feel nauseous at the same time? Easy. I'm with Drew. Add in the sun on my shoulders, a sea breeze, and dolphins popping in and out of the water in the distance, and with minimal effort, I'm okay.

What isn't so easy is keeping my motion sickness from Drew. He doesn't need to know I've thrown up in my mouth twice today. If he knows that, he won't want to kiss me again.

And I really want to kiss him again. (Don't worry, I'll drink plenty of water and I have breath mints. I'm not gross.) Last night, when I'd boldly made the first move, I had no idea it would lead to pent-up sexual desires I didn't know I had, going hog-wild in my head. I mean, I had some idea his kiss would rock my world given my attraction to him. But after having the dirtiest dream of my life last night, where Drew fulfilled my every fantasy, I'm craving more of him.

I take a deep breath and let it out slowly. Today is shaping up to be a great second date and there's no reason to think we won't kiss later.

Releasing the handrail, I turn and lean against it. I'm standing on the upper deck of the yacht. There are three small couches and ottomans, two of them occupied with party guests. At the front of the boat there's more seating. The vessel has four bedrooms, a kitchen, dining room, and several comfortable spots for lounging on the deck below. Justin, the owner of the boat and Drew's friend, is very proud of his purchase and was happy to show us every detail after we arrived.

We've been at sea for a little over an hour, the shoreline visible in the distance while we sail horizontal to the coast. Drew's been at my side the whole time until now. He needed to grab something. I'm fine standing here alone in my white Capri pants, the blue striped off-the-shoulder top I bought at Target just for today, and white tennis shoes. I hope I look like a sailor even if I don't feel like one.

A group of birds fly overhead in a V-formation. Someone laughs from across the deck. Another boat passes us going in the opposite direction, the people on board waving. I wave back.

My gaze lands on Drew next, climbing up the circular staircase, and my stomach immediately tightens. He's so effortlessly sexy in his slim dark gray chino shorts and white T-shirt. Thick watch on his wrist, athletic shoes sans socks on his feet, windblown light brown hair and thick stubble along his chiseled jawline.

I zero in on the shape of his lips. The bow on his top lip almost reaches his full bottom lip and as far as mouths go, his is a ten on the sensual scale. A ten on the lush scale. And a ten on the taste scale. Last night when I'd pressed against them, nothing had seemed more important than touching him in that way. Letting him know he affected me, but that I needed to get my feet wet before I jumped.

"Here you go," he says, interrupting my musings and handing me a tumbler of something bubbly. He lifts his sunglasses off the neckline of his shirt and slides them on.

I'd love a drink, but it's not a good idea with my queasy stomach. "Thanks, but—"

"It's ginger ale. It ought to help with your seasickness."

My mouth drops open. "How did you know?"

He takes my long ponytail between his fingers and gently flips it over my shoulder so it hangs down my back. "I saw the box of Dramamine you left on the kitchen counter."

I nod. I thought I'd put it away.

"And you look pale." He lifts my arm and places the glass in my hand. "Drink."

I do as instructed, appreciating the sweet gesture more than his bossiness. Carbonated beverages do help settle my stomach. I take a few sips.

"You came with me today even though you get sick." He takes a step to the right to block the sun from my face. "Is a boat ride on your list?"

"This definitely counts as doing something adventurous, but no it's not the reason I joined you." I take another sip of my drink.

He once again blesses me with his magnificent smile. "I'm happy you're here with me."

"Me, too."

"There you are," West says, coming to stand beside us.

Drew turns and puts his arm around my waist. On the drive to the harbor, he told me about his best friend, West. They've known each other for ten years, having met their freshman year of college. "Besides my brothers," Drew had said, "there's no one better." When Drew introduced us upon arrival on the boat, I recognized him as Romeo Number Two from the bar. His date for the day—according to Drew, West is the definition of noncommittal—wore huge diamond earrings and little else to go with her kind eyes and friendly hello. She isn't with him now.

"Here we are," Drew responds.

West tilts his face to the sky. "It's nice up here." He drops his chin to look at Drew. "I forgot to tell you I've got an investor from New York coming into town this week and I'm putting him up at your place."

"Thanks. Appreciate it. Send me his details and I'll have a bottle of Dom delivered to his room."

"That would be great. Thanks. So, Alejandra, what do you do for a living?"

"I'm the activities director at a senior community center."

He gets a funny look on his face. "Oh yeah? Which one?"

"The Davis Senior Community Center in Santa Monica. Have you heard of it?"

West runs his palm over the side of jaw. His gaze, blue and steely, flickers between me and Drew. "Yeah, I know it. Very well, actually."

"Really? That's great. Do you have a grandparent that visits? What's their name? I know all our seniors."

"No, no family member there." He cuts a look to Drew again. Something I can't decipher passes between them.

And then Drew stiffens. He drops his arm from around me and twists to look me in the eyes. "West is in real estate development. Is there someone already focused on buying the center?"

My stomach roils. I think I'm going to be sick. I stare at West. "You're the one eyeing the property?" I say to him.

"The company I work for is, yes."

"Dude, you own half the company," Drew says.

I look pleadingly at West. He's Drew's best friend. Surely that scores me some points. Gives me some leverage I didn't have before. "What do you think about investing in us rather than waiting for us to fail so you can swoop in?"

"It's not that simple."

"It never is when money's involved," I assert, not liking my tone, but the center is more than my livelihood. It's my second home. I can't believe West is the person—or company—who wants to tear down our center and build luxury condominiums instead. "Have you ever been inside the center?"

West doesn't look the least bit remorseful when he says, "No."

"Then you have no idea what you're really doing."

"I know exactly what I'm doing, sweetheart."

"Do not call me sweetheart."

He raises his hands, palms flat. *Didn't mean to insult you.* "Business isn't always pleasant, Alejandra. I need this property as much as you need the building."

I glance at Drew. He gives a barely there shrug, seemingly sympathetic to both of us.

"How can you say that? The center serves the community in ways a condo complex never could. We serve hundreds of seniors every month, offer access to programs and activities they couldn't get or afford otherwise. We're improving their overall quality of life. We're their friend, their advocate, their family."

Drew takes my hand, laces our fingers together. I appreciate his support. He's been to the center. He's witnessed the magic there. He has a special relationship with his grandmother. He might not vocalize it, but surely he's on my side here.

"Aren't there other buildings you can steal?" I say, my unwavering passion for the center clear in my troubled tone.

"So you'd throw someone else's home or place of business or life-improving facility under the bus without seeing it in person?" West asks.

That shuts me up. He has a point.

"This isn't personal," he continues. "Business like this is about profit, yes, but we also do our research, and what was good for the city twenty-five years ago isn't what's needed now."

"I politely disagree."

"I respect that and ask that you respect my position."

"Fine."

West and I exchange small, civil smiles. "I think I'll go find my date. Catch you guys later."

I put my drink down on the wood-planked deck then turn around, grip the handrail again, and contemplate the ocean. How long do dolphins live? How many fish *are* there in the sea? And lastly, if I jump overboard, could I swim all the way to shore?

"I didn't know," Drew says quietly.

"I know."

"I wish there was something I could do." He wraps his hand around mine atop the handrail.

"How are you at grant writing? Or I don't suppose you'd like to make a donation? Nothing crazy, just enough to get the center back on its feet."

He visibly flinches at my suggestions. Releases my hand and takes a step back.

"Drew—"

"Is that why you're dating me?"

"*What?* No." I shake my head. "I would never do something like that and for you to even think me capable..." I give him my back so he doesn't see how much his accusation hurts. When have I ever made him think I was using him? Yes, he's been extremely generous, but I didn't ask for any of it. *He* offered me a place to stay. *He* asked me out on a date. He came to the senior center without my asking.

I spin back around. "*You* just asked if there was something you could do," I assert. "So I answered you. Honestly.

The truth is you do have the means, but now I don't want your help. Any of it. Period."

"Shit." He jams his fingers through his hair. "I'm sorry, Alejandra. You're right. I did. And then I panicked. It's not you. I swear it's not you. It's just…"

"Just what?"

He walks over to a vacated couch and sits down. A defeated look mars his usually happy face as I pick up my ginger ale and follow, my sea legs not so steady and my stomach queasy for more than one reason now.

"Finish that and I'll get you some more," he says.

"Drew, I need you to talk, not get me more to drink."

"I know, but I need a minute first and that will—"

"Okay." I finish the last few sips so he can leave to gather his thoughts or courage or whatever it is he needs. He's never sounded so distraught before. It's unsettling. He takes my glass and returns a short time later with a refresher for me and a bottle of beer for himself. We're quiet for several minutes. A couple of other guests on the boat stop to chat with Drew.

When we're alone again, he says, "Something happened to me in college and West was there to help pick up the pieces. When I said I wish there was something I could do to help the senior center, I meant I can't because I would never go against him."

His quiet, almost secretive tone is one I've never heard before and, unable to stop myself, I immediately turn my body to his to let him know I'm here for whatever he has to say.

"What happened?" I ask softly.

Drew searches my face, his gaze warm but tentative. Whatever he's about to tell me is a big deal.

"There was a girl who took advantage of me," he says. "Miranda."

A swallow doesn't just work its way down his throat, it chokes him, his eyes empty of any expression. Emotion clogs the back of *my* throat at seeing him so vulnerable. Fallible. Of flesh and blood like the rest of us. I stay silent, giving him as much time as he needs.

"She was the whole package, or so I thought. We met at a tiny pizza place off campus when she commented on my slice of meat lovers pizza with some cute innuendo that I found I was helpless to ignore. She had a daisy in her hair, was barefoot, and I thought this girl isn't just down to earth, she's part of the earth, and I really liked that." He pauses, rubs behind his ear.

The boat rocks on the water as it turns to go back toward the direction of the harbor. I take another sip of my ginger ale.

"She didn't care about anything more than my first name and simply being with me, and I liked that, too. I worked hard at my studies so in my free time we just lazed around on the grass, at the beach, in fields, and talked for hours. She didn't want anything from me but my time. She was a psychology major and loved to do quizzes with me. Relationship ones, mostly, and we ticked off all the same bubbles. She made me feel, I don't know, alive in a way I never had before. I appreciated nature more, appreciated being with someone who liked me stripped down." He runs his hand through his perfectly messy hair again. "Literally and figuratively. We dated for three months and in that time I trusted her with everything. I was in love with her.

"Big mistake."

I wrap my arms around my stomach. I'm more afraid of what he's going to say than I am about the possibility of being seasick.

"She had me fooled. She had all my friends fooled. One night I was playing guitar at my favorite pub. I played there a few times a month and Miranda always came to watch me. After the gig, we had a drink, laughed, and left together hand in hand. I had my guitar case slung over my shoulder and I distinctly remember feeling on top of the world. I'd played great. Had a beautiful girlfriend. Was acing all of my classes.

"My car was parked on the street up a ways from the pub and as I was pulling my key fob from my pocket Miranda yanked her hand free of mine and stepped to the side. The next thing I knew I felt something hard and heavy hit me in the back of the head."

I gasp. "Oh my God."

"I woke up in the gutter, stripped of everything but my clothes."

"Drew." I wrap him in a hug. His arms stay at his sides, but he leans into me. His breath tickles the side of my neck. I squeeze tightly, holding on for a bit longer before I let go.

"It turns out I was Miranda's mark. She and her real boyfriend stole my car, my watch, my wallet, my phone, and my guitar. She knew my PIN—I once stupidly gave her my

ATM card to grab some cash while I waited in the car—so before I came to, they'd gotten what money they could, not to mention I had the three hundred dollars I'd been paid for the gig inside my wallet. They used my credit card for gas and a shit ton of mini mart food by the amount charged. Then they drove to my condo and cleaned it out with some help. My security cameras caught two guys with them, their faces hidden by baseball hats, and they had a truck."

"You're lucky they didn't steal you." My heart hammers at the thought.

"Yeah."

"I assume they were arrested?"

"No. I didn't want the police involved."

"*What?* Why?"

"I didn't want my family to know what had happened. If they knew they'd worry about me or worse, put security on me. I didn't want or need a shadow. And I wanted to forget it had ever happened. I was humiliated."

"I'm so sorry." I squeeze his arm. "Nobody knows about this?" I ask incredulously.

"West is the only person who knows. I walked back to the pub and called him from a landline. He came right away. At that point, I had no idea the extent of Miranda's deceit. West drove me home and that's when we pieced everything together."

"You didn't go to the hospital?" I fight the involuntary urge to feel for a bump on the back of his head. I know this took place years ago, but it's happening to me right now.

"I did. West insisted. It's easier to keep a trip to the ER

on the down low than it is a police report. I had a concussion, but my faith in people hurt a hell of a lot more. I couldn't believe Miranda had completely tricked me into believing she was a good person and loved me. West and I did some digging around and it turned out Miranda wasn't even her real name. She also wasn't enrolled in school. We drove to her apartment and on the way there I realized I'd never been inside the building. She always slept at my place."

I scrunch up my nose, knowing where this was going.

"Yeah, she didn't live there. The landlord had no idea who she was."

"I'm so sorry this happened to you."

He shrugs. "Thanks. I fell into a pretty deep depression after that. West helped me clean up what was left inside my condo, bought me new furniture, and besides going to class, I stayed holed up in there for months. Which brings me to the point of telling you all this. West got me through it. He made sure I didn't die in my sleep from a head injury. He helped me cancel my credit cards and close my bank account. He drove me to the DMV to get a new license. He brought me groceries when I ran out of food and refused to shop for myself. And he told me I wasn't an idiot. That Miranda had fooled him, too.

"He kept me from losing my mind and hating all women. One day he came over with his sister. She was a year older than us and I'd always had a crush on her. Little did I know, she had a crush on me, too. We never would have dated without West's blessing. If things didn't work out between us, then what, you know? But he knew I was safe in her hands after what had happened with Miranda and he wanted that for me. He knew how much I liked being in a relationship. He also knew Tracy was safe with me. West butting into my dating life is what got me to forgive myself, trust a woman again, and move on with someone new."

"You guys broke up, though, and you and West are still friends."

"Yeah. Tracy and I dated for about a year and then realized we were better off as friends. No hard feelings. She's still close to her brother and I still have my best friend. For everything he did, I owe him, Alejandra, and I always will."

I blink in understanding. Some friends are like family.

"And occasionally I let what happened cloud my judgment. Again, I'm sorry for accusing you like I did."

"It's okay."

"You'll keep all this to yourself?" That he feels the need to question my confidence hurts a little. I'm very trustworthy.

"Of course," I assure him, honored he shared something so personal with me. "Did you ever hear from Miranda again or find out anything else about her? I hate that she got away with what she did to you."

"Actually, I did. A couple of years later there was a high-profile robbery here in LA and guess who got caught? Turns out she was part of a theft ring that had been on law enforcement's radar for several years. She's in prison now, serving time for conspiracy to murder, too."

"Oh my God."

"Yeah." He lets out a breath. "How are you feeling?

Want to head below deck for something to eat?"

"Sure. I think I can handle some crackers."

"Let's do it."

The rest of the boat ride is uneventful. We hang out with other passengers and slip away for fresh air and a view of the horizon when I start to feel green around the gills.

Back on land, it takes me a while to feel back to normal again.

Not because of any lingering nausea.

But because so much happened today. With West. With Drew.

Especially Drew.

Being with him today has me more out of sorts than ever, and I'm not sure if my usual approach to life is enough anymore.

Chapter Twelve
A Jump on the Wild Side

Alejandra

THE NEXT MORNING I'm sitting in my usual spot on the couch reading a book when the hotel phone rings. To my disappointment, Drew wasn't here when I woke up, so I get to my feet and walk to the kitchen to answer it.

"Hello?"

"Hello, Alejandra?"

"Yes, this is she."

"It's Rosemary. How are you?"

"Oh, hi! I'm good. How are you?"

"I'll be better if you say you're free for the day."

The request takes me by surprise. Sundays are usually my day off, but I planned to work on another grant application today and then visit the senior center since I wasn't there yesterday. The staff can handle things without me, and my boss told me she didn't want to see my face again until tomorrow, but it's hard for me to be away two days in a row.

"Alejandra?" Rosemary's warm, strong voice cuts into my deliberation.

"Sorry. Umm, sure, I'm free. What can I help you with?"

"Fantastic. I'll be by to pick you up in thirty. Dress in comfortable pants and closed-toe shoes and bring a jacket. You're not afraid of heights, are you?"

"No," I say, imagining an amusement park in our future. I love roller coasters. The taller the better. The only thing I can't do is the rides that spin.

"Excellent. What's your cell number? I'll text you when I'm in front of the hotel."

I rattle off my number with a grin on my face. She is so incredibly vibrant for a woman who will be eighty next month.

After we hang up, I quickly shower, dress as instructed, adding my black and white STRAIGHT OUTTA THE SENIOR CENTER T-shirt then leave a note for Drew on the kitchen counter telling him I'm out with his grandmother. As I head downstairs, a special kind of joy I haven't felt in a long time fills my chest. I'm excited to spend today with Rosemary. I miss days spent with my *abuela* very much.

On my way through the lobby, I run my hand over the Baccarat vase filled with gorgeous white flowers. If I hadn't made the gutsy move of pretending to steal it, I wouldn't be where I am right now. One day I'll tell Drew what I was really doing that morning. Speaking of Mr. Hotel Owner, I catch sight of him in my periphery just as my phone chirps with a text. He's speaking to someone behind the registration desk with a serious expression on his handsome face. He is beyond good-looking in his dark suit and white shirt, open at the collar. His hair is neatly combed; sexy stubble continues to surround his mouth and cover his jawline. A sigh unconsciously slips through my lips.

With a nice visual of Drew tucked in the back of my mind, I step outside the hotel to find Rosemary waiting for me in a fancy black SUV. The valet opens the back passenger door and I slide inside.

"Good morning," I say.

"Good morning." She eyes my shirt. "I'll need an explanation on that as we drive."

"You got it." I'm happy to tell her about my job. "Can I ask where we're headed?"

The car pulls away from the curb. The soft sound of classical music plays through the speakers. "That's one of the things I really like about you, Alejandra. You joined me without asking about what we were doing. That tells me you're here for my company and I appreciate that."

"I am definitely here because of you. In fact, I really like being with people of your age group. You could even say I'm more comfortable with seventy-somethings than I am with twenty-somethings."

"Hence the T-shirt."

"Hence the T-shirt," I echo. "I work at the Davis Senior Center as their activities director."

"How wonderful. Tell me about it."

I do. I tell her about our programs and our seniors and I invite her to visit anytime. Conversation flows easily back and forth after that on too many topics to recount. She is funny and opinionated and sharp-witted. Finally, I get back to my question from an hour ago. "What are we doing today?"

"We're going bungee jumping," she says calmly.

I, on the other hand, immediately fight for breath.

She's almost eighty years old! How does the idea of jumping off a tall structure connected to nothing but a large elastic cord not scare the crap out of her?

Like it does me. I grip the door handle and contemplate flinging myself out of the moving vehicle, but that would be impossible since I'm pretty sure an invisible elephant is sitting on my chest.

"Breathe," Rosemary says, putting her delicate hand on my arm. "Deep breath in—" she inhales slowly and looks to me to do the same "—slow breath out."

I don't feel even marginally better on the exhalation, but it was nice of her to try.

"If you don't want to jump, you don't have to," she says. "You can be a spectator, but I'm told there are two bungee jumping platforms so we can jump at the same time, if that makes you feel better."

She is amazing, attempting to put me at ease while she is gung ho to do something I bet very few seniors do. I'm reminded of what Drew said to me, about her hurting herself, and his worry about Rosemary worms its way into my thoughts. "Drew is going—"

"To be sorry he didn't come. I gave him a chance; he blew it." She sits taller. "I'm glad, too, because I don't need anyone fussing over me. Just think about the look on his face when we tell him what we did."

"Aren't you even a little afraid?"

"Fear is something we invent and so I refuse to let it exist. Want to know what I do instead?"

"Yes, please."

"I say to myself, 'What would Thor do?' and we both know Thor would jump in with both feet, so that takes care of that."

I chuckle. And those five little words ring in my ears. *Jump in with both feet.* This would be the biggest adventure of my life *and* be considered a walk on the wild side. *Take that, Gabriela.*

"You're picturing Chris Hemsworth now, aren't you?" Rosemary asks.

"Yes."

"So, if we die today at least it's with that hottie on our minds."

"Rosemary," I admonish. "No one is dying today."

"Atta, girl."

We arrive at a campground in the Angeles National Forest. There are several other cars parked in the lot and a group is gathering at a Forest Service gate. Rosemary is stylish as can be in a pair of jeans, hiking boots, and a green cashmere cardigan. The sun is shining in a clear sky, but the air is much cooler up here in the mountains. Our driver, Carl, carries a large backpack and joins us. From his size and easy way with Rosemary, I gather he works for her in many different capacities.

We hike a couple of miles to a historic arch bridge that's as beautiful as it is scary. An ice-blue lake glistens one hundred feet below. (Our guide gave us the history of the bridge and all of the particulars.) My heart gallops as I stare at the notable structure. It continues to beat heavily against my rib cage through Jump School, where we learn everything we need to know and are given a 'jump menu.' As if I'd do anything but a regular jump, thank you very much. My heart is careening out of control by the time I'm standing on the edge of the platform, safety gear on and triple checked. I feel like a nervous Nelly, not an adrenaline junkie. The teeth chattering is a major giveaway. But despite all this, I'm doing it. I'm going to jump, even if it kills me. It's not going to kill me. I promised Rosemary. And speaking of Rosemary, I look over at her on the other platform. She looks over at me. I'd return her smile, but my face is frozen in fear. *What would Thor do, Alejandra?*

Thor would smile and jump his ass off, so that's what I do.

What *we* do—jumping simultaneously.

Rosemary shouts, "Yippee ki yay!"

I shout, "Holy shit!"

In the blink of an eye, gravity pulls me down. Adrenaline, excitement, anxiety, and terror rush through me as I free-fall. The feeling of weightlessness only lasts a few seconds, though, and then I bounce up and down a couple of times and boom! I'm done. I survived. *Aleluya! Nunca lo volvere a hacer.* Hallelujah. I am never ever doing that again.

A small boat drifts underneath my dangling legs and a staff person pulls Rosemary, and then me, down. The experience was super quick, but my body won't stop shaking. I also can't keep the smile off my face, proud of myself for what I just did.

"That was incredible!" I high-five Rosemary.

"It was," she agrees. Her short dyed-blond hair is wind-blown. Her cheeks are pink. But her temperament is serene as ever. The woman is remarkable. "I'm glad you jumped with me."

"Me, too." I give her a hug, grateful she lets me hold tight for as long as I need.

A guide leads us back to the campground where Carl is waiting with a full picnic lunch. My nerves finally settle while we eat and laugh over the digital photos taken of each of us when we jumped. Rosemary's expression is one of complete composure, while my face is filled with terror. We're talking slasher-film-level horror. It's embarrassingly funny, and I don't care. It's proof I jumped. Proof I've lived on the wild side. Spread my wings.

I can't wait to tell Drew.

"Chloe is going to love this," Rosemary says, her fingers busy on her phone. We were each emailed our photo, so I'm guessing she's in the process of posting hers to social media. "In addition to being my granddaughter-in-law, she's my social media manager." Rosemary's fingers stop for a moment. She looks up in consideration. A grin follows, and she resumes her task. "Hashtag YOLO."

"You only live once," I say.

"Exactly."

On the drive home, she talks animatedly about her family and I learn more about Drew's brothers and their significant others. Ethan's girlfriend has a daughter, Rylee, whom Rosemary is quite taken with. She shows me a picture

Ethan texted her yesterday of Rylee at Wrigley Field for a Chicago Cubs game. She's in the visiting team's dugout with Finn, dressed in full Landsharks attire, and grinning.

The closeness between the Auprince family is almost tangible. It reminds me of what it was like when my grandparents were still alive. When me, Gabby, and Diego would happily spend all day at home watching telenovelas, playing cards, reading books, and sharing meals. As I stare out the car window, lost in thought, I can smell my *abuela*'s asopao. She made the delicious Puerto Rican stew every Sunday.

I miss those days more than ever when around close-knit families.

And I long to one day have my own.

By the time Carl pulls up to The Surfeit to drop me off it's almost five o'clock. "Thank you so much for today," I tell Rosemary. "I'll always remember it."

"It was my pleasure. And I will, too."

I give her a hug goodbye.

"Alejandra?"

I pause before stepping out of the SUV to look over my shoulder. "Yes?"

"How about we hang glide next?"

"You talking a tandem glide where we're hooked in with an instructor?"

She blinks. "Hooked with a hottie sounds right up my alley."

I laugh. "You're too much."

"So I've been told. I'll look into it. You in?"

"I'm in." Even though I have no idea if I'll still be in contact with Drew and his family when the time comes. It's selfish, agreeing so readily, but all I can think is I want more of this. More adventures with Rosemary. More feeling like I belong, that there's a place for me among this devoted family.

My relationship with Drew may have started out on the wrong foot, but we've righted it now. There's a tingling under my skin whenever I'm around him. His smile makes me forget what day it is. It's Drew's smell and touch and taste emblazoned in my memory while Matthew's has faded.

I take the elevator up to the penthouse. Alone in the small space with my overactive imagination, I may not be ready to give up on Matthew entirely, but one thing is crystal clear.

It's getting harder and harder to keep feelings out of my attachment to Drew.

Chapter Thirteen
Sexy Sorry

Drew

I CAN COUNT on one hand the things that matter most to me in this world. My family. My friends. The Surfeit. As a kid, I worshipped the ground my brothers walked on. I still do, to a certain extent. (Don't tell them I said that or I will never hear the end of it.) I've also revered my parents, even during my teens and early twenties when the last thing I wanted was to be around them.

Then there's my grandmother.

Mémère is remarkable, exceptional, incomparable. She's also nosy, trouble-making, clever, and too perceptive for her own good.

We love her unconditionally and would be lost without her, and I pray to God she's got another twenty years in front of her.

So, when Alejandra walks through the door of the penthouse after spending the day doing something I explicitly told her not to do with the matriarch of our family, I'm aching for a fight. (I may have also had to put out more than one work fire today and that's put me in a bad mood, too.)

"Hi!" she says, meeting my gaze from across the room.

I stagger back, knocked for a loop. I swear she brought sunshine inside with her, a halo of light brightening her beautiful face.

"Guess what I did today with your grandmother?"

I blink away her heavenly beauty and cheerful voice and remember I'm pissed. "I don't need to guess. I know."

Alejandra stops walking toward me. Frowns. My tone left no room for misunderstanding. She looks out the window behind me, hurt replacing joy. Without another word, she spins around to leave.

"Do not walk away."

She spares a glance over her shoulder. "I'm not. I'm getting the last piece of lemon meringue pie." She opens the refrigerator door, pulls out the pie.

I didn't have the heart to tell her I don't like lemon meringue pie when she was sweet enough to tell me she'd saved me a piece, but my heart has left the building so... "Good. I don't like it anyway. It's my least favorite pie."

"I don't know what crawled up your butt, but it's very unattractive." She lifts a fork out of the utensil drawer, doesn't bother with a plate, and leans against the counter to eat her pie.

"I told you not to go bungee jumping with my grandmother." I'm fully aware I'm acting like a petulant child, but I don't care. Who does she think she is, risking my grandmother's safety?

"No, you didn't."

"Yes, I did."

"No, you told me not to tell her I wanted to add some adventure to my life. Something that gives me an adrenaline rush. And then you said she'd been bugging you to go bungee jumping with her for her birthday."

I stride across the suite to close the space between us and stand my ground across the counter from her. She swallows a bite of pie then licks the fork. In slow motion. Savoring the crumbs left behind. Her tongue slides under the prongs, then she flips the fork to glide her tongue over the top of the prongs. Her innate talent for turning the mundane into something sexy sends my mind straight to the gutter. I imagine her licking me. Taking my cock in her hand and licking me from base to tip, then sucking me off.

"For your information, your grandmother called me. She invited me to spend the day with her. She didn't tell me what we were doing until we were almost there so I had no choice in the matter." She points her fork at me. "So there."

"You should have stopped her then." I adjust my pants, grateful for the countertop between us.

Alejandra stabs the pie with her fork. "*Eres un idiota!* You're being such a jerk. I should not have stopped her. She is her own person and can make her own decisions. No one likes being told what to do, Drew. I just had one of the most exciting days of my life with an amazing woman, who also had an unforgettable time, and you're ruining it with your control freak issues."

"I'm not a control freak."

"That's what all control freaks say."

"Wanting to keep my grandmother safe does not make

me a control freak. I care about my family. I don't want anything bad to happen to them."

"Like it did you?" she says, voice lowered.

For the second time since she walked into the room, I stagger back, only this time it doesn't feel good. It feels shitty and stifling. I pull at the collar of my shirt, my neck hot. I hate that Miranda left a mark on me I can't seem to erase completely.

"Drew." Alejandra hurries around the counter, hoists herself to sit atop it so we're eye level, and then pulls me between her legs. "I'm sorry. I didn't mean to upset you."

I'm not sure 'upset' is the right word. Stunned, maybe. No, that's not right either. *Seen.* That's how I feel. Alejandra cut through my suit, my skin, and my vital organs, to my soul. The fight in me diminishes. She's right. I do give orders. I like to be in charge. I don't leave much—if any—room for negotiation. If I'm in command I can protect myself and those I care about.

"You care with your whole heart and that's admirable," she says. "But your grandmother doesn't want to be ordered to avoid something because of her age or risk factors. She won't listen anyway."

"That's true," I murmur.

"She's made of tough stuff." Alejandra cups my cheek. "So are you. I can say that since I'm one of only two people who knows about she who shall not be named or thought about ever again. *Entendido?*"

I raise my brows.

"Got it?"

This woman never gives up on anyone. Her faith and compassion are wildly attractive.

"Got it." I catch her wrist as she drops her arm away from my face. "And I'm sorry for being a jerk." I kiss the back of her hand.

"A big jerk."

"A big jerk," I agree.

"Apology accepted."

"Is it?" I turn her hand over and gently kiss her palm. "Because if you wanted to hold it against me, I'd be more than willing to earn your forgiveness." I place my hand on her leg, grazing my fingers along the inside of her thigh.

"What, uh, did you have in mind?" Her breathy voice tells me she's on board with me working for it.

"Starting here…" I touch her mouth with the pad of my pointer finger then slide it around her chin, down her neck, to the top of her breastbone. I pause there. Her eyes—sparking with heat and approval—stay steady on mine. There's no evidence of indecision. No doubt. With her wordless go-ahead, I resume my mission, drawing my finger lower, between her breasts, over her stomach, to the button of her jeans.

"…And finishing inside here," I conclude.

Her chest rises and falls. Her eyelashes flutter. "Okay."

"You sure?"

She makes me wait for the longest second of my life. "Yes."

"I was really hoping you'd say that." I unfasten the button.

"Hey. Aren't you getting ahead of yourself? I was prom-ised—"

I take her face in my hands and crash my mouth against hers. She squeaks in surprise, and we share a split-second smile before our lips get down to business. This kiss is not like our first one. This kiss is insistent, reckless. Wild. Alejandra is soft and warm under my palms, under my mouth. She curls her hands in my shirt to bring me closer, to lock her legs around my hips. I lick the seam of her lips, leading her to open for me so I can take the kiss deeper. Kissing her like this is better than I imagined.

A sexy sound comes from the back of her throat as our tongues tangle and duel. Warmth invades my body. My dick grows impossibly hard. This sexy, kind, smart woman who was reluctant to date me at the start, is now kissing me back with enthusiasm I feel everywhere.

And not just physically. Alejandra's kiss surpasses every single one I've had before this. My blood is on fire. My head is in the clouds. My feelings are magnified. She is everything pure in this world. She sees beyond my prominent name and business suits to the man I am underneath.

I slant my mouth over hers to change our angle, to ex-plore with longer, slower strokes of my tongue. I kiss her until I'm in danger of coming in my pants. Then I run my thumbs over her delicate cheekbones and step back.

Her legs fall away from my hips. She releases a shaky breath. I take a minute to admire her. Her well-kissed, wide mouth, lips slightly parted. Her heavy-lidded almond-shaped eyes. Light brown satiny skin so pretty and feminine, it's like looking at a work of art.

I slide my finger over her lower lip, then drop down to the words on her adorable T-shirt. I trace each letter—every single one. She sucks in a breath now, her gaze on the movement of my hand as I track across, over, and under her tits, spending an extra second or two around her rigid nipples. I can't wait to strip her naked, discover what color those nipples are, feel the weight of each round breast in my hands as I play with and knead them. Next time. This time I'm going for driving her wild without undressing her completely.

I'm doing a pretty good job so far if her shallow breathing and wiggle is any indication.

Before she wiggles off the counter, I unzip her pants. She lifts her bottom so I can pull her jeans down. I make quick work of ridding her of her shoes and socks and tossing them over my shoulder before I slip her body free of the denim and then look my fill. Her limbs are long. Her skin smooth. I've seen her legs uncovered before but seeing them like this, bare while she sits on the edge of the kitchen counter waiting for me to taste between them, is something else.

"Drew," she whispers. "Please stop looking and start doing."

"Are you wet for me already, Alejandra?"

Her eyes widen. *Interesting.* I grab the thick dish towel that's within reach and slide it under her bottom so she's more comfortable.

"Are you dripping with anticipation of having me lick and suck you until you come on my tongue?"

Lust sparkles back at me.

"Fall apart on my face?"

She squirms. Grips the edge of the counter as her legs fall open. "*Yes.*"

The small triangle of material covering her is pale yellow. A small strip of dark curls is visible through the thin fabric. It takes all my willpower not to rip them off her and show her just how out of control I can be. Instead, I toy with the string at her hip.

"Do you like to be fingered at the same time you're being tasted?"

"Yes."

"One finger or two?"

"Surprise me."

Jesus. Every word out of her mouth turns me on more than the last one. I love how uninhibited she is. Candid. Honest.

"Now, Drew. Before I take matters into my own hands."

My dick is about to break through my zipper at that impatient announcement. "Would you really, Al?"

"Drew!"

I nudge her panties to the side.

"You're not going to take them off?" she asks, a restless edge to her voice.

"Nope. There's something forbidden about leaving them on, don't you think?"

"Drew, this isn't—"

She doesn't get to finish that thought because my mouth is on her. Lips, tongue, I latch on. She immediately bucks against me, runs her fingers through my hair. She tastes so good I'm going to eat her out until she can't take it anymore. Until her juices no longer coat my face and her sexy body goes limp.

"Oh my God, that feels so good," she croons.

It's about to feel even better. I finger her opening. Rub her wetness around her folds then slide slowly inside. She's tight and warm and when I touch the right spot, she lets go of my head to slap her hands down on the counter.

I devour her with my mouth. Suck and lick. Fill her with a second finger. She about flies off the counter, but I've got her. With my free arm around her thigh, she's under my ministrations and my protection.

A harsh cry accompanies her first orgasm. I taste and finger her through her climax and then I change my angle, withdraw my fingers, and keep going.

"Drew," she pants.

It's not, *Drew, I'm a one and done girl.* It's *Drew, you sex god, make me come again.*

To make sure she gets her point across, she palms the back of my head to keep me in place. No problem, gorgeous, having you come apart again will be my pleasure.

I drag my tongue through her slickness, happy to exist between her legs for as long as she needs. There's no other place I'd rather be than right here, buried in Alejandra's most intimate spot.

She moans, the sultry sound filling the air around us. Feeling, seeing, and hearing her turned on has me hornier than I've ever been. I grip underneath both her thighs and push her knees up, spreading her wider. Giving me more to see and taste. Her hands slip free of my head and she hooks a finger in her underwear to keep it from getting in the way. Then she sweeps the pie out of the way with her other arm and falls onto her back. I'm vaguely aware of the pie hitting the floor somewhere.

I slant my head to taste her more deeply. She arches her back off the counter and I regret not stripping her shirt and bra off her. She is so fucking sexy, curving and bending in pleasure, her knees practically at her ears, while I work to bring her a second release.

My pants feel two sizes too small. My skin hotter than Hades. Alejandra pushes against my face. I pull. She pushes. I pull. "Don't stop," she whisper-sighs. "I'm so close."

The hotel could be falling down around us and I wouldn't stop. I'm laser focused on lashing her with my tongue and brushing my lips across her sensitive skin. *I'm addicted to you, Alejandra.*

She calls out my name this time, when she comes. I continue my onslaught until she presses her knees down and wiggles away from my reach. Her shirt slides up, exposing her midriff. To my surprise, there's another tiny tattoo on her hip bone. This one two interlinking hearts.

I straighten and stare down at her. With her legs dangling off the counter, her arms spread wide, and her face pointed to the ceiling she says, "I'm dead."

"Took you to heaven did I?"

She cracks one eye open. "Maybe."

I grin. I absolutely did. "Let me help you up." I get her

to a sitting position with one hand on her lower back, the other holding her elbow. "You doing okay?" A hard counter-top isn't the most comfortable spot to lie down on and I silently scold myself. Next time will be more luxurious.

"Yes, but…" She looks to her left, to the upturned pie box on the floor. "It looks like my pie isn't."

"I'll buy you another one."

"Two orgasms *and* pie. You are completely forgiven." She glances down at the obvious bulge in my pants. "Need a hand with that?"

I slowly step away from temptation. It takes strength I didn't know I had, but tonight wasn't about me. "While I'd love your hands on me, this time was about you and an in-depth apology." I pick up her jeans, pass them to her.

Our fingers brush on the hand-off as she slips down from the counter. "Thanks." She doesn't put them on like I was hoping. Nope. She stands there in her T-shirt and scrap of underwear, with her flushed cheeks and tousled hair, tortur-ing me. "Pretty confident of you, thinking there's going to be a next time."

"Al, there are going to be many more next times."

Chapter Fourteen
Third Date

Alejandra

I S IT NEXT time yet?

This question is way more troublesome than 'Are we there yet?'

It's been six days since Drew kissed me then buried his face between my legs. Did he not say there would be multiple more times? Does he not know I've been on edge? Waiting and hoping.

I close my book and sigh all dramatic-like for the empty room. I can't concentrate on a single word knowing he will be walking through the door any minute to have dinner with me. My *abuela*'s stew is cooking on the stovetop. The table is set for two. I haven't made asopao in over a year, and I hope Drew enjoys it. I glance over at the flickering candlelight. I found two taper candles in the cupboard so I put them on the table between our plates.

It's our official third date tonight.

We've both been crazy busy with work this week. I'm desperately trying to come up with a plan to save the senior center. Silent auction? Casino night? Raffle? Crowdfunding?

But nothing is meeting with approval for one reason or another. Drew and his marketing team are trying to come up with something to 'wow' hotel guests and make The Surfeit *the* hotel on everyone's mind.

I walk to the kitchen to stir the stew, putting my book down on the counter. I have very fond memories of this counter. In fact, I'll never be able to look at a kitchen counter the same way again. My cheeks heat and it has nothing to do with the steam rising from the pot on the stove.

"It smells amazing in here."

I jump at Drew's announcement. I didn't hear him come in, so lost in imagining his mouth on me.

"Sorry, I didn't mean to scare you." He puts his hands on my waist, kisses the back of my neck. "I didn't know you were cooking."

Tingles shoot across my shoulders and down my arms. His lips are warm. His voice low. Powerful. "I thought you might like to stay in. This is a special recipe of my *abuela*'s."

"Alejandra," he whispers against my ear. "Thank you."

"You're welcome." I lay the large wooden spoon back on a paper towel.

He turns my body to face his. Today's dark suit is paired with a white shirt and pale yellow tie. A five-o'clock shadow lines his jaw and circles his full lips. Fathomless blue-green pools of intelligence and warmth stare down at me. I wish I could say for certain I knew where our relationship was going, but I can't. In the meantime, it won't stop me from enjoying right now.

From being the carefree girl I didn't allow myself to be growing up.

That I care for Drew a great deal makes it that much more thrilling.

"How much longer does it need to cook?" he asks.

"It's ready whenever we are. A little longer definitely won't hurt." *You know, in case you want to Next Time.*

"I was hoping you'd say that."

"I thought you might."

"Oh, you think you know me, do you?"

"A little."

"It's more than a little, Al," he says with reverence. But before I get a chance to enjoy his admiration, he picks me up and tosses me over his shoulder like I'm a sack of potatoes.

"Hey! Put me down!"

"I will."

"Drew! Please."

He laughs. "Was the 'please' supposed to make me listen to you?" He carries me toward his room. Okay, so maybe I don't mind where this is headed.

"I can't help my good manners," I say honestly. I'm the kind of girl who even when I'm alone and I burp I say 'excuse me.'

"How about putting that please to better use then," he commands as he casts me onto his bed. He's in bossy-pants mode and I've got to say, I'm cool with that in the bedroom.

I lift up onto my elbows. My blush-pink shift dress is bunched around the tops of my thighs, and Drew can't seem to decide where to look first, his roving eyes moving all around my body. I'm wearing two articles of clothing: the dress and a pair of white G-string panties. All part of my master plan for tonight.

"You mean like 'please get me naked, Drew.' Or 'please kiss me, Drew.'"

He loosens his tie.

"Wait." I scramble onto my knees. "Let me do that... Please," I add with a simper.

I want to enjoy every moment, every minute, every aspect of my time with Drew, including having my hands on his sexy suit and then *not*.

He drops his arms and steps within reach, giving me the okay to have my way with him. Our eyes never leave each other as I unknot his tie and let it drop to the floor. Next, I slide my palms under his coat and over his shoulders and guide the expensive cloth down his arms until it slips free of his hard, well-toned body. He breathes a little harder. A little faster.

"This is fun," I say.

"The longer it takes you, the longer it's going to take me."

"Doubtful." I work the buttons of his shirt from top to bottom. I think he means to return the favor, but I'm pretty sure he can't wait to lift my dress off me.

"Are you questioning my patience, Al? Because I can and I will take my sweet time with you if that's a challenge."

"Hmm..." I push his shirt off him. It's beautifully clear Drew takes care of himself from the carved muscle detailing his arms and abs. I want to lick him. The thought is so foreign, and animalistic, that I almost cover my face in embarrassment.

Instead, I stick my tongue out and slide it over his pec. His skin is warm. Soft, but hard. The muscle there flexes in response, boosting my confidence. My impact on a man I'm hopelessly falling for.

I pull back. Last weekend Drew got to know me intimately, but he didn't get to see all of me. I've never been shy about my body, but I've only shown it to one other man. Everything I've done and learned in the bedroom has included a safety net: a person who explored with me and shared the same firsts. A person who loved me. Who might still.

There is nothing safe about this time.

I lift my dress up and over my head and toss it to the side. My nipples are hard points. My breathing is ragged. My stomach quivers in anticipation.

Drew looks at me like I'm a snow cone in the middle of the Mojave Desert. His gaze sweeps over every inch of me, sparking goose bumps to pop up on my skin.

"You are gorgeous, Al."

"You are, too." I reach for him again. I can't help myself.

Only he's faster. He slams his mouth against mine in a kiss that sets off fireworks behind my eyelids. He brings me flush against him with one hand on my butt and the other curved around the back of my neck. His heart is pounding as hard as mine. His erection presses between my legs.

The hold is possessive. I melt beneath his touch.

We kiss until we need a breath and then he lays me down

on my back. His hands make quick work of his belt. I watch as he unbuttons and unzips his pants, pushes them down. He tries to take off his shoes and socks and kick off his slacks at the same time and loses his balance.

I laugh. "What was that you were saying about patience?"

"It's overrated," he growls, righting himself.

I lift my arms above my head. Curve slightly at the waist. Press my legs together and bend them at the knees. Bite my lip. My seductive pose works. He loses his balance again.

"You want to play, huh?" His husky voice is laced with warning.

"It seems I do." I love the playful side Drew brings out in me.

His eyes glitter like light on water. And God, I don't care if I sink.

He removes his boxer briefs and stands at the foot of the bed to let me visually explore every inch of his six-foot naked body. Except his shins and feet. I can't see those from my position. Which is more than fine since I'm currently much more interested in his erection. His beautifully thick, long length is standing at attention. For me.

Drew strokes himself. It's the most erotic thing I've ever seen. I like how unabashed he is. I like staring at his fist wrapped around his shaft as he moves slowly up and down.

I shift on the plush comforter, slide my hand down my stomach to rub myself over my panties.

"Jesus," he rasps.

I'm wet. Achy. Dying for him to come inside me. But

I'm also lost to this moment of naughty surrender where we watch each other with lust and abandon. I've never felt sexier. Never craved someone so much.

Time passes at a snail's pace, gifting me the pleasure of Drew's body and dirty act. Soon, though, it's not enough. I need his hands on me. His mouth. His body.

"Drew."

"Yes, gorgeous?"

I stop touching myself and lift up onto my elbows. "Get over here."

"Or what?" he teases, staying right where he is. He wins the patience game, damn him.

Rather than answer, I use brand-new ninja skills I didn't know I had to grab him around the waist and pull him down on top of me. He comes willingly, bracing his elbows on either side of me so he doesn't crush me.

We laugh.

And then finally, he kisses me. His mouth devours mine, but only for a moment before his lips move to my jaw, my neck. He kisses his way down to my breasts where he lavishes each one with a gentle touch, like he already knew how much the soft brushes of his lips over my nipples would make me even more needy for him.

I run my fingers through his hair then lift his head back up to mine.

"Tell me what you want," he says.

"I want you inside me."

"Which part of me? My tongue? My fingers?"

I shake my head at the same time I take his length in my

hand. He's hot and slick at the tip and I don't care if he pushes my underwear to the side again. I just need him thrusting inside me. "This part," I urge.

He smiles, part playful part depraved. "Say no more." He slides my G-string down my legs while he regards my body with appreciation. "I could look at you all day," he whispers.

The feeling is mutual.

Reaching over to the nightstand, he opens the drawer to retrieve a condom. He's got my full attention as he rolls it on. And my full attention when he parts my thighs and enters me. Slowly. Giving me time to adjust to his size.

I lock my legs around his waist, thrust my hips against his. I'm done with the leisurely state of our lovemaking.

Drew kisses me on the mouth as he buries himself all the way inside me. I cry out in bliss. It's heaven all over again, only this time there's something more to it. Being connected like this cracks open my carefully maintained dedication to the past. It gives way to new feelings. Deeper feelings. Afraid of what that means, I focus on Drew's body. The rhythm of his thrusts, the smell of our arousal. I press my heels into the backs of his thighs. Dig my fingernails into his shoulders. I'm lost to every delicious stroke, sensations blooming hotter and more intense.

We move together in oneness.

And it's that sneaky thought—being in total harmony with Drew—that sends me over the edge.

Drew keeps a steady pace through my orgasm and when my body goes molten, he drives into me harder, faster, chasing his release on the heels of mine. He pushes in deep, deeper than I've ever felt before then goes rigid, groaning in pleasure before collapsing on top of me.

Our bodies are slippery with sweat. Our breathing rapid. He kisses behind my ear then rolls onto his back. I immediately miss his warmth.

Side by side, our gazes on the ceiling, he laces his fingers with mine. The small gesture of keeping us connected means more than he'll ever know.

"I'm going to need to repeat that after dinner," he says.

I grin so big my cheeks hurt. "Okay."

"With a few changes. But don't worry, the outcome will be the same." His cocky, yet lighthearted tone is a ridiculously sexy combination.

"I have no doubt."

What is in question is my ability to not be affected more than I already am. As much as I worry and wonder if I should run away from Drew, I want to stay.

Chapter Fifteen
Lessons in Affection

Drew

"THE TATTOO ON your hip, does it have significant meaning?" I ask, eating asopao across the table from Alejandra. It's one of the most delicious foods I've ever tasted and I've tasted a ton of great food given Ethan owns the hottest restaurant in LA. Not to mention my restaurant downstairs and the others in my family's hotels. The best way to describe Alejandra's dish is a cross between soup and paella.

"Gabriela has the same one on her hip. We wanted something simple to bond us when we turned eighteen. To us it means our hearts are always interlinked." She puts her spoon down, dots the corners of her mouth with a napkin. "Have you ever wanted to get a tattoo?"

I register her question but I lose focus for a moment. That mouth. The wavy shape of her lips that drives me wild with want. Alejandra steals my concentration on a regular basis. She's unlike any woman I've been with before. Sweet, but argumentative. Kind, yet resolute. She's comfortable with who she is and couldn't care less about impressing me.

Side note: At the moment, she's wearing nothing but a hair tie to keep her messy bun in place and my white dress shirt and it's very impressive.

"Drew?"

"I almost did in college. One night after a fraternity party a few of us went to a parlor to get our Greek letters inked on our arms, but it was late and there wasn't enough time to do West and me."

At mention of West, a faint line bisects her brows before she looks across the room. Candlelight throws a shadow across her cheek. I'm a dumbass for saying his name. Tonight is strictly about the two of us.

"What books are you reading?" I ask, to get her mind off my best friend. If there's a way to bridge the gap between them that works in both their favor, I will do it. I just haven't had time to think on it.

She rattles off two titles, her favorite hobby erasing her frown. "The second one is a Reese's Book Club pick, and it's soooo good."

"How good is it?" I tease.

"It's almost better than sex," she says matter-of-factly.

I laugh. That's another thing about Alejandra. She makes me feel lighter.

"I'm serious." Her earnest expression is damn cute.

"So, you're saying for all intents and purposes, the book can give you as good an orgasm as I have?"

"That's not what I said, but some books have that potential, yes." She takes a bite of her stew.

"Got it. Who's Reese?"

She looks at me like I'm from another planet. "Reese Witherspoon."

"She has a book club? How does that work?"

Alejandra pushes her stew to the side. "She recommends a book every month and posts it to social media. She has a huge following. She's made books into bestsellers."

"Wow."

"You know," Alejandra puts her elbow on the table, her chin in her hand. "Reading is something a lot of people do when on vacation. In hotels."

I nod, taking my final spoonful of stew.

"You've been looking for something different to make The Surfeit special."

"Mmmhmm," I mutter through a closed mouth.

"You're kind of famous and probably know people in Hollywood. What if you reached out to Reese and formed a partnership? Whatever book she picks you could buy and put in every room for hotel guests to read during their visit." She sits taller; excitement twinkles in her eyes. "Instead of chocolate or whatever else you might put on the bed for new guests, you could leave the book! You'd be promoting reading, helping authors, and I imagine having Reese's name attached to your hotel could only help. Granted, there's a big cost involved, but think of all the publicity. Reese puts a book club sticker on the book she picks so maybe she could put a Surfeit sticker somewhere? I'm thinking the sky's the limit here."

I stare at her as I let that all digest. "That's a brilliant idea."

"You really think so?"

"I do. To the best of my knowledge no other hotel does anything like that. We supply a curated publication on local shopping and activities, but you might have hit on something next level."

"Probably," she boasts. "And think of all the pictures guests will take with the book. On *your* property. You could come up with a special cocktail to go with each book. Oh! And you could make Surfeit bookmarks. Even someone who might not be interested in the book will probably take and keep the bookmark." She makes a sour face. "That is the one downside. Not everyone will be interested in the book. On the flipside, the book selection changes every month so you'll most likely have some winners and some less favored reads. Your marketing people probably have tools to track that kind of thing and gauge your customers' habits. The book club has been around for a couple of years so if one month you want to do a throwback because you think the current selection might not be as popular, you could."

If I thought Alejandra was hot as hell before she started spouting a plan to put my guest services on a new trajectory with crazy new potential, imagine how smoking hot she is now. I'm so blown away, I don't know what to say. And it's not her smarts that have me tongue-tied, because I've admired her intelligence from day one. No, it's her honest-to-goodness desire to help me. Hell, to gift thousands of people with a program like this.

"Beautiful, smart, and altruistic. If you're not careful, you'll never get rid of me, Al."

She quickly looks down at her lap. I'm not sure which parts of what I said bother her most, but I don't regret a single word. I lean over, lift her chin with the back of my hand. "Thank you. I can't wait to share your idea with my team. Now, I need to do something for you. I know it's technically something you want to do on your own, but if you'd like a guitar lesson, I'm at your service."

"You have a guitar here?"

"Yes."

"Could you teach me how to play a whole song?" Gone is her apprehension and in its place is the pure, unguarded radiance that makes it hard for me to breathe.

"Did you have a certain song in mind?"

"No, not at all. I wouldn't even know where to start. Obviously, I need something easy. I've never even held a guitar before."

"Tonight's your lucky night, then." And yes, I mean that in more ways than one. I get to my feet. "Come on. I'll clean up the dishes later." I pull out her chair. She stands and walks with me to my bedroom. I'm playing with fire here, opening myself up in a way I haven't since that horrible night in college, but with Alejandra I'm operating on instinct.

"How long have you played?" she asks.

"Since high school." I pick up the straight-backed desk chair in the corner of my room and put it down facing the foot of the bed. My mind wanders back to an hour ago when we watched each other touch ourselves before I buried myself inside her. My dick twitches remembering how tight she was, how perfect, how her muscles clenched around me when she came. Being with her in that way rocked my world and there is no going back. I want her in a way I've never wanted anyone else, and yet there's her ex looming over our heads in a way I'm not sure how to remedy. *He's coming back.*

If I come on too strong, I'm afraid she'll run. If I don't come on strong enough, I'm afraid she'll leave.

"Have a seat," I tell her, pushing aside what comes next. We've got two weeks until my grandmother's birthday party so she's mine at least until then.

As she sits, I walk into the closet and retrieve my guitar. Alejandra tracks my every move as I walk back out, around the bed, and sit at the foot, facing her, our knees almost touching.

I take a moment to admire her in nothing but my dress shirt, the top two buttons unfastened, the hem hitting the middle of her pretty thighs. She's sitting up straight, hands clasped in her lap, her legs pressed together, feet flat on the floor. A few wisps of hair have escaped her bun and frame her face. Her student pose is sexy as all get-out, and I'm ready to teach her every fucking thing I know.

"First rule of guitar playing," I say. "Relax and have fun."

"I can do that."

"Quick rundown of the parts. Neck, bridge—" I touch each part as I go "—headstock, turning pegs, frets. You hold the guitar like this." I rest the bridge of the guitar on my right thigh under my arm, the neck in my left hand. "The back of the guitar should touch your stomach and chest so that your body cradles it. Your right hand will strum and your left hand should be able to move smoothly up and down. Like this." I demonstrate then pass the guitar to Alejandra.

"Give it a try and don't be discouraged if it's uncomfortable. It takes time to get used to the position."

She hits it out of the ballpark on the first try.

"That's great," I tell her.

"It's awkward but with practice, I guess you get used to it."

"You do."

"Can I ask you something?" She holds on to the guitar, making slight adjustments to get more comfortable.

"Anything."

"When I first met your grandmother, that morning in the lobby, she said it was a shame you didn't play anymore. But here's a guitar, here with you, rather than at your house."

We gaze at each other. As always, I see compassion. Kindness. I'm not sure what she sees.

"I'm guessing you stopped playing after what happened in college, which is completely understandable."

I nod.

"But you loved it too much to quit forever, and I'm glad. That would have meant that bitch won and that's unacceptable." She hands me back the guitar. "Play something for me?"

I take the instrument back, too choked up by her intuition, protectiveness, and request to answer aloud. After Miranda, I thought maybe I was looking for something I didn't deserve. That in some twist of fate, I couldn't have a good family, a good job, wealth, and also love. Sometimes you just don't get to have it all. But then West told me to stop beating myself up, and I dated Tracy, and I told doubt to suck it. I'd try for everything until I succeeded.

Alejandra is my gold medal. My cherry on top. My silver lining.

The song I play for her flows through my fingertips without thought. I play the music and sing the song, never taking my eyes off her. She's unable to hold my admiration, glancing away a time or two, but always coming back.

'Brown Eyed Girl' by Van Morrison.

As I strum the last few chords, I realize it's a simple song, one I could teach her. I like the idea of sharing this music with her, knowing it's the first song we've shared—the first one I've shared with someone else since that awful night.

When I'm finished, she claps. Her brown eyes shimmer, her lips are slightly parted. She takes the guitar out of my hands and puts it down on the floor. Then she crawls onto my lap, straddles me, and kisses every other kiss in my memory bank but hers out of my head.

She grinds on me, rubbing her center over my growing erection. My cotton sleep pants are a thin barrier between us so the friction turns hot in a matter of seconds. Her arms go around my neck. She presses closer.

I cup the back of her head with one hand. My other hand finds its way under her shirt to her lower back. I press my palm there, keeping her tight against me, but letting her set the pace.

She moans into my mouth, kisses me harder.

Out of control, no-holding-back humping and kissing continues until she murmurs expletives that sound more like terms of endearment coming out of her sweet mouth and her body jerks then stills then melts against mine.

"I can't believe I just did that."

"You can use my body to get off anytime you want."

She buries her face in my neck. "Watching you play guitar and sing…"

I rub my hand up and down her back, palm her ass cheek, dip my fingers lower. She lifts her head. We make eye contact.

And then clothes fly off, protection is put in place, and our bodies become one until we're both spent and satisfied.

A little while later we sit against the headboard to resume the lesson. She's wearing the cotton T-shirt I had on and I'm back in my pajama bottoms. My guitar rests in her arms. She's struggling with playing the chords I taught her, her finger placement frequently slipping.

"Oops," she says, catching herself when she once again touches the wrong string.

She strums with a loose, relaxed motion for a few seconds, but then her wrist gets tired and her elbow starts to move more, which makes the sound uneven and less rhythmic. She lets out a frustrated sigh.

"Hey, get over here," I say, taking the guitar and motioning for her to sit in between my straight legs.

She looks at me quizzically for all of a second before settling in with her back to my front and stretching her legs out in front of her.

I put the guitar in her lap, wrap my arms around her, and place my hands in playing position. It's tedious, but my long reach allows it to work. "Can you look down and see my hands?" I ask.

"Yes."

"Great. Do that and as you do, feel the music. Feel the vibration of each chord as I move my fingers against the instrument but also with it, if that makes sense. I'm not fighting to make sounds, I'm welcoming what this instrument can do with my assistance."

I play 'Brown Eyed Girl' again, singing softly in Alejandra's ear with my eyes closed. It's not as flawless a rendition this time, given I'm working solely off touch, but Al won't necessarily know the difference.

Having her cocooned in my arms like this, after a night of good food and fantastic sex, is something I will always remember. I strum the last chord and kiss the slope of her neck.

She takes the guitar and reaches over to lean it up against the nightstand. I literally bite my fist to keep from biting her luscious ass.

"Thank you," she says, facing me with her legs crossed in her lap.

"You did great. If we keep practicing, I bet by the end of the week, you'll have the entire song down."

"We?" She blows a piece of hair off her forehead, and I get a whiff of the fruity vanilla scent of her shampoo.

"I'm here every night, Al," I say when what I really wanted to say was, *I'm not going anywhere.* "But feel free to use the guitar whenever you want. This was your solo wish so I certainly don't need to be around for you to play. You've got the basics down."

"I'll keep that in mind."

I lift her hand and kiss the tip of her pointer finger. "How do your fingers feel?"

"They hurt."

"Shit. I'm sorry." I kiss the tips of each one, then move to her other hand and repeat. "I should have cut you off sooner. It's normal, though, and will get less painful with time."

She kisses the back of my hand. "Please don't be sorry. Tonight was...tonight was so much more than I imagined it to be."

"So, you've been dreaming about me?"

She swats my upper arm. "You're incorrigible."

I'm also falling in love.

Chapter Sixteen
Sunday, Monday, Tuesday

Drew

W E SPEND SUNDAY in bed, playing guitar, eating leftover asopao, and reading. I figure if I'm going to pitch the book club idea to my marketing team at our Tuesday meeting, then I better know what I'm talking about.

Monday night, Alejandra gets home from work and excitedly announces a meteor shower is taking place sometime around two a.m. "Would it be okay if I slept outside at the pool tonight?" she asked. "I know it's asking for preferential treatment, and I'll understand if you say no, but—"

"It's fine," I told her. "I'll let security know."

She flung her arms around me and kissed me in thanks.

"Do you...do you want to join me?"

I did, but I also knew she wanted to do this by herself. "Next time," I told her, and she hugged me again in appreciation. At one a.m. I had a thermos of hot chocolate delivered to her. Around three a.m. a chilled body crawled into bed with me and tucked herself against my chest. "Is this okay?" she'd asked.

"It's more than okay," I'd whispered back, but I'm not sure she heard me, the sound of her soft snore filling the space a split second later.

Today's marketing meeting is a long one. The team loves the book club idea and Luna reaches out to Reese's people. Emails go back and forth and we set a date to discuss further. I'm beyond stoked and want to take Alejandra out to dinner to celebrate, but I'm called out of town to take my father's place at an important meeting in Vancouver. He's stuck in New York due to a delayed flight and as one of the VPs of Auprince Holdings, I'm happy to go.

I text her I'll see her tomorrow night.

And already miss her like hell.

Chapter Seventeen
That Night

Alejandra

THIRTY SECONDS FEELS like thirty minutes when you're in star pose.

I know this because I'm currently sitting in a chair in the exercise room of the senior center with my arms and legs out wide in V shapes. I'm in serious danger of looking weaker than the group of seventy-somethings around me. Chair yoga is a lot harder than you think it is. My core is protesting. My muscles are quivering. And as soon as the thirty seconds are up, we have to repeat this pose two more times. I liked candle pose much better. The seconds flew by with that one because my feet stayed on the floor and I kept singing 'Walk Like an Egyptian' in my head.

"And release," our instructor says.

Finally. I drop my limbs like they each weigh a hundred pounds. The running I've been doing is zero help with this activity.

Lu, the center's director of finance and operations, waves to me from the wide doorway and I want to run across the room and tackle her with gratitude. Adios, chair yoga! "Nice job," I tell Mrs. K. as I vacate my chair and step around hers.

"You too, sweetie," she says.

"Keep up the good work," I say to Gloria when I pass her striking the second star pose.

"I will. Now hurry back, okay? You're my inspiration."

Aw, how sweet and wonderful is that? I pause, tilt my head to the side, and look down at her gently wrinkled face. "It's definitely the other way around, Gloria."

She waves me off.

"Hey," I say to Lu, wrapping her in a quick hug. "Thanks for saving me."

"You only looked mildly constipated," she teases.

"Ha! Lucky for me everyone else's vision isn't what it used to be."

"We should only hope we're in as good a shape as they are when we're their age."

We peek back at the class and nod in tandem. "I'm guessing we need to talk," I say. I've been dreading speaking with her and Karen, our executive director, since our meeting two days ago when we discussed the center's survival.

"Yes."

I follow her to the office-slash-conference room she shares with Karen and the three of us sit at the round work table.

"We were denied the Madison Grant," Karen says, never one to beat around the bush. Lines of disappointment crease her forehead. "They took a magnifying glass to our entity structure and weren't satisfied with what they found."

My shoulders sag. "We've still got one more to hear back

on."

"Yes, but I don't think we'll hear in time," Lu says. "If we don't fulfill our financial obligation by the first of next month, then the bank will foreclose." Her lips tremble. "I'm so sorry my budget strategy got us here."

"It's not your fault," I say. "Sometimes even the best plans just don't work out."

"West Landry did reach out again," she says. "His company has the means to buy the land from the foundation in cash and with the tax revenue the city will receive on their proposed new development, we're fighting an uphill battle."

I clench my jaw. I'd like to push West *down* a hill right about now.

"But. He's offered to help us relocate."

"He has?" Did Drew ask him to do that?

"The problem is there is no place for us to go. Not in the same zip code. Not even in a ten-mile radius, maybe more," Karen says.

"Which means our seniors would have to travel a lot farther and many won't do that. Plus, we'd have to make sure we're not encroaching on another senior center. I doubt West Landry is thinking like that," I contend.

"True."

"I think we need to give everyone a heads-up," Lu says.

I truly adore every single one of our seniors, but I do have a few favorites I'm not sure I can live without.

You're my inspiration.

"Give me a week," I say. "I'm not ready to give up."

Karen and Lu look at me with kind, but doubt-filled

eyes.

"Please," I implore.

"One week," Karen says.

I jump to my feet before she changes her mind. Back in my office, I check my phone and find a text from Drew. He's going out of town for the night and will see me tomorrow. A funny feeling worms its way into my chest. I'll miss him. A lot. I type a quick reply back with a heart emoji at the end. Delete the heart emoji. *Send.*

"Got a minute?"

I startle at the question and look up to see Mrs. K. and Gloria standing in my doorway. "Always. Come on in."

The two of them look adorable in their yoga pants and graphic tees. "Age before beauty," Gloria teases, motioning for Mrs. K. to take my only guest chair.

"What are you talking about? You're older than me." Mrs. K. still takes the chair.

"Yes, but you look as if you're older than me."

"Says you. You're only as old as you feel, you know."

"Which makes us…" Gloria trails off.

"Thirty-nine!" they say simultaneously.

I grin at them. "What can I do for you, ladies?"

"We'd like to invite you to a Galaxy soccer game on Friday," Mrs. K. says. "My daughter was supposed to make it a threesome, but now she has to work. Think you could play hooky and be our chaperone?"

My heart squeezes. In appreciation. And so much more. "I'd love to take you to the game." Friday is kind of a holiday given tomorrow is July fourth, so I can definitely sneak away.

"Wonderful. We'll meet you here at ten. There could be traffic," Mrs. K. says.

"There will be traffic," Gloria corrects good-naturedly.

My phone rings on my desk. Gabby's name appears on the screen. "Sorry. Mind if I take this? It's my sister."

"Not at all." They say goodbye and thank you and leave me to my call.

"Hey, Gabs."

"Allie." Gabby's voice sounds crestfallen. She sniffles, and I picture her holding a tissue under her nose.

"What's wrong?"

"Landon and I broke up. He broke up with me and kicked me out of his place and said terrible things and—" she cries "—I hate him and I have nowhere to go and I need you. I need my sister."

"I'm so sorry, Gabs. Come to the hotel. I'll meet you there in thirty and you can stay with me. Park in the underground lot in space number one. Are you okay to drive? I can come get you if you're not."

"I…I'm okay." She hiccups. "See you in a few."

"Love you. Take your time and pull over if you have to. You know what? Why don't I just pick you up?"

"No. Really. I can drive myself. Thanks, though. Love you."

We hang up, my heart hurting for my sister. On the way to the hotel I make an emergency stop at the supermarket for ice cream, chocolate chip cookies, potato chips, Ritz crackers and spray cheese, and two bananas. We have to eat something healthy before we pig out on junk food for dinner while we dissect what happened. I've been secretly hoping Gabby would break up with Landon, but I never expected it to go the other way around.

Breaking up is painful and hard, not matter what. Even if it's amicable. In only nine days I'll be face-to-face with Matthew again. When we agreed to break up, all I could think about was getting to this point. Getting through a year of separation then reuniting under a star-filled sky at one of our favorite spots and announcing we still loved each other. That no one else compared.

Only now there is someone who compares.

Who is maybe beyond compare.

But do I feel that way because I haven't seen Matthew in almost a year and I've forgotten about all his good qualities? Has my attraction to him faded because we haven't stood in the same air space, but as soon as we do, all my feelings will come flooding back?

We didn't end on a bad note. We didn't end because we no longer loved each other. We didn't end because of mistrust or miscommunication or a mistake. In fact we didn't *end*. We paused to pursue our own lives for twelve months. Seeing each other again was always in the plan. *No matter what, I will meet you at eight o'clock on the rooftop of the Observatory on July twelfth and if we're both still single, then we'll pick up where we left off.* Those were Matthew's exact words, and I've carried them with me every day since.

A man doesn't say *no matter what* unless he plans to keep you in his life.

The question is, in what capacity? And what happens if

our ways of thinking don't mesh?

Gabby is leaning against her car, her arms wrapped around herself, when I pull into the parking spot beside her. I barely have my car in park before I'm jumping out to hug her. I may not have been a fan of Landon's, but my sister means everything to me.

She cries on my shoulder while I rub her back.

"Come upstairs," I say a couple of minutes later. "I've got sustenance and Drew is out of town so we have the place to ourselves."

I grab the groceries. She grabs a duffel from her front seat. We're quiet in the elevator. Once in the suite, we throw the comforter from my bed, extra blankets, and bed and couch pillows onto the floor in front of the window in the main room so we can watch the sun fall asleep and see the ocean in the distance. When we were young, we loved to make forts in the family room when one or both of us were feeling unwell. This makeshift arrangement isn't exactly the same, but it's close enough.

"He said he didn't like how Alan looked at me," Gabby says, sitting identical to me with her legs crossed in her lap, and spraying cheese on a cracker.

"Doesn't Alan have a boyfriend?" I ask, putting my banana peel down. Alan is a hair stylist and works at the same salon as Gabby.

"He does, yes, but then Landon goes, 'He swings both ways you know,' and I said, 'Yes I know that; he's my friend, and nothing more.' *Then* he has the gall to say, 'That's not how I see it.' Like I purposely flirt back or something."

"He was a jealous jerk a lot, but that's on him and has nothing to do with you."

"I was so pissed, I told him he was clingy, which he pretty much is, but I chose to ignore, and that's when he decided to tell me I'd put on a few pounds and having sex with me was a chore." Her eyes fill with tears.

"He's an asshole," I say, squeezing her arm. "Your body is beautiful."

She sniffles. "I know." She wipes a tear off her cheek. "So I asked him why was he so mean and he said he wasn't mean he was breaking up with me."

"You're so much better off without him."

"I am, but it still hurts." She waves her hand in front of her face and lets out a deep breath. "Okay, that's it. No more crying over that douchebag. Tell me about you and Drew."

"I've told you everything." I pop a potato chip into my mouth. Gabby and I talk or text every day, sometimes at length, sometimes not, and since the past few days have been busy for both of us, we've been brief with each other.

Gabby studies me like she can read my thoughts, damn her. She often can. "Have you?" she challenges.

"Mostly." I can't lie for anything.

"Alejandra Cruz, *derrame ahora*." Spill right now.

"I'm a little conflicted," I admit.

"A little?" She raises her sculpted eyebrows.

"Okay, a lot. I tried to keep my feelings to a minimum, but Drew made it impossible. He's...he's..." I struggle for the right words because whatever I say out loud will make it more real and less imagined, and because I don't want to say something that isn't true. Something that is too much, but not enough.

"Making you doubt what you had with Matthew?"

I weigh that statement in my mind. Matthew has and always will deserve my respect. "No, not doubt. I was really lucky to have Matthew as a boyfriend. You know that. He was—he is—a great guy. But the way my heart pounds when I'm around Drew is unlike anything I've felt before. He feels like home *and* an adventure. He gives me wings and a safety net."

"You love him," Gabby says.

Now *I* want to cry. Because I do. I love him. But it's only been a month. And how can I love him and still feel something for Matthew? How can I put seven years in the same category as several weeks? What if I tell Matthew I'm seeing someone and he isn't and he wants me back? What if—

"Stop with all the what-ifs." Gabby lightly pushes my shoulder to shake me from my contemplations.

What if Drew isn't in love with me?

I fall back onto a pile of pillows, torn up inside. Life is too hard at the moment.

"Matthew left," Gabby says softly. "And I know your breakup was friendly, but it wasn't even. He wanted it more than you did—you have to remember that." She crawls over and lies beside me. "I don't think you should even consider his feelings anymore. Think of yourself and what *you* want. Don't stop dating Drew, or feel guilty for having feelings for him just because you feel a sense of loyalty to Matthew. Matt gave up any right to you the minute he got on that airplane."

"I know." I turn onto my side. "But we did promise each other we'd meet."

"That doesn't mean you have to."

"It does. He's still my…friend. And I can't move forward without seeing him."

She rolls to her side to face me. "Actually, that's a good point."

"I can't decide if I want time to speed up or slow down," I say.

"I wish I hadn't ruined that night for you."

"What night?"

"The first time you met Drew at the bar. If I hadn't wrecked that night for you with douchebag Landon, you would have gone home with him."

"Might have," I correct.

"Oh, you would have because I would have made you." She gets a wicked look in her eyes. "Or gone home with him myself."

"Gabby!"

"Aha! See, that right there confirms you've got it bad for our resident hotelier."

I bury my face in the pillow. When I'm finished grinning into the cotton, I peek at her. She's sitting up and eating a cookie. She hands me one.

"I do," I admit as I sit up, too. "And I wish I had all the answers."

"You will soon enough."

While we eat our weight in junk food in easy silence, my mind wanders to Drew and his grandma's birthday party.

I've been meaning to buy her a gift. Something for her to remember me by.

"Ready for a movie?" I ask and Gabby nods. I grab the remote to find a chick flick on the television just as Gabby's phone, face down in the center of our blanket, chimes with a text. She lifts the phone so I can see the face and says, "If it's him I don't want to know."

"It's not him. It's Alan."

She reads the text. "He and some friends have rented a house in Newport for the long weekend and he wants to know if I'd like to join them. This is perfect! I have clients on Saturday, but I can drive up and back." She thumbs a reply.

"How did he—"

"I texted him when I was waiting for you in the parking garage." She finishes her text and puts the phone down. "And I forgot to tell you, the house is supposed to be done next Friday so I'll just move back in a little sooner. It should be fine."

"I don't think Drew would mind if you stayed here."

She plucks a chocolate chip off a cookie and places it in her mouth. "He would *so* mind. I am not getting in the way of your sex-capades, little sister."

I roll my eyes at 'little sister.'

The 'sex-capades' remark puts Drew front and center in my mind again. I swallow hard, my head and heart overflowing with different emotions contending for dominance. Drew is so many good things, I can't count them all, and I can't wait until he's back tomorrow.

He's important to me.

Arguably more important than Matthew.

But what has mattered for the past eleven months and twenty-one days, is seeing Matthew again and finding out where we stand, and I can't ignore that.

Chapter Eighteen
Fireworks

Drew

T HE SUITE SMELLS like strawberries.

I close the door behind me, anticipation beating down my exhaustion. The room is quiet, dark except for the glow of light coming from the direction of my bedroom. I walk toward the illumination and the scent of my favorite fruit, hoping I find Alejandra in my bed. I don't even care if we get naked, I just want to hold her in my arms and whisper how much I missed her. How I can't stop thinking about her. How my days drag on so much longer when she's not in them so she should always be in them.

Outside the floor-to-ceiling windows, one final beam of red-yellow sunlight smolders on the horizon. I narrow my eyes to extinguish it. I've got my own personal ray of sunshine waiting for me around the corner, her soft singing of 'Brown Eyed Girl' hitting my ears and alerting me to her presence.

Ever have a dream about the most beautiful person you've ever laid eyes on taking a bubble bath in your bedroom, candles lit around the tub, their head reclined back so you can stare at their profile while their voice, very much off-key but it doesn't matter, croons to an imaginary sound-track?

Not a dream, my sleep-addled brain says.

I let out a deep breath and take a minute to enjoy the perfect reality in front of me. Alejandra has a folded towel underneath the back of her head. Bubbles float atop the water. But lucky me, the whirlpool tub with blue chromo lighting features a glass-front panel design so I get glimpses of her naked body lounging in the circulating water. It's sexy as hell and all the invitation I need. I slide off my suit coat. Peel off my tie.

She's singing with her eyes closed, her arms resting on the sides of the fiberglass.

I pull my belt through the loops of my slacks then drop it on the floor. The buckle clanks lightly on the rug, but Alejandra doesn't acknowledge it. I should probably call out a hello—I don't want to scare her—but I'm enjoying watching and listening to her too much. If that makes me a creeper, so be it.

My shoes and socks come off next. Then the rest of my clothes hit the floor.

I'm about to let her know I'm here when a loud boom sounds from outside. Her eyes fly open. She registers the Fourth of July fireworks outside at the same time she sees me.

"How long have you been standing there naked?"

"Long enough to check you out and then get undressed." I step closer. "Hi."

"Hi."

It could be argued that right now the brilliant energy between Alejandra and me is more substantial than the display lighting up the sky.

The air is crackling.

With heat. Desire. Affection. And…eagerness. Or maybe it's delight. Delight that we're back together in the same room.

"Mind if I join you?"

She taps her chin. "Hmm. I don't know. Are you going to behave?"

"Do you want me to behave?"

She glances at my dick, getting harder by the second, and shakes her head. *No.*

"He'll take that under advisement." She giggles at my ridiculous comeback before I kiss her soundly on the mouth and then climb in behind her. The medium jet pressure and hot water is a welcome sensation. The soft body in my arms an even better one.

She settles between my legs, leans back against my chest. Tilting her head up and back, she smiles at me. *This. This right here is everything.*

In a matter of weeks, Alejandra has become the woman I can't live without. Most people would tell you love at first sight is bullshit, but I'm here to tell you it happens, because I knew she was someone special nine months ago when I saw her across a crowded bar. And I knew when I saw her again in my hotel lobby that I'd been given a second chance, and I'd do whatever it took to make her mine.

The boom of fireworks draws her attention to the windows. We've got a great view of the annual display taking place over the Pacific. A multitude of color exploding for our enjoyment.

I cradle her closer, kiss the curve of her neck. Her long, dark hair is piled on top of her head so I've got easy access to the delicate skin there.

She drifts her hand over the surface of the water, displacing bubbles. "I could stay like this for the rest of the night."

"We'll soak as long as you want, but you may want to take the pruning factor into consideration."

"I don't care. I can count the number of baths I've taken on both hands, and this is by far the best one." She softens even further, completely melting against my body, her bottom no doubt feeling the continued effect she has on a certain part of my anatomy. A string of fireworks decorate the sky, one clap after another reverberating against the window. "And it's not because of the fireworks show."

"Good to know." I slide a hand across her collarbone, over her breasts, circling one nipple then the other with the tip of my finger.

"I'm not a big fan of fireworks."

"You're not?" I ask surprised. "I thought everyone liked them."

She gives a tiny shake of her head. "When I was eight, my brother and some of the other boys in the neighborhood got their hands on some illegal fireworks. Gabby made me sneak out of the house with her to see what Diego was up to. He was right outside in the street so we hid behind a tree to watch them. I was worried about my brother. He was only thirteen, but some of his friends were older. One of them burned his hand when the firework went off before he let it go. I ran into the house crying and told my grandparents."

"Was he okay?"

"Yes, but my brother was furious with me. He called me a tattletale and didn't talk to me for a week. That's how long he was grounded for."

I continue to touch her with light caresses, over her breasts, across her stomach, between her thighs. "When I was eight my brothers had the bright idea to carry our bike ramp into the backyard and put it at the deep end of the swimming pool. Then they grabbed their skateboards to jump off the ramp into the pool."

"If I didn't know both your brothers were alive and well, I'd ask you to stop telling me this story."

"With some of the shit the three of us pulled, it's a miracle we never got seriously hurt. Like you, I tended to worry, and when Ethan and Finn told me I was too little to skateboard off the ramp and flip into the pool, I marched into the house and told my mom. She was already aware, and on her way outside since she was watching us through the kitchen window, but my brothers still gave me shit about it and said it was my fault Mom put a stop to it. Even though she sat on the ramp so it wouldn't slide and they could each launch off it into the deep end one time."

"No way. Your mom seriously did that?"

"She did. She's pretty remarkable."

"Did you get to jump?"

"Yep. It was awesome."

She carefully turns her whole body, braces her arms on my thighs, and kisses me, openmouthed, hot. Significant. I'm thinking, *yeah baby*, but then she turns back around like that was not the start of something insanely enjoyable.

"What was that for?" I ask, clearly misreading her intentions.

"I had an urge." She takes my hand and places it back on her stomach, presumably so I can continue my delicate mapping of her body under the water.

I laugh. "Feel free to act on your urges anytime."

"I will."

"I think a little quid pro quo is in order here." This time when I slip my hand between her thighs, I keep it there. "I have the urge to make you come," I whisper in her ear.

She answers by allowing her knees to fall open as wide as they'll go within the confines of the bathtub. As a rainbow of lights flash in the sky outside, I stroke her center with one hand and play with her boobs with the other. She lifts her hips, arches her back. Soft moans fall from her lips; her breathing speeds up. I slip two fingers inside her, find that magic spot, and slowly bring her to release.

I love having her fall apart in my arms. Once she's still, she hugs both my arms to her chest.

I'm content to hold her just like this for the rest of the night. As long as the jets are running, the water will stay warm. Several minutes pass, the fireworks stop. Eventually she lifts away from me and blows out all the candles but one.

We climb out of the tub and dry off. She leads me to the

bed, pushes me down. My cock bobs between us, leading her to smile at it. I'm very glad she likes what she sees. I'm very, very glad she reaches into the nightstand for a condom.

"There's something I need to tell you," she says, stopping our progression.

"Is it a matter of life or death?"

"No."

"Then tell me later. I need you to ride me, Al, like I'm a wild-fucking bronco."

Seconds later she mounts me and it feels like my first rodeo.

Alejandra

"*YOO-HOO.* ALEJANDRA?"

I track the hand waving in front of my face. "Sorry. What did you say?" I pause the daydreams about Drew. About his slow hands all over my body, making my legs quiver, my breasts tingle, my stomach tighten. Last night in the bathtub was the sweetest, sexiest time of my life. Afterward in bed, it was red-hot. Exciting and so addictive. There was only one tiny snag. I'd realized while soaking in the tub waiting for Drew, that I'd told him Matthew was coming home, but I hadn't told him that Matthew and I had a "date" to meet. As soon as I registered the oversight, I was racked with guilt again. I hadn't meant to keep it from him, and I wanted to get it off my chest, but then Drew asked if it was a matter of life or death and then, well, other things took over my brain.

"We said we want to get on camera, so stand up and

wave your arms, would you? You're much taller and prettier than we are."

"Oh. Okay," I say getting to my feet and waving in the direction of the cameraman. *Do not zone out on Mrs. K. and Gloria again.*

We're sitting midfield for the Galaxy game. It's a warm day, but there's a nice breeze and puffy white clouds in the sky that occasionally block the sun. I don't follow soccer, but I love being at sporting events. Sports fans are the best, with their T-shirts, hats, jerseys, chants, smiling faces, and fun signs.

My two sidekicks have a piece of poster board that's cut into a frame so they can hold it in front of their faces. Around the edge of the poster board they've written, PLEASE PUT US ON TV. It's adorable and I hope they get their wish.

Across the aisle, I notice a boy holding a sign that says, IF THE GALAXY WIN MY DAD'S BUYING ME A PUPPY. There's a drawing of a dog and an arrow pointing to, I'm guessing, the boy's dad.

I look at Mrs. K. and Gloria. I look back at the boy. I look up a few rows at another fan holding a sign, and an idea formulates. There are thousands of people here and maybe some of them can afford to help me out. I haven't come up with any other plan to raise money quickly, so I reach for my tote bag and pull out the large notebook inside. I'm glad I didn't have time to switch to my smaller purse this morning as I sit down and get to work writing my own sign: HELP SAVE THEIR SENIOR CENTER ~ VENMO @ALEJANDRA-CRUZ

It's a long shot, but at this point, what have we got to lose? This is definitely thinking outside the box. I draw an arrow on the bottom of the paper, pointing to my wonderful seniors, and hope the next time there's a break in the game, we can get the cameraman's attention.

"What's going on?" Gloria asks.

"Is the center in trouble?" Mrs. K. asks.

Crap. I forgot they didn't know yet. "I'm sorry to tell you this, but we're in jeopardy of closing at the end of the month."

They lend a sympathetic ear as I share with them what's going on and how upset I am about it. I also tell them how much they mean to me. "So, maybe a plea for aid will help. You two are the perfect poster seniors—literally—right now."

"It's on," Mrs. K. announces with authority.

"If I have to fake a heart attack to get attention, I will," Gloria says.

"Oh no, please don't do that," I say.

"Choking. You could fake choking," Mrs. K. suggests. "That's less offensive."

"No one is faking anything," I assert. "I'll hold up my little sign, you two will hold up your poster and smile, and if *I* have to, I'll flash the camera guy or something." I won't really. Or, maybe I will. I'm learning I'm capable of anything when I set my mind to it. I'm also wearing my cute yellow bra.

"We're a team," Mrs. K. says. "If one flashes, we all flash."

"Oh, I haven't flashed in ages," Gloria volunteers. At my stunned expression she adds, "Mardi Gras."

This is one of the many reasons why the senior center has to stay open. I need to hear more stories from these ladies. "Let's agree to skip the flashing. We don't want security escorting us out of here."

"I don't know," Mrs. K. says. "It's one way to get attention."

"I have faith we'll get it done without risking our clean records."

"Who says I have a clean record?" Gloria smiles with pride. She is too much.

We watch the game, though we're mostly watching the camera guy stationed to our left. Finally, he turns in our direction.

"Time to try again!" Mrs. K. gets to her feet. Gloria quickly follows. "And, Alejandra, whatever happens with the senior center, we know you've tried your best and the years we've had there with you have been wonderful."

"Thank you," I say, too choked up to say anything more.

The cameraman looks out to the crowd for his next fan close-up. I hold up my sign with one hand and wave my other to get his attention. Mrs. K. and Gloria put their heads together and put their "frame" in position.

And then all of a sudden, we're on the jumbotron. We're on the big screen with our signs and our smiles for at least five seconds. Holy shit!

The fans around us take notice. This sparks lively conversation and soon the people in our row and those near us are sending me money to help save the center. The camera guy walks over to us, eyes on Mrs. K. "Are you Mrs. Kindred?" he asks.

"I am." She casts an affectionate gaze at him.

"You were my favorite teacher. A long time ago." He looks more closely at my sign. "How about we get you three on camera again?"

"That would be amazing. Thank you."

The cameraman catches up with Mrs. K. for a few minutes before he's given the signal in his earpiece to record again. He counts down with his fingers. Three, two, one.

I glance up at the giant TV screen to see us before I drop my gaze to look right into the camera and mouth, *Please.*

"Seniors rock," someone shouts.

"We got you," someone else yells.

Sitting back down, I check my phone. My Venmo account is blowing up. The donations are small, but they are numerous. "It's working," I whisper, so as not to pop whatever magical bubble we've created this afternoon. I doubt it will be enough to save the center, but it will definitely go to something nice for everyone there before our doors close.

We're on cloud nine when we leave the game. The Galaxy won and so have we, with three thousand dollars in donations. While it's not enough to save us, it was fun and heartwarming to have so many people take interest. Mrs. K. and Gloria get several high fives on our way to the parking lot. I drop them off at the senior center then drive to the hotel. It's close to six o'clock and I'm hungry and in need of a shower.

There's a car parked in my usual spot next to Drew so I

valet park. It's close to impossible to find parking on the street on a Friday night.

"Hi," I say to the valet.

"Hey. How's the training going?"

"So far, so good. Thanks for asking." I've seen the valet several times when I've left the hotel to go for a run. He's around my age and totally Gabby's type. I wonder if he has a girlfriend. "Have a great night."

"You, too."

I always get a little tingly when I walk through the lobby, a combination of residual embarrassment over the vase fiasco and butterflies over meeting Drew again. Tonight, through large, shuttered sliding doors, the pool area is hopping. Lounge-style music is blaring. It's the first time I've been around to see the Friday Pool Party so rather than take the private elevator up to the suite, I walk out onto the patio to check it out.

Today's theme is in keeping with yesterday's holiday. Classy red, white, and blue decorations are everywhere from umbrellas to lounge cushions and shimmery curtains around the cabanas. Cocktail servers are dressed in all-American swimwear. A woman walks by me holding a drink that's electric blue.

I people-watch for a few minutes and am about to leave when I catch sight of Drew stepping out of a cabana, a beautiful woman in a barely there black bikini right on his heels. I track their every step to the pool bar. He's dressed in his usual dark suit pants and a white dress shirt, the sleeves rolled to his elbows. No coat or tie. The woman stands very close to him. She angles her head to say something in his ear.

Sharp, stinging pain slices through my chest, the likes of which I've never felt before. It takes me a few more moments of staring at Drew and the woman to put meaning to this most unwelcome sensation.

I'm jealous.

This is what being jealous feels like.

Seven years with Matthew and the emotion never reared her head. I don't know what it means to suffer it now, but there's only way to fix it. Go say hello.

I'm definitely overdressed for this function, and a mess with a ketchup stain on the center of my shirt, but I don't care. I have to fix this ache.

About halfway to the bar, doubt creeps in. Maybe I should go take my shower and see Drew when I see him. But as I've come to learn these past weeks, time drags when we're apart, and I imagine it would be a thousand times worse knowing the company he's keeping at the moment.

My decision is made for me when Drew turns to lean his back against the bar. Our eyes meet. He smiles that devastating smile of his from ear to ear, destroying any doubt I had. Turning it into confidence, instead.

He waits for me to come to him. "Hi," I say.

"Hi." With one arm around my waist, he kisses me. "How was the game?"

"Amazing."

"This is my friend, Tracy. Tracy, this is Alejandra."

Tracy? His ex, Tracy? Some of my jealousy returns and I don't like it. Not one bit. (The emotion part, not the part where he's with his ex. He told me they were better off as friends.)

"Hi. Nice to meet you." I shake hands with her.

"You, too." She looks at Drew with questions written all over her pretty face.

At my frown, Drew takes my hand. "Come on. Let's get out of here." He kisses Tracy on the cheek. "Take care, Trace. Say bye to West for me, okay?"

"Will do."

As Drew leads me back toward the lobby, I wonder if Matthew and I could be the kind of friends who kiss each other on the cheek. "I noticed the way Tracy looked at me seemed to upset you," Drew says. "Sorry about that. West was in the cabana with some other friends of theirs, and I didn't want to talk about you with him there. He's been a little touchy lately. Nothing that won't smooth over eventually."

Like when he gets his property.

"You've spoken to him about the center, haven't you?"

"Some, yes. If there's a solution that can make you both happy, I want to find it."

"Thank you. I know you're in a tough position."

"You hungry?" he asks.

"Starving, actually. I've only eaten a burger today."

He takes me into the hotel's kitchen where he asks the chef to wrap us up some lasagna, to go. We take the delicious-smelling bag of food to a table on the second floor veranda. The terrace is beautiful with ivy-covered stone columns and iron furniture with sapphire-blue cushions.

"Speaking of the center," I say once we're situated and I've taken a few bites of my meal. "Something happened today." I reach into my bag to check the final number raised, but my phone is dead. I wanted to show him the picture someone took of me, Mrs. K., and Gloria, too.

"Tell me."

"You know how people are always holding up signs at sporting events? Well, I…" I relay the whole story, reliving it all over again with a grin on my face.

"That's fantastic," Drew says. "And I wonder…" His stares over my shoulder.

"What?"

"When you get your phone charged, send me the picture and I'll ask Chloe to share it. She's got a big following on social media, and a far reach when it comes to promo. Maybe she can do something that gets you even more donations."

I touch his forearm. "Drew, you don't have to do that. I completely understand your position on the matter."

"Thanks, but I want to. West has a whole company behind him. He can't fault me for having your back with something *you* initiated."

"That means a lot, thank you. And I don't know if you know, but West did offer to help us find a new location."

"He's a good guy."

"So are you." I dance my fingertips up his arm. "How about we go upstairs and I initiate something else entirely."

"I've said it before, but I'll say it again. I like the way you think."

For the rest of the night the only thing we think about is bringing pleasure to each other with our hands and mouths and when that isn't enough, Drew moves inside me until a shudder racks both our bodies.

Chapter Nineteen
Broken

Alejandra

T HE NEXT MORNING I wake up in Drew's bed to find him absent. Peeking through one open eye, the digital clock on the bedside table reads 7:57. Drew is an early riser so I'm not surprised I'm alone, but I do miss his warm body and the comfort he brings.

I put on one of his shirts and pad into the main living area. Drew is tinkering in the kitchen wearing his black sleep pants and a plain gray T-shirt that clings to his broad chest, muscled biceps, and flat stomach. I take a moment to admire him.

He mumbles a few curse words under his breath.

"Morning." I step up to the counter to find a mini disaster. An egg carton sits open with broken eggs inside it, flour coats almost every inch of every surface, spilled milk makes a sticky paste, and the collection of dirty mixing spoons, bowls, and frying pans is abundant. "Can I help you with something?"

He lets out a frustrated sigh and runs his fingers through his hair.

Now there's flour in his hair, too.

"Making pancakes should not be so difficult."

My heart swells. He's cooking breakfast for me.

I step around the counter to give him a hug. "It's the thought that counts." I take his hands in mine and wash them in the sink with soap and warm water. I dry them with a clean dish towel I pull out of a drawer.

We leave the kitchen disaster for later and sit on the couch—or rather I sit on his lap on the couch, my arms around his neck, my lips pressing soft kisses to the stubble on his jaw, his neck, his temple. "I don't need no stinking pancakes."

"Good, because I'm pretty sure they aren't edible." He rests his hand on my thigh under the hem of his shirt.

"There's Pop-Tarts in the cupboard."

"You bought some?"

"Frosted strawberry ones if that's your jam." I giggle at my joke.

"It is and I haven't had one in forever." He places me on the couch. "Don't move."

My eyes are glued to his backside as he walks to the kitchen to retrieve the sugary filled toaster pastry. It takes him three tries before he opens the right cupboard, which has him grumbling under his breath again. Frustrated Drew is very cute. He opens the box and returns with one foil package for each of us in his hands. By silent agreement it seems we aren't toasting them. Okay by me.

"Oh! Mind grabbing my phone off the counter?" I ask before he's taken too many steps. He pulls it off the charger.

"Thanks." I turn my cell back on then inhale the sweet scent of Pop-Tart goodness before sliding one of the tarts out of the wrapper and taking a bite. "I knew these would come in handy one morning."

"Good call." Drew breaks his in half before biting into it.

I glance at my phone to find several notifications and missed calls from Mrs. K. I put my Pop-Tart down and unlock the screen. I listen to my voice mail first.

"Alejandra," Mrs. K. says, "the channel five news posted a picture of us from the soccer game! I don't know how they learned it was the Davis Senior Center, but they did, and they shared the name of the center on television, as well as a report on the vital importance of senior centers in a time when people are living longer." There's a pause. "Tell me we did it, sweetheart. Tell me *you* did it."

I quickly check my Venmo account.

"Oh. My. God. Ohmigod. Ohmigod. Ohmigod." My hand starts to shake. My heart is bending like Beckham, curving, twisting, *pounding*. I fight back tears of utter joy.

"What is it?" Drew asks. "What's wrong?"

I can't tear my eyes off the number on my phone screen. "Nothing is wrong. Everything is great! The local news posted a picture of me with Mrs. K. and Gloria at the soccer game yesterday. They talked about the senior center and did a report on how necessary they are." I look up at Drew. "And guess what?"

"What?"

"There's one hundred and thirty-three thousand dollars in my Venmo account."

"Holy shit, that's amazing." Drew wraps me in a hug, squeezing my arms to my sides. "You did it."

"I can't believe it," I say.

"I can. Congratulations, Al."

"Yes!" I pump my fists in the air then jump to my feet to do a happy dance. When I plop back down on the couch, Drew is staring at me with noticeable heat and adoration. It's heady and meaningful and...I can't wait any longer to tell him that I'm meeting Matthew. I have to tell him now.

"Drew—"

"Alejandra—"

We smile at each other. "You go first," Drew says.

"No, you go," I counter, suddenly struggling with the right words to tell him I'm meeting my ex next weekend. Maybe I'll ask him to go with me because—I take a second to listen to my heart—because Drew is who I want. In all honesty, he's been who I've wanted all along. I only needed to accept that Matthew was my first, but not destined to be my last.

Drew turns to face me on the couch. "I think you know this, but in case I haven't been clear, I don't want this to end, Alejandra, and after my grandmother's birthday party next Saturday night, I—"

"Wait." I hold up my palm. "Your grandma's party is a week from today?"

"Yes."

"Next Saturday?"

"Yes." A line bisects his eyebrows. *What's the big deal?* that crease says, and I want to scream, *It's a huge, ginormous, monumental deal!*

"July twelfth? Your grandma's birthday is July twelfth?" All the happiness from a mere minute ago is gone. Disappeared. This can't be happening.

"Yes," he repeats again with kindness and confusion. "What is going on? Why did the color just drain from your face?"

Out of all the days in July, why does Rosemary's birthday have to fall on the same day I'm meeting Matthew? The universe is supposed to be on my side here.

"What time?" I ask.

"Eight o'clock."

Of course it is. I shift uncomfortably, miserable on the inside. Elbows on my knees, I cover my face with my hands. It never occurred to me to ask Drew the exact date of the party. And for that I'm truly sorry. That date has always belonged to Matthew so I never gave it a second thought. I've been caught up in my own selfish head, dwelling on Matthew, then falling in love with Drew and being unsure about our future and his feelings for me and puzzling over what-ifs I have no easy answer for.

"Is that a problem?" Drew's question pulls me from my thoughts. I turn to face him again.

"Yes."

"Because…?"

I wrap my arms around myself. "It has to do with Matthew."

"Okay." Drew's expression is blank. His eyes void of emotion. "I sense I'm not going to like what you have to say?"

"I don't think so."

"Go ahead, anyway."

"Matthew is coming back that day. He was always coming back that day. When he left, we agreed to meet one year later. On July twelfth."

Drew clenches his jaw.

"Since we broke up amicably and were together for such a long time, we promised each other we'd meet after his work assignment ended, no matter what, and see if we still had feelings for each other."

The devastated look on Drew's face kills me. Silence falls between us like a brick wall.

When it's clear he's not going to say anything, I apologize. I will apologize a hundred times if I have to. "I'm sorry I didn't tell you sooner. It honestly slipped my mind until recently."

"It slipped your mind?" he says harshly.

"Yes," I say softly.

"When were you going to tell me? The other night before I was buried deep inside you and then you screamed *my* name?"

"Yes," I say, ashamed of myself.

"So, this whole time we've been together, you've been what? Biding your time until you see your ex again?"

"What? No," I quickly say. "That's not true at all. I'm with you because I want to be. Because I can't imagine not spending time with you. I care about you. About *us*." *I love you.*

"You care about me." He rubs the back of his neck. "How am I supposed to believe that when you've been lying to me?"

"I've never lied to you."

"You still have a fucking boyfriend, Alejandra. How is that not lying?"

"He's not my boyfriend. I told you that. I told you that we agreed to break up. And then I told you that he was coming back."

"But you conveniently didn't mention he was coming back *for you*. Big difference between coming back home because it's where you're from and maybe running into each other, and setting a date to actually meet."

"I'm sorry. I'm sorry I didn't tell you that I was meeting him. That was wrong, I see that now, but please forgive me. You mean something to me."

"I guess the question is do I mean more to you than Matthew?"

"It's not about who means more." Can't he see it's about a promise I made to a person who was an important part of my life for a very long time? I owe Matthew a face-to-face. Don't I?

"It kind of is," Drew says, exasperated.

"You don't understand."

"You're right. I don't. I don't understand how someone I trusted completely and told things I haven't told anyone else, kept something this important from me. You had plenty of chances to come clean, and you didn't."

"I suck, okay?" I hug one of the pillows on the couch to

my chest. "I was caught up in you, Drew. In us. And deep down—" I hate the truth that just popped into my mind "—deep down, I think I knew telling you might push you away and I didn't want that." I take a shaky breath. "Everyone I've loved has left me. I lost my parents. I lost my grandparents. I made this agreement with Matthew because I didn't want to lose my first love, too."

"I have no idea how I'm supposed to take that."

I shrug. "I don't either. I just wanted you to know where I was coming from."

Drew moves his gaze to the window. "Have you talked to him?"

"No. We've texted, nothing significant, just quick hellos, really. We agreed not to mention our love lives."

"Do you think he's been faithful?"

"No."

Drew's eyes slowly find mine again. "Why not?"

"Because I know Matthew. If he was going to stay faithful, we wouldn't have broken up. He might even be in love with someone else." Like I am. "I don't know yet."

"Then he's an idiot."

Tell him, Alejandra. Tell Drew you love him.

"Again, I'm sorry and I hope you can forgive me for leaving this out."

He looks back and forth between my eyes for a long time before he says, "Apology accepted, but you still have a choice to make. My grandmother's party or Matthew."

"I told you, I already promised Matthew." My word means something to me, and I don't think I could live with myself if I broke it.

"Then there's nothing left for us to say. No reason for us to prolong this." He stands up. "I'll have another room in the hotel ready for you in an hour. You can stay until your house is ready. No charge."

"Drew." I catch his arm before he walks away.

He jerks away from me like I burned him. "What did you think was going to happen here? That you could continue to string me along until boyfriend number one shows up and sweeps you off your feet? Because rest assured, Alejandra, the guy knows what he lost and I have no doubt he'll want you back. So, save us both from further humiliation and pack your stuff and please get out of my sight." He turns so I'm staring at his back.

It's the 'please' that reaches inside my chest and squeezes the life out of my heart. He's imploring me to leave before I hurt him any more than I already have.

I hurry to my room to gather my things. I deserve his anger and shunning and anything else he wants to dish out. Closing the door behind me, I lean against it, sink to the floor, and cry. How could I be so stupid? I'll tell you how. Fear. Fear of loving and losing. Fear of a new love replacing the old one. Fear of putting my heart out there and it being rejected—by both men.

Without meaning to, I was pushing Drew away at the same time I was drawing him closer. I'm a terrible person! It was never my intention to disrespect Drew, but I did. I made him feel like he was my second choice. My backup plan.

I cry harder. I'm a snotty mess.

Now, even if I wanted to pursue a future with him, I've lost my chance.

He won't forgive me, and I don't deserve it.

Chapter Twenty
Three's a Crowd

Drew

"JESUS, YOU SCARED the shit out of me. What are you doing here?" Ethan says, padding into his kitchen in pajamas, thank God.

It's early Sunday morning and I'm sitting at his breakfast bar. Make that passed out at his breakfast bar since I pulled up to this spot at around five a.m. after zero sleep. I lift my head. "I wanted to be the first one to welcome you home." I lift my now cold cup of coffee. "Welcome home. Coffee is made and everything."

"You made coffee?" he asks astounded.

"Took three tries."

Ethan laughs. "Thanks, little brother, I appreciate it. Now what's wrong?"

"What makes you think something is wrong?" *Everything* is wrong.

"I got back into town last night after a month away and the first thing I see is you, looking like someone shredded all your suits and ties and stole all your hair product."

"I don't use hair product. My hair is naturally this good."

"Have you looked in a mirror?" He sets down his cup of coffee and takes mine to dump out and refresh.

"Fine. I look like shit. I feel like shit, too. It's because of a girl."

"I figured."

"Not just any girl. *The* girl."

Ethan stares at me, trying, no doubt, to figure out how sincere I am. "I haven't been gone that long, and this is the first I'm hearing about it, so what makes this girl special?"

"First, you fell for Pascale immediately, correct?"

"Yes."

"Okay, so you know what it feels like to be gobsmacked by a pair of incredible eyes and then feel like your blood is on fire and there's an electric current binding you to this person for reasons you haven't figured out yet, but you don't care because it feels so good."

Ethan leans his elbows on the counter. "Okay, I'm convinced. What happened?"

"She broke my heart, that's what happened."

"And it can't be fixed?"

I stare at my brother this time. Pascale broke his heart once and now they're madly in love. I suppose if it is the love of your life, then there's always the chance it can be fixed. However, there's a third person in my relationship with Alejandra, and I have no control over what happens with him. "I—"

"Drew!"

At the sound of Rylee's high-pitched little voice, and the pitter-patter of her feet on the floor, my mood lifts. I spin around in my barstool. She's in princess pajamas and her hair is an uncombed mess. "Hi, monkey butt."

She jumps up into my lap for a hug. It's exactly what I needed, and I hang on until she's squirming for me to release her. Before I do, though, I say, "The tickle monster missed you!" I tickle her sides until she threatens to pee in her pants. I free her with a kiss on the cheek and she climbs up onto the stool next to me.

"How was your trip?" I ask her.

"Super good. Ethan bought me a camera and I took a million pictures. I want to be a wildlife photographer when I grow up."

"Wow." I glance at my brother. He's beaming with pride. "Will you show me some of your pictures?"

"Uh-huh." She swivels in her seat. "Are you gonna make pancakes with chocolate chips?" she asks Ethan.

"Would you like that?" he returns.

"Yes, please."

At mention of pancakes, my thoughts race right back to Alejandra and yesterday morning. "I'll have some, too," I tell my brother.

Ethan moves around the counter and picks Rylee up off her seat. "I need my morning hug first," he says to her.

She snuggles into his chest, and mine aches at the sight. I want that. I want a family.

"I need a few minutes to talk to Drew, too, so how about you go wake up your mom and see if she'll take you outside to see the chicks. I don't think they're babies anymore."

"Okay," she says, her little feet hitting the floor and taking off toward the stairs.

"You're a lucky man," I tell my brother as he sits in the stool left vacant by Rylee and reaches across the counter for his coffee.

"I know." He puts his hand on my back. "Talk to me."

I start at the beginning with the night I first met Alejandra and how she stayed in the back of my mind until we met again. I tell him about my stupid lie to Grandmother and how I couldn't help myself. I needed to do something to keep Alejandra from disappearing on me again. He listens and nods and takes in everything I'm saying. I tell him we didn't immediately jump into bed, that we got to know each other better first, but that once we did sleep together it was explosive.

"Alejandra is the complete opposite of every girl I've ever dated. No girl has ever made me feel like *I* matter, that if I was stripped down to nothing, she'd still care. She's never tried to impress me either. She's confident in who she is. She's genuine. And I am hopelessly in love with her because it turns out, I was wrong. She lied to me."

"About?" Ethan asks.

"She has a boyfriend. Or rather, someone else in her life that she neglected to tell me she was going to see again." I go on to explain the situation, chipping away at my heart as I do. This sucks. And the worst thing is I want to hate Alejandra. But I fucking can't.

"So, let me be sure I've got this straight. She and her boyfriend broke up with the caveat that they would meet a year later with the possibility of getting back together, and the night they're meeting is the same night as Grandmother's party?"

"Correct."

"Does she still love this guy?"

"I don't know."

"You didn't ask her?" Ethan says like, *Duh, that should have been your first question when she dropped this bomb on your head.*

"No."

"Did you tell her you loved her?"

I rub my fingers across my forehead. "Could you please stop with the questions?"

"I'll take that as a 'no.'"

"I didn't want to scare her off. She wanted to take things slow and I thought if I told her how deeply I felt, I'd push her away. I wanted to give her time because I thought we had plenty of it. I told her I wanted to keep dating her but then she told me about her meeting with Matthew and everything went to shit."

"What's the big deal if she misses the party? It's not the end of the world. You guys could still—"

"It's not about the party. It's about her seeing her ex. It makes me sick to think about them together."

"You've got to trust her, Drew."

"That's just it. She hurt me, Ethan. Completely blind-sided me and I haven't felt that way since—" fuck! "—I trusted we were on the same page when she had her ex in her back pocket the whole fucking time."

"She didn't *set out* to hurt you," Ethan says. "It sounds

more like she got in over her head and then got confused about what to do."

"Whose side are you on?"

"Yours, of course. That's why instead of bashing her, I'm trying to make you see things from her point of view. Not that she's in the right, but just so you can understand her way of thinking. From what you've told me, I honestly don't think she set out to break your heart. And most likely, her own heart isn't feeling so great either.

"If she's as kind as you claim she is, then she's hurting, too. People make mistakes, and you have to decide if her mistake is forgivable."

"That's if I'm even still part of the equation."

"Oh, you're still part of the equation." He bumps elbows with me. "We Auprince men are pretty stellar."

"What should I do?"

"You should talk to her. Ask her some of those important questions. Don't count yourself out of the race unless you really don't want to be in it."

"That's the problem. I don't know what I want."

"I think you do and you're just letting your pride get in the way. But hey, what do I know?" He stands and rounds the counter. "You want chocolate chips in your pancakes, too?"

I drag my sorry ass to his side. He's right. I am letting my pride interfere. But damn it, I gave chase. I let her set the pace. And then I loved her with my body and admired her with my words and she still felt the need to see her ex. Right or wrong, it stings. "Teach me how to make them?"

His stunned expression makes me laugh. "Don't look so surprised," I say. "One day I want to cook them for my daughter."

My brother is a great cook and he tells me about his trip across the country while giving me a lesson in the fine art of pancake batter and pancake flipping. Pascale and Rylee come in from checking out the chickens in the backyard, and the four of us sit down to breakfast. It's obvious who made certain pancakes, but they all taste the same so I count it as a win.

On the drive back to the hotel, I mull over what my brother said. I also reflect on everything that's happened between Alejandra and me. We've talked. We've fought. We've laughed and teased. We've shared stories. We've had sweet sex. And dirty sex. We've made love. Could it be I took her transgression as a way out because she is *the one*? And that means she has the power to break my heart for good, so before she did, I bailed?

Maybe.

But maybe not. Maybe I'm setting her free to decide for herself what future she wants. After all, she's accused me of being controlling. So, if I storm into her hotel room and demand the answers Ethan mentioned—like I really feel like doing—then I'm the overbearing guy taking charge of the situation and that won't help me.

Alejandra is the most decent and caring person I know. I've seen it with my grandmother, the seniors at the senior center, the staff at the hotel. She doesn't give up on people either. Not strangers, and certainly not family or friends. So it makes sense she would see this through with Matthew. She wouldn't be the woman I love if she didn't. A promise is a promise.

I park my car and take the public elevator to the lobby. If nothing else, I need to make sure she's okay with her new accommodations. Yesterday, I ignored the feeling in my gut telling me to check on her, too upset and angry about her confession.

Stepping behind the reservation desk, I wait until Marty is done with a guest before asking her to let me know which room Alejandra is in.

"I'm sorry, Mr. Auprince, there's no Alejandra Cruz staying with us."

"Could you please check again? I arranged for a room for her myself."

Marty shakes her head. "She's not under any reservation. Let me just check under... Here she is. She was a no-show."

A no-show. "Thanks, Marty." I march to my office and shut the door. Alejandra left the hotel to go where? She told me the other day work was still being done on her house. Now I feel even shittier for kicking her out of the suite. I pull my phone from my pocket, place it on my desk.

She. Left.

Without a word, a note, a text, *anything.*

If that doesn't shout *goodbye*, I don't know what does. Clearly, she wants nothing more to do with me. My fault, but common courtesy would dictate a small measure of acknowledgment, wouldn't it? I open my desk drawer and pull out the napkin, frayed around the edges from so much handling.

Drew,
Maybe some other time...
Sweet dreams,
Alejandra

Apparently, our time is up. We're done.

I rip the napkin in half, ball it up, and toss it into the trash. Looks like I'm odd man out and if she's still in love with Matthew, I won't stand in her way.

Chapter Twenty-One
The One That I Want

Alejandra

F OR THE FIRST time in two years, I call in sick to book club. I can't pretend to be happy when I'm heartsick and split in two. Half of me in love with Drew and wanting to tell him as much and beg him to give us another shot. The other half of me loyal to Matthew and our shared history and the promise we made to meet up with each other. I'm definitely not *in* love with him anymore. I know that. Those feelings have faded into memories I'll always cherish. As far as first boyfriends go, he was the best.

But if we see each other and there's still a spark, could I fall for him again? If he sweeps me off my feet like Drew thinks he will, can I love him as much as I love Drew?

I bury my face in my pillow just as my phone rings on my nightstand. Hoping it might be Drew, I reach for it so fast, I practically pull my shoulder out of the socket. It's not him. It's my brother.

"Hey, Diego," I say miserably.

"Hey, what's wrong?"

"Life."

"Some days are like that. Care to narrow it down for me?"

"Sure," I mutter, because maybe he'll have some words of wisdom or advice. I put the phone on speaker. Being my older brother, he doesn't want to hear anything about my sex life, but he's a good listener when it comes to all the other relationship stuff. I previously mentioned to him I was dating Drew so narrowing it down doesn't take too long.

"He thinks I used him," I complain. "But I swear I didn't. Not deliberately. And it kills me that I've hurt him like that."

"From what you've told me, I think he's smart enough to realize that's not true. In the heat of the moment, people say a lot of things they don't mean."

"I guess."

"Have you put yourself in Drew's shoes?" Diego asks.

I roll onto my back and fling my free arm over my forehead. "No."

"Do it now."

"Okay." I picture Drew meeting an ex who he spent seven years with and who might still love him, and my stomach clenches. It clenches painfully. It clenches in extreme anger. I would hate if he met her. Hate, hate, hate it. I sink further into my mattress with a heavy sigh.

"Doesn't feel very good, does it?" my smarty-pants brother asks.

"No. In my defense, I was thinking about asking him to come with me, but he didn't give me the chance."

I hear the front door of the house open and close and the

click-clack of Gabby's heels grows louder the closer she gets to my room. The new hardwood floor is finished. The baseboards and drywall and paint, too. Old and new furniture is in the garage, and the damaged bathroom is almost repaired. I dragged my full-size mattress inside and dropped it on my bedroom floor last night so I'd have somewhere to sleep. I'd noticed Gabby had done the same.

"Hey," I say as she walks past the doorway.

She jumps so high she almost hits her head on the low ceiling. "Christ, Alejandra. You scared me half to death." Hand over her chest, she comes to sit next to me. "What are you doing here? Why aren't you at book club?" She looks around the room. My suitcase and duffel bags are piled in the corner. "And why have you moved back home already?"

"Oh, Gabby." I drop my phone beside me and swing my arms around her.

"Hey, Gabs." Diego's voice startles Gabby again and she practically jumps out of my hold.

"Diego? What's going on?" she asks softly, hugging me back.

"I messed up," I say.

We keep Diego on speaker while I tell her everything that transpired between me and Drew yesterday.

"I'm sorry, Allie, but sometimes things happen for a reason. Maybe this happened to clear the way for you and Matthew."

"I don't want Matthew," I half cry, half whine. The words fly out of my mouth without any hesitation.

"I know that," Gabby says around a smug smile. "You

just needed to remind yourself."

"Agreed," Diego says. "And uh, now that Gabby's there, I'll talk to you guys later, okay?"

"Thanks, D," I say.

"No problem." He disconnects.

The honest-to-God truth is I don't want Matthew back. I want a future with Drew. The thought of not seeing him ever again is more painful than anything else I can imagine, even being covered head-to-toe with poisonous spiders.

"I still have to see Matthew, don't I?" I ask.

"Yes. But only because the two of you are friends. You're something special to each other and if you're lucky, you'll always have that."

"That might be hard for Drew to accept. That is, if he even gives me another chance."

"There's only way to find out."

"Love is so hard," I grumble, a mixture of hope and new awareness filling my chest. I messed up, but I know in my heart Drew and I are meant to be together.

"If it wasn't it wouldn't be worth it."

"Since when did you get so smart?"

She yanks on my ponytail. "You're not the only one who lives and learns."

"Thanks, Gabby. How are you doing? How was Newport?"

"I'm good. It was fun."

"*Really?*"

"Really. I met a guy." She gets that gleam in her eye that tells me she's under the spell of a Romeo. Again.

"Gab—"

"And this time I had some fun with him and then I said goodbye."

"That doesn't sound like you," I challenge. Gabby is quick to fall in love every single time.

"It's the new me. I figure if you can step out of your comfort zone, then I can step out of mine. No more boyfriends. Not for a while anyway. This single girl doesn't need a man to make her happy."

I lift my hand for a high five. "Amen, chica. I'm proud of you."

"I'm proud of you, too. Want to order pizza and start getting the house back in order?"

"I'd love to."

We spend the rest of the night talking, laughing, and organizing furniture and knickknacks. Mr. Hernandez helps us move the heavier items and tells us the neighborhood hasn't been the same without our cheerful faces. He and our other neighbors want to plan a block party for our return. I know, no one has block parties anymore, but our street does.

Gabby and I are beat by the time nine o'clock rolls around so we go to sleep, joking that we're too young to be hitting the sack so early, but once in a while is okay.

One guess who I dream about when I finally doze off. I'll give you a hint: His name starts with a D and ends with a W. I wake up with renewed energy and dress for work.

I get to the senior center with a giant box of donuts in my hands. Monday being Monday, some glazed or chocolate goodness will help us through the day. I drop the box off in the kitchen then go to my office. A balloon bouquet is waiting for me. White and yellow balloons surround a huge Mylar balloon that says *You Rock!* I smile. Donations have continued to land in my Venmo account and the total is now up to one hundred and sixty thousand dollars.

I did it and then some.

Or rather, I instigated it, and the generosity of strangers saved us. It's inspired me to think of more ways to help senior citizens. Not just in my city, but across the nation. I'd like to start a foundation with some of the money. I'd like to work more directly with the National Institute of Senior Centers for ways to make the voices of seniors heard.

I pick up the framed picture of me, Gabby, and Diego with our grandparents. They gave everything to us. Taught us to be good people. The elderly deserve goodness in return.

"Good morning, rock star," Karen says, striding into my office and taking the chair across from me.

"Pretty cool, isn't it?" I say.

"You don't know the half of it."

"What do you mean?"

"Alejandra, we've been receiving private donations all weekend directly to the center."

A buzz charges through my veins. "*What?*"

"After the news broadcast, people started phoning the center asking where they could donate." She leans across the desk to give my hand a squeeze. "We've received an additional hundred thousand dollars."

My jaw drops. "That makes two hundred and sixty thousand dollars."

"Actually," she says, "Venmo got in touch and said they would match the donations to your account."

"Shut up!" My pulse pounds in my ears. *No puedo creer que esto este sucediendo.* I can't believe this is happening.

"We are in business for a long time to come thanks to you."

I'm overcome with emotion. I blink back tears until I can't. Karen can't either. We're a giggling, crying mess when Lu walks in. "I'm not crying, you're crying," she says, joining us.

The entire workweek is a celebration, for which I'm grateful. I've little time to think about anything but the center as we plan and strategize.

On Friday, I'm sitting at my desk working on a proposal when an unexpected guest knocks on my open door.

"West?" I scramble to my feet. The only reason I can think of for him to be here is because something happened to Drew. "Is everything okay? Is Drew okay? Please tell me he's all right." I almost trip moving around my desk. West catches me by the elbow.

"Hey, slow down. Drew is fine. Well, he's surviving, let's say, but I'm glad to see this reaction from you." He releases my arm.

Now that I know I don't have to run out of here to see if Drew is still alive, I settle back behind my desk. West barely folds himself into my guest chair. I hadn't realized how tall he was. "Oh, okay, good." I release the breath I was holding. "I mean not good that he's surviving, rather it's good that he's not hurt or something."

West raises an eyebrow.

"Physically hurt." I pinch my arm under my desk. *Get it together, Alejandra.* "And my reaction is perfectly normal given he's someone I care about."

"Is that all? You just care about him?"

"I think that's between me and Drew."

"Fair enough. It's not why I'm here anyway. I stopped by to say congratulations."

My neck stiffens. Like a bird in surprise. "You did?"

"You don't have to sound so stunned. I am a good guy. And yes, I came to say what you did was genius and I'm happy to see the senior center continue."

"Truly?" I ask around a smile. West is a nice person. He's only been doing his job.

"Okay, somewhat happy. But I like to acknowledge defeat with class rather than any ill will, so again, congratulations."

"Thank you. I appreciate it."

"For what it's worth, your boyfriend is very happy for you."

"Drew's not my boyfriend." I want him to be. I hope when the weekend is over he will be.

"You sure about that?" He stands up, puts his arm out for a handshake. "I'll see you around, Alejandra. Take care."

He walks out of my office like he did not just drop a bomb on my day. Was he hinting that Drew could forgive me seeing Matthew? That Drew still cares about me, too, and there's still a chance for us? God, I hope there is.

I drop my head onto my desk. Tomorrow is the big day.

I've known Matthew for eight years, loved him for seven, missed him for one.

I've had a plan to win back Drew for two days.

Wish me luck.

THE VIEW OF Los Angeles is stellar from the roof deck of the Observatory. It's especially beautiful at night when the city is lit up with lights against the backdrop of a black sky. Matthew and I came here often to stargaze, picnic, or just hang out. The last time we were here—the last time I was here—was about a month before he left.

I fiddle with the brooch on my dress, keeping my hand on the vintage glass bead and diamond flower-shaped pin in hopes it will bring me luck. At the very least, it helps me feel connected to my grandmother, and in some small way, my mom. Whenever my grandmother wore it, she always said my mom wore it better. I wish I could remember seeing her wear it, but I can't.

A slight breeze carries the scent of jasmine and I try to relax the nerves inside me. I'm tempted to look at my phone for the time, but I don't. I know he'll be here.

My hands are slippery on the railing. My leg won't stop bouncing. A couple next to me leans against the guardrail and takes a selfie. "Would you like me to take a picture for you?" I offer.

"Would you?" The girl gives me her phone. My small purse dangles from the bend in my arm as I snap the photo.

"Thank you," she says.

"You're welcome." I smooth my hand down my midnight-blue lace maxi dress and resume my position against the railing. The breeze ruffles my hair so I tuck it behind my ears.

"Alejandra?"

At the sound of Matthew's voice, I turn around. This is it. The moment we've waited three hundred and sixty-five days for. Will it be awkward? Easy? Feel like no time has passed? "Hi, Matthew." He looks the same, like I just saw him yesterday. There's the answer to one of my questions.

"Hi." His face lights up with a smile. "It's good to see you."

"You, too."

We lean in to hug, but don't know how close to get so it's cumbersome and brief. There's the answer to another question.

"You look beautiful," he says.

"Thanks. You look exactly the same. Maybe your hair is a little longer?"

"A little, yeah."

"How was your flight?" He came directly from the airport for me.

"Long."

"Dumb question," I say. "Want to sit?" I motion to a bench.

"Sure."

We leave a little space between us as we sit down. He's wearing jeans and a polo shirt and his knee touches mine as he gets comfortable. It doesn't spark even the tiniest bit of electricity.

"So," we say at the same time then laugh.

"This is weird," he says.

"It is," I agree. "But then it's been a while."

"We never had trouble immediately connecting." He takes my hand in both of his and turns it over in his palm like he's testing our bond, checking to see if there's anything still there. "I guess time and distance have had an effect."

I cover his hand with my free one. "I think so." Touching him again doesn't trigger the slightest desire to touch him more.

He continues to hold my hand in his, placing our linked fingers on his thigh. "I've dreamed about a lot of different scenarios here."

"Me, too."

"Yeah?" His brown eyes meet mine and I look really hard into them. I don't blink. I don't think. I just want to feel. Something.

And I do. Familiarity. Comfort. Friendship.

"I've missed you and thought about you every day," I say. "But..."

"You've met someone else."

"Yes. Did you?"

He squeezes my hand as if to take the edge off what he's about to tell me. "I met a few someones."

I nod. I'd be lying if I said there wasn't a twinge of hurt, but it's okay. I'm okay with this news. "Anyone special?"

"Not as special as you." He takes a strand of hair at my

shoulder and twists it around his finger.

"Matthew."

One word. Just his name and he knows. He was always good at reading my tone. And he was always good at guessing my emotions with little to no help from me.

"It's okay, Allie. I knew what I was risking. And I was willing to take that risk because the bottom line is I want you to be happy."

My eyes fill with tears. My breathing flutters. This is Matthew. My Matthew. The boy who meant everything to me and I love him. But not the same way anymore. I'm not *in* love with him. I could watch him walk away and go back to New Zealand for another year, another five years, and my heart would remain perfectly intact.

I can't imagine going one more day without seeing Drew. The ache his short absence has left is gigantic.

"I'm sorry," I mutter.

"Why are you sorry? You have no reason to be sorry."

"I didn't want to hurt you."

"I'm not hurt. Disappointed, yes, but that's on me, not you. We promised to meet, nothing more. And now we can truly move on. As friends."

"Thank you." I cup his cheek. "That's the best thing you could have said. You will always be one of my most important friends."

He smiles.

"Are you back in California for good?" I ask, dropping my arm and withdrawing my hand from his.

"For now, yeah. But who knows. Adventure awaits,

right?"

What perfect parting words. I hope I'm not too late for my biggest adventure of all. I get up from the bench. "I'm sorry to cut this short, but I need to go."

"To see him?"

"Yes."

"Is that why you changed our meeting time to six?"

"Yes."

"And the dress is for him, too?"

"Yes."

"Do you love him?"

"More than anything."

Chapter Twenty-Two
Perfect Match

Drew

THERE COMES A time in a person's life when they can do whatever they want and say whatever they want. Things like, "Drew, if you are going to be an idiot, then you've got to be tough."

This from my eighty-year-old grandmother.

It's her birthday today so I can't talk back and tell her I'm not an idiot. Not that I would if it wasn't her birthday. She gets away with saying anything she wants because she's of that age. Normally the unpleasant things she says make me laugh. Or cringe. This, however, makes me mad.

Because she's right. I need to toughen up.

She's cornered me in the kitchen as I drink a beer to drown my sorrows. My mom and the party planners are in full prep mode for this evening's celebration, moving swiftly around the house and the backyard without need for further help from me. I glance at my watch. Start time is one hour.

"You're right," I say and kiss her cheek. I also need to put on a happy face even if I don't feel it. Tonight is special. My grandmother is special. And the fact that Alejandra isn't here should not ruin it.

When I mentioned to my grandmother yesterday that Alejandra had something come up and wouldn't be my date, my grandmother had stayed unusually quiet. I guess she needed time to formulate an opinion. That happens, too, in later years. You need more time to think. (Don't tell her I said that.)

"Can I get you a drink?" I ask, pressing my shoulders back and giving her my best smile. "Or escort you to the bar?" I put out my elbow.

She takes my arm. I lead her out of the kitchen toward the backyard. "What do you think of the decorations?"

"They're terrific," she says sincerely, then she tugs me in a different direction.

"Where are we going? The bar is out back."

"I need a word with you in private." She deposits us on the front porch, just in time to greet Finn and Chloe, a small gift box in Chloe's hand. So much for privacy.

"Hi! Happy birthday!" Chloe says, wrapping Grandmother in a big hug.

"Happy birthday, Grandmother," Finn says, kissing her cheek. "How is it you keep looking younger?"

Grandmother preens at the compliment.

"Hi, Drew." Chloe gives me a hug.

Then Finn and I do the one-arm guy hug. "Hey, Bro. It's good to see you."

"You too," I say. "We'll be right in," I tell them.

The front door closes behind Finn and for some reason my Spidey senses start to vibrate now that my grandmother and I are alone and away from everyone else. "It's just you and me," I say. "What's up?"

"I need to come clean," she says.

"About what?"

"I knew you were fibbing when you told me Alejandra was your girlfriend."

I run my hand along my jaw. I didn't exactly see that coming, but then I'm not surprised either. I also feel guilty for not telling her before today. "You did?"

"Of course I did. I wasn't born yesterday."

I laugh. "No, you weren't." I step off the porch so we're slightly closer to eye level. "I meant to come clean to you. But then Alejandra and I are—*were*—actually dating so it slipped my mind. What gave it away?"

"Funny story."

"I'm all ears." She's had some good stories over the years.

"The morning you and I had breakfast, I actually got to the hotel early to have coffee with my friend Margaret. And as it turns out, we were sitting at a table next to Alejandra— and I believe her sister and sister's boyfriend if my eaves-dropping skills are correct."

"Holy shit."

Grandmother grins. "I wasn't there long since you and I had a date, but it was long enough for me to be smitten with that girl. She spoke so kindly to her sister. She treated the waitstaff like they were friends. And she wore a brooch on her dress that she touched more than once, as if it was the most important thing on her body. Even more important than a limb. So, when I saw you talking to her, well, it didn't matter if you knew each other or not."

"Holy shit," I repeat.

"Just call me the greatest matchmaker of all time," she says with pride.

"But we really did know each other. Not exactly like I alluded to, but we had met once before."

"And that made my job a little easier."

I walk in a small circle, digesting everything my grand-mother just said. She's a tough critic and for her to see something rare in Alejandra means I am the idiot she called me if I don't fight for the woman I love. If I don't at least tell her I love her before she chooses between me and Matthew. I stop pacing and meet my grandmother's affectionate gaze.

"There's some things you don't know," I say.

"I don't care what I don't know. I care about what I do know. And Alejandra is meant to be with you."

"What if I told you she might be happier with someone else?"

"I'd tell you to ask her yourself." Grandmother nods over my shoulder.

I spin around and drifting down the red carpet the party organizers laid down for tonight, is Alejandra.

All the air leaves my lungs as I stare at her. She is breath-taking in a spaghetti-strap blue dress that flows from her waist to her feet. Her hair is a mass of loose waves around her shoulders and down her back.

The brooch is pinned to the form-fitting bodice.

I glance back at my grandmother, but she's gone. I didn't even hear the front door open or close.

"Hi," Alejandra says.

"Hi. What are you doing here?" My heart is about to pound its way out of my chest and that's the first thing I say to her? *Jesus, Drew. Get back on your game, man.* "You look incredible," I quickly add.

"Thank you. You do, too." She smiles, almost shyly, and it reminds me of the first time she smiled at me in a bar ten months ago. "I thought maybe your grandma told you I was on my way?"

"She didn't, no."

"Oh. We've been texting back and forth so I thought you knew I was coming. Should I..." She thumbs over shoulder. *Go.* No, she shouldn't. She's here. She came to the party. To see me.

"You should stay right where you are."

"I can do that. And please don't be upset with Rosemary. I reached out to her first with my plan."

"You have a plan?"

She rolls her bottom lip between her teeth. "Could we go somewhere else to talk? Guests will be arriving soon, right?"

I lace our fingers together—hello live wire under my skin—and lead her around the side of the house to my mom's rose garden.

"This is beautiful," she says as the stone walkway curls through brightly colored rose bushes. We stop at a concrete bench built for two.

I wipe my hand across the seat to clean off any dirt before she sits down and places her small purse in her lap. I straddle the bench so I can face her.

For the first time in a week, I'm at peace.

"If we weren't at your parents' house I would lift up my dress and straddle this bench, too. But I want to make a good impression and wrinkling my outfit before the party has even started isn't the best way to do that."

"I have no objection," I say. "To the wrinkles."

"I'm relieved to hear that."

We stare, soaking each other in. I've missed her to distraction this past week and now that we're together again, I hope it means what I want it to mean.

"Since you're the one with the plan, why don't you tell me what happens next."

"You have questions, I have answers. Go."

How the hell she knew that, I don't know, but I'll take it. "How are you here?" I ask. "It's almost eight o'clock, which I guess means..." I trail off, wanting—needing—to hear her say she chose me over him.

"I met Matthew at six." Okay, not what I expected, but I'm the one inches from her kissable lips right now so I'm okay with this turn of events. It never occurred to me she could change her meeting time. "I had to meet him before seeing you. Not because I needed to be sure about you, but because I owed it to Matthew to tell him in person that I'm in love with someone else."

"How did he take that?" Yes, I'm playing it cool. Give me a minute.

"Pretty well."

"So, he's in love with someone else, too?"

"No. He's still in love with me."

My hands ball into fists atop my thighs. Alejandra notices and covers them with her soft, warm palms. "But I repeat, I'm in love with you, in case you didn't get that the first time. And I'm sorry for how I treated you. So, so sorry, and I will spend the rest of my life making it up to you if you'll let me. If you can put this behind us, I promise you will never doubt how much you mean to me ever again."

Best. Apology. Ever.

"I can do that. I can do all of that." I lift her hand and press it to my chest, over my heart. "Do you feel that?"

She nods. "FYI, mine's pounding too," she says.

"This is your beat. Your melody. You own it. And for the rest of my life the love it holds is yours. I've been waiting for you, Alejandra, only you." I cup the back of her head and bring her lips to mine. We kiss and we kiss and we kiss. It's not sloppy or hurried. It's slow and controlled. Open-mouthed, closemouthed, I pour everything into it so she knows I'm hers.

The sound of party guests arriving in the distance pulls us apart.

"I love you, Drew."

"I'm really happy to hear you say that. I love you, too."

Her grin is almost as big as mine.

"So, I'd like to ask you out on a date," she says, a sparkle in her eyes.

"A date, huh? I may have to check my schedule."

"What?" She lightly pushes my chest.

"Kidding. I'm in."

"Do you want to know what we're doing?"

"Don't care. There's nothing I won't do for you."

She flutters her eyelashes. "What if it's to pose nude for the art class at the senior center?"

"Shit. Is that it? Can I wear a sock puppet?"

She laughs. "Oh my God, would that be funny."

"Hey, now," I say, but I'm laughing, too. The level of happiness I'm at right now is off the charts. There's a comfort I only feel when I'm with her. Contentment I feel in my bones.

"My seniors love you, you know. The book club ladies think you're dreamy. Which does bring me to our date." She levels me with a serious look. "Drew, will you be my plus-one to Mrs. K.'s seventy-fifth birthday party?"

"Alejandra, I would escort you to the ends of the Earth, so yes."

We seal the deal with a quick kiss.

"Speaking of the senior center, I hear you're kind of a celebrity there now. I'm really happy everything worked out. Mostly because the seniors get to continue to have you in their lives."

She brings her hand to her chest. "Thank you for saying that."

"We should probably head into the party now. I'm sure my grandmother is dying to see us. And wait until I tell you what she told me. That woman is a mastermind, and I am eternally grateful." I help Al to her feet and take it upon myself to assist her in smoothing down the back of her dress.

"Drew."

"Not sorry."

She shakes her head and sighs. I look forward to a lifetime of her responses to my touch.

Holding hands, we stroll back through the rose garden. "What did Rosemary do?" she asks.

"You know, I think you should ask her yourself. Ask her about the morning you met in the hotel lobby."

Alejandra looks puzzled, but nods. "I'm kind of nervous to meet everyone here tonight."

"Don't be. They're going to love you."

"I've been doing some studying on your family in preparation."

"Was that part of your plan? Which by the way, is stellar so far." I pause in the middle of the path—it's my turn to properly apologize to her. "I owe you an apology, too, Al. I'm sorry for the way I treated you last weekend. I never should have doubted your integrity and issued an ultimatum. And I shouldn't have spoken so harshly. I was blinded by jealousy and, honestly, fear. It hurt to think of you seeing your ex."

"It's okay. You were right to feel the way you did."

I smile at her and we resume walking. With the strong scent of roses in the air, I think back to that morning we fought and some of the words she said. *I was caught up in you, Drew. In us. And deep down I think I knew telling you might push you away and I didn't want that. Everyone I've loved has left me.* She'd basically told me then she loved me and I didn't hear it. I hold her hand tighter. I am never letting her go.

"Your mom's name is Liza," Alejandra says. "Your dad is

James. Ethan is your oldest brother and his girlfriend is Pascale and she has a daughter named Rylee. Finn is the baseball player and he's married to Chloe. She's the one I talked to on speaker phone that day at my house, right?"

"Right."

"Anyone else I should know?"

"Chloe's dad will be here. His name is Casey. If you get stuck near him and Finn, plan on talking baseball. Casey is an umpire for Major League Baseball. Pascale's mom and dad and sister will be here, too. Her parents are Paula and Thomas and her sister's name is Paige. I should warn you, Paige has a crush on me."

"Oh, she does, does she?"

"It's a pretty big one."

"How old is she?"

"Twenty, almost twenty-one, I think."

"You are pretty crushable so I won't hold it against her. Who else?"

"Are you remembering all this?"

She points to her temple. "I have a great memory for names."

"My aunt Helena and uncle Wayne will be here with their daughter, Meredith. You'll like Mere a lot. Besides being my cousin, she's a good friend. My grandmother will have plenty of friends here too, and I'm sure I'm forgetting someone, but I can't think of anyone else off the top of my head."

We arrive back on the red carpet and pivot to walk up the step to the front door.

"Thank you," I say, "for being my date tonight."

"Thank you for inviting me," she quips. We both know it wasn't your ordinary invitation. But then it might not have turned into something extraordinary.

I touch my nose to hers and delicately cup her cheeks in my hands. "You ready to do this?" And by *this* I mean tonight and everything afterward.

"I'm ready," she says.

LIGHTS, CAMERA, ACTION...

IT'S ROSEMARY'S 80TH BIRTHDAY!

Please join us in celebration
Saturday, July 12th
8 o'clock

#CheersToEightyGreatYears

Epilogue One

Alejandra

T HE BACKYARD HAS been transformed into an outdoor movie wonderland. Back in the day, Rosemary briefly consulted with a Hollywood film company and she's loved movies ever since. Her favorite is the 1978 French film *La Cage aux Folles* so that's what we'll be watching on the big screen set up on the expansive grass area in a few minutes.

I'm curled up next to Drew on a cozy little couch, a blanket in our laps. There are more plush couches and oversized pillows, blankets, and lawn chairs for viewing comfort. Five-foot-tall gold Oscar floral arrangements with red and white roses are spread around the yard and on the patio behind us. Stars like those on the Walk of Fame are scattered around, too, each with something nice to say about Rosemary. Antique film reels, an old-fashioned popcorn cart, tuxedo cake pops, and strings of white lights add to the homey but lavish ambience.

Servers are dressed like ushers. The food is upscale casual. Fancy grilled cheese sandwiches. Gourmet impossible burgers. Mashed potato pancakes with sour cream and chives. Grilled bacon-wrapped asparagus. I've made it my mission to eat everything.

There's also a party hashtag. *Cheers to eighty great years.* Between Rosemary and Chloe alone, the party is getting a lot of likes on Instagram. This time when Rosemary asked for a picture with me and Drew, I posed with my lips pressed to his cheek. Drew Auprince is off the market for good, ladies and gentlemen.

"Hey, you two," Liza says, kneeling down. "Drew, do you mind if I borrow Alejandra for a minute? I promise to return her before the movie starts."

"Sure," he says, slipping his arm out from under me.

Drew's mom takes me to a quiet spot on the patio. We were only briefly introduced earlier since she's been busy playing hostess, but I immediately liked her. You know how you can just tell someone is a genuine and nice person and you feel like you could spill your guts to them? That was Liza. And when I later noticed her speaking and laughing with her husband and Rosemary, my heart gave a little squeeze. It's clear this is a close-knit family.

"I'm sorry we haven't had a chance to talk," she says.

"That's okay. The party is wonderful."

"Thank you. Rosemary speaks very highly of you and I know she's thrilled that you're here."

I swallow the knot of emotion in the back of my throat. "I'm happy to be included."

"Well, I think we both know it's more than that, and I just wanted to tell you I look forward to spending more time together and getting to know you better."

"Me, too." Having women like Liza and Rosemary in my life is the icing on the Drew cake. I've come home to something new and wonderful and I will cherish it always.

She hugs me. "I've never seen Drew look so happy. You've warmed my heart, Alejandra. Thank you."

"I love him," I tell her. "Very much." I said the same thing to Rosemary when she scooped me up for a quick conversation. The two most important female figures in Drew's life are aware of my feelings, so in my book he's stuck with me.

The lights blink, signaling it's time to start the movie. Liza gives me one more hug. "I think the feeling is mutual. Enjoy the movie," she says.

The feeling is.

I nestle next to Drew again. He's warm and snuggly and I could stay curled beside him forever. "I just told your mom I loved you."

He covers us with the blanket. "I suppose this means I'm stuck with you now."

"My thoughts exactly." I kiss his cheek.

"Sexiest ball and chain ever."

I punch him in the stomach.

"Just kidding. Sexiest *and* fiercest."

"You better watch it, mister." The sound of the movie projector pierces the air and the movie begins on screen.

Drew nuzzles the side of my neck. "Think anyone would notice if I slid my hand between your legs?" He slips said hand under the blanket and over my thigh.

Tingles cannonball through me. I slap my hand down over his. "Drew, don't you even think about it," I whisper.

"Too late. I'm thinking it." His voice is husky. He tugs

my earlobe between his teeth.

"Drew," I warn, pushing his hand off me. "Later. You can do whatever you want to me later."

"Okay. I'll be patient." He sits taller and tucks me under his arm. "It won't be easy, though."

We watch the movie in blissful comfort, our bodies bundled together. There's a cold breeze tonight, but Drew keeps me pleasantly cozy. The film is heartwarming and hilarious and everyone claps when it's over.

A little while later, Rosemary blows out all the candles on her Hollywood-star-shaped cake, and when the guests are down to just immediate family, we sit in the living room to watch her open the gifts from her grandsons.

Rylee helps her rip through the wrapping paper on the present from her, Ethan, and Pascale. She is the cutest, most precocious little girl ever. When the paper is all over the hardwood floor, she clasps her hands under her tiny chin and bounces up and down on her feet while Rosemary lifts the lid off the box.

"It's us!" Rylee shouts before the gift is even out.

Staring into the box, Rosemary's expression is one of absolute affection. "It is and it's magnificent." She lifts an ornate frame out of the box then turns it to show everyone. It's an incredibly detailed and accurate black and white drawing of Ethan, Pascale and Rylee.

"We had it done by an artist in Chicago," Ethan says.

"I love it. Thank you." Rosemary's voice is the softest I've heard it. The love she has for her family is so clearly etched on her face as she draws Rylee in for a quick hug.

"Here's the next one," Rylee says, lifting a small box off the coffee table.

"Hang on there, squirt," Finn says, leaning off the couch to snag the box. "We'd like to save ours for last." He shares a look with Chloe before sitting back down.

"Okay," Rylee says. "Here, Nana Berry."

Rosemary delights in the special name Rylee has given her and accepts the large gift bag that Drew brought. Before she lifts out the tissue paper, Rosemary's eyes meet mine—a brief look of thanks for the gift I gave her earlier. She and I are going hang gliding. It's our little secret for now.

She pulls out the handbag from Drew. "Love it," she tells him with a wide smile.

"Look inside the pockets," he says, and my heart almost explodes for this man. He wrote the sweetest things. I peeked at them when I helped him wrap the gift.

Rosemary reads the first note. "There's more like this?" she asks, clutching the note to her chest.

"Handwritten notes about how awesome you are? Yes." Drew beams.

"Kiss-up," Ethan mumbles under his breath.

"I think we've got you both beat," Finn says, passing the gift in his hand to Rosemary.

"Boys, this isn't a competition," Liza reprimands.

Rylee helps once again with the wrapping paper then leans over to inspect the contents after Rosemary has lifted the top off the small box. "What is that?" Rylee asks, her nose scrunched up.

"That," Rosemary says, "is my second great-grandchild."

She lifts out an ultrasound picture.

Tears, cheers, and congratulations explode around the room. Chloe is ten weeks pregnant, is nauseous all the time, and she and Finn are so in love it's palpable.

"There's a baby in here?" Rylee asks, her hand on Chloe's stomach.

"There is," Chloe says.

"Mommy, when are you going to have a baby in your tummy?"

Ethan puts his arm around Pascale. "Sooner rather than later, I hope."

"Ethan," Pascale says, *knock it off* in her tone. "Would you like to have a baby brother or sister?" Pascale asks Rylee.

"I would like to have one of each, please."

Everyone laughs before conversation returns to more neutral topics.

Drew picks up my hand and we slip away. He takes me down the hall, opens the door to a room, and flicks on the light. It's a study. But also a library. One entire wall is filled with book shelves. The ceiling is vaulted so there's even a sliding ladder.

"Wow," I say. "It's a good thing I didn't know this room existed or I would have snuck away earlier to hang out in here."

"This will be our escape room when we need a break," Drew says, playing with the spaghetti strap on my dress. "My mom likes to entertain and have family gatherings so plan on frequent trips to Casa Auprince."

I wrap my arms around his neck. "Sounds like a plan."

"Speaking of plans. Did yours go the way you wanted?"

"It went better." I kiss him. "Tonight has been really special, for so many reasons, and I'm so very grateful and lucky to have you."

He kisses me. "The feeling is mutual."

"Think it's okay if we left now?" I ask. I want to be alone with him. I want to fall into bed and stay there until tomorrow afternoon.

He walks me backward until my butt hits something hard. "What? You don't want me to do you on top of this desk?"

"Not with your entire family down the hall, no."

"You sure?" He grinds his hips against me so I can feel how much he wants me right now. "The fear of getting caught is a pretty powerful aphrodisiac."

Drew looking at me like he is right now is pretty powerful. "Does the door lock?"

"It does."

"Do it," I say, a little breathless and a lot turned on.

He locks the door. Then he does me. I come embarrassingly quickly, but so does he. Later that night when we're in bed, we make love. Whisper words of love.

Pledge our love.

For always.

Epilogue Two

One year later...
Drew

I ALMOST BURNED down the house. Do not laugh. The no-fail, easy recipe Ethan gave me for tonight was not easy or fail proof. And then the jerk laughed in my ear when I called him to say smoke was coming out of the oven and what should I do? He was no help there either.

So, I called our housekeeper, and she saved the day.

She also told me it didn't matter what food I surprised Alejandra with; tonight was not about the food.

Which is absolutely true and why I'm pacing around the family room and kitchen like a nervous wreck. Tonight is about the two of us, our love, and our future, and I know the only thing that really matters to Alejandra is the honest and genuine simplicity of that.

Still, I want it to be perfect for her. Make that *wanted* it to be perfect. She's an hour late. Dinner's probably been warming in the oven for way too long. And the house smells a little smoky.

She moved in with me six months ago, when renovations on the house were finally finished. Since then it finally feels like home. In hindsight, it wasn't remodeling that I needed, it was her.

It's impossible to count the ways Al has made my life better.

She feels the same way about me. I know this because every day we tell each other one thing we love about the other person. Every. Single. Day. We can fight. We can be mad as hell with each other, but we must share one good thing before our heads hit the pillow.

"Hello!" she finally calls out, stopping me in my tracks. Suddenly, I don't know what to do with myself. I hear her getting closer. Fidget. Closer still. Fidget. She'll round the corner from the hallway in three, two... "Hi! What are you doing?"

Standing like a goofball doing robot moves.

"Nothing." I get my feet to move so I can greet her properly with a kiss. "How was your day?"

"It was good. Did you burn something?" she asks, putting her tote down on the couch then turning to peer into the kitchen.

"Yes, but don't worry, Martha helped me out."

"You cooked for us?"

"I got home early." Lame excuse, and I'm pretty sure she doesn't buy it.

She steps toward the dining table where I've set out two place settings, a vase with ranunculus, and a small side gift to go with the one burning a hole in my pocket. "Drew," she says lovingly. God, I love the sound of her voice.

I pick up the book on her plate and give it to her. "It's next month's book club pick. Reese sent it to me early." She turns the book over to read the back copy. "You are officially one of the first to know."

"Thank you!" She wraps her arms around my waist and kisses me. "I'm so excited to read it."

She turns to put the book on the table and when she twists back around, I'm down on one knee. I can't wait another fucking second. Her hand flies to her mouth as she gazes at me.

"Alejandra, you are the magic in everyday things. You are the sunshine that makes every day bright. You're precious. Beautiful. Kind. I love you with all my heart and want to keep yours safe and happy for the rest of our lives. You're the best thing to ever happen to me. Will you marry me?" I take the velvet box out of my pocket and open it to reveal the oval-cut diamond ring I had specially made.

"Oh my God! Yes! Yes, I'll marry you." She drops down to her knees before I can stand up. "I love you. I love you so much."

I put the ring on her finger. We admire it for a moment, her arm braced out, and then she's kissing me. I'm kissing her. We're kissing like we're about to win the world record for most passionate kiss.

"I love you," she murmurs into my mouth.

"I love you." I stand and lift her into my arms. I need to be inside her more than I need my next breath. I start toward the bedroom but only make it two steps when the doorbell chimes. Damn it. With Alejandra getting home late, I completely forgot to push back the celebration.

I place her on her feet. "I've got one more surprise. Come on."

We open the front door together. There, smiling from ear to ear with cake, champagne, and balloons (I'm sure it was Rylee who wanted those) is our family and close friends.

"Congratulations!!" they shout.

Alejandra beams at me. "You did this?"

I nod.

She takes my face in her hands and kisses me.

Cheers erupt and everyone files inside. Grandmother, Mom, Dad, Gabriela and Diego, Finn and Chloe and their baby girl Willow, Ethan and a pregnant Pascale (they tied the knot in Hawaii a few months ago) and Rylee, cute as a button with a missing front tooth.

West follows behind them with Al's friends Sutton and Jane. If I'm not mistaken, Sutton is definitely giving my best friend an interesting look.

Next up is Mrs. K., Gloria, Ethel, Claire, and Rhoda. I had a car pick them up and as they hug my fiancée in congratulations, they thank me and tell me to take good care of their girl. I promise them I will. Alejandra's co-workers, Lu and Karen, join us, too.

Lastly is Matthew and his girlfriend Pippa. He shakes my hand. It took me a little while to welcome him into our lives, but he means a lot to Alejandra and after spending time with him, I discovered he's a good man. "Congratulations," he says.

"Thank you."

He and Alejandra share a look. Of friendship. Respect. "Congratulations, Allie." He glances at me. "You picked a great guy."

She wraps her arms around my biceps and gazes up at me

with unmistakable love and admiration. "I did. I picked the best guy for me, and I'm so lucky he chose me back."

Four years after that...

"GRANDMOTHER," I SAY, "you may be turning eighty-five next week but there is no way my wife is getting on that thing with you. Not when she's five months pregnant."

Alejandra giggles. "Drew, it's a Ferris wheel."

"I don't care. It's not safe." I scrutinize the carnival ride. It's way too rickety. How Rylee's school approved all of this is beyond me. I happily gave a donation and don't need anything in return.

"Momma," Isabella murmurs, waking up in my arms. She fell asleep while sitting on my shoulders as we wandered around the fair so I slid her into my arms to carry her against my chest. She reaches for Alejandra and this is one of the rare times I happily pass my two-year-old over because now Al definitely cannot ride the Ferris wheel.

"Hi, Bella Bug." Al cradles our daughter atop her beautiful round belly and kisses her forehead before moving Bella over her shoulder and rubbing her little back.

"Okay, then," Grandmother says to me. "You're coming with me. Let's go."

"Me?" I protest. I'm not afraid of heights, but I don't exactly like the way this ride looks. Did I not make that clear?

"Yes, you. Are you losing your hearing already?"

"No, and I'd rather not lose my lunch." We haven't eaten lunch yet.

"Nice try," Grandmother says. "I thought you were some hotshot hotelier, not some wimp."

"Fine. Let's go." I kiss my girls goodbye.

"You're adorable," Alejandra whispers in my ear. "Take care of her."

Grandma Rosemary is not quite as spry as she used to be so I place her arm inside mine and walk steadily beside her. I still admire the hell out of her. Her adventurous spirit hasn't waned one bit. Her mind is still sharp as ever.

We climb shaky stairs to get on the ride. "Is this thing safe?" I ask the attendant. "Because I've got some precious cargo here."

He nods and tucks us into a passenger carrier. "Enjoy the ride."

"I haven't enjoyed a ride in a long time," Grandmother says. It's clear in her tone she does not mean this kind of 'ride.' I groan.

The wheel jerks then starts to move. "You know, it's good to lose control sometimes," she says as we go higher. "It puts hair on your chest."

I smile. She used to tell me and my brothers that all the time when we were young, only it had to do with eating our vegetables.

That's not the part she wants me to zone in on, though, and the reminder hits home.

So, when our carrier hits the top of the wheel, I raise my arms in the air and shout, "I love you, Alejandra and Isabella!"

The End

If you enjoyed this book, please leave a review at your favorite online retailer! Even if it's just a sentence or two it makes all the difference.

Thanks for reading *Hot Shot* by Robin Bielman!

Discover your next romance at TulePublishing.com.

TULE
PUBLISHING

If you enjoyed *Hot Shot,* you'll love the other books in....

The American Royalty series

Book 1: *Heartthrob*
Finn's story

Book 2: *Sweet Talker*
Ethan's story

Book 3: *Hotshot*
Drew's story

Available now at your favorite online retailer!

More books by Robin Bielman

The Palotays of Montana series

Book 1: *Falling for Her Bachelor*

Book 2: *Once Upon a Royal Christmas*

Available now at your favorite online retailer!

About the Author

Robin Bielman is the USA Today bestselling author of over fifteen novels. When not attached to her laptop, she loves to read, go to the beach, frequent coffee shops, and spend time with her husband and two sons.

Her fondness for swoon-worthy heroes who flirt and stumble upon the girl they can't live without jumpstarts most of her story ideas. She writes with a steady stream of caffeine nearby and the best dog on the planet, Harry, by her side. She also dreams of traveling to faraway places and loves to connect with readers.

Thank you for reading

Hot Shot

If you enjoyed this book, you can find more from all our great authors at TulePublishing.com, or from your favorite online retailer.

TULE
PUBLISHING